PARADISE
FARM

PARADISE FARM

BRENDA WEBSTER

State University of New York Press

Published by
State University of New York Press, Albany

© 2000 State University of New York

Printed in the United States of America

For information, address State University of New York
Press, State University Plaza, Albany, N.Y., 12246

Cover photo: The Farm in the Early 1930s.

Production by Diane Ganeles
Marketing by Fran Keneston

Library of Congress Cataloging-in-Publication Data

Webster, Brenda S.
    Paradise Farm / Brenda Webster.
        p.   cm.
    ISBN 0-7914-4099-0 (hardcover : alk. paper). —
ISBN 0-7914-4100-8 (pbk. : alk. paper)
    I. Title.
PS3573.E255P3   2000
813'.54—dc21   98-26875
                                                         CIP

10 9 8 7 6 5 4 3 2 1

To Lisa, Michael, and Rebecca
And, with special gratitude, to Ira

❦ 1 ❧

When she pulled back the curtain that darkened her father's bedroom window, Lara could see straight down the maple-lined road almost to the pinkish brown pillars half a mile away that marked the entrance to the farm. There had been a freak spring blizzard on April Fool's Day—some wit had forecast more unpleasant surprises for 1929—and there was a thick coating of snow on the arching branches.

"Why haven't they come yet?" her father Eugene asked, looking at the log that was sputtering on the grate. He was stretched out on the carved four-poster bed, his wasted body propped on a mass of pillows. Lara could tell from his face he was hurting, but she knew better than to stroke his head and ask if she could give him something for the pain. He'd refused to take his morphine until after he'd talked to their new tenants about the rental agreement.

"Why don't I read to you some more?" she asked instead, gesturing at the neat pile of books next to his water pitcher— "Want to try *The New Yorker* cartoons?" He looked incredulous. No chance he was going to laugh at jokes about flappers and what he called their silly modern views. But she couldn't stand reading any more Marcus Aurelius. Her father needed no encouragement to be flintily stoic.

1

She turned to the window again, holding back the corner of the heavy curtain, glad of an excuse to look outside—anywhere but at the bed. She didn't want to see his hands moving nervously on the counterpane, eager to scratch his signature on the lease and vacate permanently.

A black car broke through the white V at the road's end where the snowladen trees came together.

"Oh, there they are," Lara said, feeling an irrational sensation of hope at the car's steady progress. For a moment she forgot the suffocating room and let herself enjoy the way the sleek double curved front of the car cut the space as it swam toward them, setting up ripples of movement in the trees.

She was hungry for movement, tired of this awful, static waiting. "They have one of those new Packards," she said to her father, "a touring car."

"I don't know where all this speed and racing about is going to get people," Eugene said. "Death is still the last stop." He looked suddenly anxious, his thin nostrils flared. He sniffed. "Does it smell too bad in here?" he asked. "Of disinfectant, I mean."

"The flowers cover it," she lied. Her mother had filled the room with forced narcissi and pots of herbs, but underneath you could still smell the decay—like a compost heap. She hated it. This degrading, painfully slow process of hunkering in the dark, eaten from the inside.

The car pulled up with a screech in front of the house. Lara saw Muriel and her companion get out and stretch. Muriel was unstylishly hatless, but Lara saw that her coat was nicely cut and she'd turned up a fur collar around her ears. She didn't look any more pregnant than when Lara had seen her last month in New York. The slender man in the belted overcoat with the homburg must be her husband, David. Muriel caught her looking and waved awkwardly.

A few minutes later, Lara heard the creak of the front door hinges, murmured greetings, then footsteps up the wood stairs as her mother, Agnes, swept their new tenants into the bedroom. The first thing Lara noticed about David was that his pomaded hair—he'd taken off his homburg—threatened to break into curls. His eyes moved rapidly from face to face. A restless fellow, she thought. Not exactly the husband Lara would have imagined for Muriel, who had turned her gray luminous eyes toward Lara's father and was looking at him with steady concern.

Eugene visibly gathered himself. "You've come," he said to them, holding out his hands. "I'm so glad. I was afraid you'd get lost. Excuse the curtains, the bright light hurts my eyes. It's too bad, the view is stunning from here." He looked around. "Lara, open the drapes a bit, would you?" Lara saw her mother make a gesture of distress, knuckles to her mouth, and hesitated. "Go ahead, I'm all right."

"It's not necessary," Muriel put in quickly.

"My brother John's room has almost the same view," Lara said smoothly. "You can see it when we look around." She didn't want Muriel and David to think her mother was miserable about renting the house to them. What point was there in making them feel bad, especially when they were going to have to live here together cheek by jowl? Muriel and David in the big house and Agnes, Lara and Johnnie in their old guest house.

"Agnes, could you bring me a glass of lemon water, dear? Someone has to be realistic," he said when she went out. "She keeps insisting I'm going to get well. She seems to think if I just had sufficient willpower, I could stay alive." He stroked his pale moustache. "I've asked Lara to talk to her but she won't listen. It'll be a shock to her when I die. My partner, Sol, will handle all the financial arrangements."

Lara reflected wryly that her father wouldn't listen either. When her mother had asked why they had to move out (Didn't they have enough money?), he didn't even pretend to answer her, simply went over what he'd already told them about their allowances.

Now he leaned over stiffly, opened the drawer of his bedside table and drew out a document. What he did, was doing, wanted to do, was always the center of their lives. He'd always acted as if they needed his constant surveillance. Lara had the disloyal thought that they might flourish without him.

"I have the contract here," he was saying to David, "but of course you'll have to look at the place first to see if it suits you."

David scanned the papers. Lara noticed he had a good profile. Enough nose to look interesting, not just pretty. Muriel had a stronger face, framed by her long black hair, the free-falling kind her father certainly disapproved of. Determined cheekbones. An insistently unmade-up face.

"There was one thing I was going to ask you," Muriel said hesitantly. "What about structural changes? We're technically just renters. But if we're going to have a clinic here eventually, we'll probably need to remodel. I'm sorry to bother you. . . ."

"Why be sorry? I'm a lawyer," Eugene answered simply. "You're right. Things ought to be crystal clear. *Cuique suum.*" Skeletal, his pajamas flapping on his bones, he was still sharp, Lara thought.

"Why don't you look around," her father said, "see what changes you might want to make and then come back and we'll work out something that's satisfactory to both of us. I don't think there will be any problem unless"—he gave them an engaging smile—"you're planning to tear the place down and put up a nursing home."

Agnes came back with the lemon water and poured it for Eugene, holding it to his mouth. A wisp of hair came loose from her upswept hairdo and straggled next to her ear. She pushed it back distractedly, just as she was pushing back her tiredness, Lara thought, and making an effort to smile.

When Eugene had finished drinking and lay back, resting, Agnes offered to show Muriel and David the rest of the house. Lara went along. After a perusal of the bedrooms and Eugene's library they went into the living room, the biggest and most impressive room in the house. Lara noticed Muriel's instantly suppressed motion of distaste at the sight of the heavily draped wall of French doors and the dark, massive furniture, elaborately carved with scrolls and fruit. Every surface, except the grand piano at one end, was covered with crocheted lace and small ornamental objects.

Once Lara had overcome the embarrassing urge to weep, there was something perversely funny about the whole situation. Two investigators of the mental underworld in a shrouded room filled with oppressive furniture and fragile ornaments.

The strange, dissonant furnishings of the collective Kamener soul.

Lara lounged against the piano, her cigarette holder clamped in her teeth. "Imagine it empty," she told Muriel. "The lines are good. It's simple and spacious. I don't know why Mother insists on keeping it dark."

"You do too," Agnes said indignantly, "the sun fades the oriental rugs."

"Maybe Muriel and David won't have any. Maybe they'll have rush mats." Lara walked quickly along the wall of French doors, drawing back the heavy curtains—by the last she was almost running in her eagerness to let in the light.

"It makes all the difference, doesn't it?" she said and saw Muriel smile with pleasure as the dazzling white of trees and snowy lawn burst on them, glittering with reflected sun.

Her mother shrugged as if to say, you see what I'm burdened with, and went on with the tour. "This is where we have our afternoon tea," she said, indicating a highly polished mahogany table with claw feet. Her tone suggested Muriel and David were going to be her guests, not take over her house. It was pathetic really, but Lara felt she couldn't start pitying her or there might be no end to it. She frowned, not liking herself. After all, Agnes wasn't asking for compassion, was she? If anything, her demeanor suggested that nothing unpleasant was occurring, certainly nothing tragic. Lara wondered if she was trying to trick fate, or did she imagine this was only a whim of Eugene's that would pass when he got better?

"I'll take them over the grounds, Mother," she said, going to the closet in the front hall and coming back with their coats. "I know you don't want to leave Daddy too long." When they'd put their things on, Lara took them out through the screened porch.

As soon as they got outside, she brightened up considerably. She always felt like a different person when her mother wasn't around. They stood in front of the screened porch for a minute while Lara pointed out the snow-blown tennis courts, pool and gardens—now just long white mounds—on the west side. Then Muriel said she'd like to see the outbuildings. There was a gravel drive running along the front of the house and the rustic outbuildings were strung along it: water tower, game room, garage, caretaker's house, greenhouse, barn. Then, across from it, set alone on the edge of the field, the windmill. Behind the game room and water tower, like the point of a triangle, was the guest house.

They strolled along through the soft snow looking out at the rolling fields just beyond the drive and beyond them to the woods and bluish hills in the distance. Lara took them to the game room first. As they went inside she noticed that David was taking copious notes. While he paced around the knotty-pine room tapping walls and estimating square feet, Lara looked at the battered ping-pong table, her old victrola, and the vividly colored croquet mallets in their rack under the big window. Let them refurbish the place, she thought, let it all go.

After the greenhouse and the caretaker's house—which Muriel wanted to turn into a dormitory—they went on to the big barn. Lara showed them the cows placidly ruminating in their headlocks, and the hayloft with the huge rough beams high above the floor that she had crawled across when Johnnie dared her. Looking up at their cobwebby underside, neck craned back, the muscles of her arms and legs contracted, her body remembered the feel of the splintery beams. Even very young, she'd known if she slipped she'd crack her skull.

"You could use the threshing floor under the beams as a theater," she told Muriel. She had always wanted a theater as a child.

They seemed so pleased, so hopeful, Lara thought as they walked along in the sun, after their tour, looping back across the snowy lawns behind the outbuildings, toward the farmhouse. She heard Muriel say to David in a low voice that it could do with a coat of paint. Was it naïvete or bravery, thinking they could change things for the better, not just buildings, but badly damaged children? She remembered herself and Johnnie playing in the game room—that would be the new craft room—playing doctor, playing torture the prisoners, and shivered. It would be such a relief to believe that somehow things could change.

"I don't mind moving here," she offered as they passed the guest house with its cockeyed chimney and the cozy porch that caught the sun in the winter. "It wouldn't be good for Mother to be locked up in the big house with her memories. Besides," she added, "this way she'll have to get rid of some of that awful furniture and the porcelain bric-a-brac."

Muriel seemed to be studying the resolutely closed green shutters. "She may not see it that way."

"She doesn't. But that's because she can't think ahead yet. She wants everything to stay the same."

"And you?" David asked. She saw him looking her over.

"I need a cigarette." She laughed, took off her glove and extracted a pack from her bag.

David flicked his lighter and Lara bent her face toward the light. When she lifted her head, she saw Johnnie's kite beneath the shoulder of the pool hill. It had a red tail like a streak of blood against the snow. Muriel looked at her questioningly.

"It's Johnnie," Lara said, puffing out with a note of bravado, "the invisible man."

"He looks quite visible to me," Muriel said, as a young man in a greatcoat and cap appeared higher up on the hill next to the bathhouse.

"That's because you don't know him yet," Lara answered. "I'd introduce you but he likes to be alone when he tries out a new one. That's Free-soaring Tiger." She gave an apologetic laugh. "He has quite a collection, all shapes and sizes. It's the only use he's made so far of his engineering degree." She imagined her mother's face listening to this and sighed. "Actually, that is something of an exaggeration. He taught a course two years ago at NYU."

"Maybe he just wants to have some fun, take some time off," David suggested.

Lara shrugged. "It's more like time out," she said, "in a different zone entirely, but maybe with your training you can cross time zones more easily than other people."

David frowned, not sure whether she was mocking him, but Muriel laughed.

"If there are enough clues to the route."

Lara kept watching Johnnie out of the corner of her eye.

"There's no need for you to go upstairs again unless you want to," David said to Muriel when back in the house they stood in the front hall. "I've got the list."

He kissed Muriel lightly on the cheek and headed up the big staircase, running his hand along the mahogany banister.

"Why don't you come into the kitchen and have a cup of tea with me?" Lara offered, anxious to stay out of the sickroom as long as she could.

"I'd love to. It's probably easier on your father just to have David to deal with. He was so welcoming to us both, but I'm afraid he's in a lot of pain."

Lara led the way into the big kitchen just off the front hall. "He is," she said, glancing over at the kitchen table. Muriel followed her glance and saw an open sketch pad, full of faces and hands, some with a light wash of color over them.

"Don't look. They're not very good. I've been trying for days to do Daddy's portrait, while I still can. But I can't get him, there's no life to what I'm doing. I don't know why." She picked up her sketch pad and regarded it grimly, her mouth shut in a tight line. It wasn't just these sketches; she'd been stuck for months not seeming to make any progress.

"Maybe you don't have much energy to spare just now," Muriel said.

She thinks I'm suffering, Lara thought, finding it too painful to think of losing him. But the truth was, she wasn't feeling that at all. She was losing the last chance to show him what she was capable of.

Muriel picked up a blue pastel and held it toward a sheet of empty paper. "May I?"

"Sure. . . ."

Muriel took a breath and drew the chalk full across the page leaving a bumpy blue track behind her.

"You can use the edge too." Lara took a yellow one and scrawled a quick sketch of a wildly pregnant Muriel all belly and long hair. Muriel laughed, turned hers on edge and drew a square house with a columned entry.

"The second floor windows have such a nice rhythm," she said, "but I've made them look like cement blocks." She tried again, sticking her tongue between her teeth. "The children will love these," she said.

"In your clinic, you mean? Poster paints might be easier at first."

"I'd like to have everything—paints, crayons, pastels, watercolors, clay. I want to have a real art program—not just the diddly little crafts programs they've been trying at some clinics—caning chairs and making doilies." Muriel tossed back her hair energetically. She was a big woman, Lara thought. She'd be full bodied even when she wasn't pregnant.

"Aren't you going to do the talking cure?" Lara asked, not sure if that was what the doctors called it or only a sort of nickname.

"That's more for a certain kind of patient. . . ."

"A very rich one," Lara quipped, and they both laughed.

"I work with children who are more disturbed," Muriel said when she caught her breath. "They don't have much use for talking. They need the physical stuff. The holding, stroking. They need someone they trust near them when they wake up."

Lara looked at Muriel's large hands with their short, unvarnished nails, and an image of her own endless succession of white uniformed nannies flashed through her mind. She grimaced.

Paradise Farm: a model for the country. Lara thought that would be the perfect irony.

"Do you have any prospective patients?" she asked.

"We'll start with a little girl named Robin. She's been mute for a year."

"Aren't there lots of patients who never get better?"

"This is a special child. She has a spark." Muriel leaned forward emphatically. "And then I'll have a whole different way of treating her." Her eye caught sight of Lara's scissors and she picked them up, opened and closed them quickly. "I'm even going to let her—them—handle scissors and palette knives, to show them we trust them."

"What if the children decide to cut each other up?" Lara asked. "Or the teacher?" She eyed Muriel's stomach wondering when it would start to show. Or hurt the baby? Wasn't Muriel worried about that?

Muriel passed a hand over her belly as though she were communicating with what was inside. "Maybe it won't work— even David thinks I'm going a bit too far. I could be wrong," she said. But her whole stance, even the way she carried her head,

∽2∾

I look ghastly, Agnes thought, frowning at herself in the bedroom mirror. The black mourning dress that she'd thought was so elegant when she bought it for the funeral a month ago seemed unrelievedly drab. Her freckles stood out above the high neck like pox and her kinky hair made her look like Topsy. "Everything about your face is too large," her mother used to say, "especially your nose. Why couldn't you have been beautiful like your sisters?" Since she hadn't been, she'd tried very hard to be good. But it hadn't worked. Being polite and obedient hadn't gotten her the love she wanted. Or praying either. Now she felt tired of trying. Maybe being wicked would be better, she thought angrily, sucking in her cheeks, at least maybe I'd feel something.

She remembered how alive she'd felt when she'd thrown the Christian Science prayer book out the window the day Eugene died. His eyes were barely closed when she'd been seized by a fit of rage, opened the window so hard the sash broke and hurled it right into those bushes there. The rabbi would have gloated to see her. God, how she disliked being Jewish. It was almost as bad as being an ill-favored woman. Maybe if Eugene hadn't insisted on calling in Rabbi Citron that last week, her prayers would have worked. Maybe it was bad

11

animal magnetism. She peered out the window into the bushes looking for a glint of gold lettering. But the bushes were dense and full of prickles and she couldn't see anything. Strangely relieved, she turned away from the window and began to walk briskly around the house, checking to make sure that everything was packed for their move to the cottage.

Two days before the movers were coming, Agnes was still looking methodically through Eugene's desk drawers for something that could make sense of the clock moving forward when he wasn't there. She hoped that somewhere in the drawers there would be a message for her. She secretly hoped for a letter—a sort of codicil to the will that was so cold and formal—that would tell her what he liked about her—besides her hair; she knew he loved that—so she'd know better what to like about herself. Or give her instructions. She would have liked it if they were very practical. Crochet a blanket with four colors of velvet and put it at the foot of our bed. Brush my suits. Engrave my headstone with a verse from Shakespeare or "He was a scholar and a gentleman." She considered going to a medium to ask what Eugene wanted her to do with all this time that was left her.

She took out some things from a lower drawer—his pen, his pipe, an hourglass, his opera glasses, a French dictionary, a German dictionary, a verse he'd translated from Horace, a bullet from the war, his moustache cup, a novel. The objects seemed so incomplete, she couldn't understand how they could be there, pretending to be real when he wasn't there to use them.

She took the moustache cup—blue Egyptian glass—in her hand and tried to meditate on it, was bored, was horrified at her boredom, tried again, promised him in her thoughts to be faithful forever, got flustered, looked into a cubby-hole and found what she knew all along was there—a photo of Lara's nursemaid with a lock of her blond hair—and burst out crying.

What she was really looking for, though she didn't know it, was a reason not to stay in mourning for the rest of her life. She really wanted something to slice into her like a surgeon's blade. Cut off the part of her that belonged to her husband and put it aside so she could go on. Like an operation, this was painful. The photo and the lock of hair hurt her physically. Betrayal hurt worse than giving birth. But the fact that he betrayed her—and she guessed that betrayal was constant—didn't mean she didn't have to mourn. She mourned doubly hard. She wanted him back and she wanted back the part of him that wasn't hers.

She held the lock of hair between her first and second fingers making it move back and forth like a snake—it was electric and lithe—and remembered the laugh.

When she first heard him laughing like that she had thought it was someone else. But he had been talking just a minute before to Lara's young nursemaid, Marie. Agnes had heard the familiar murmur of his voice and then suddenly that laugh. It was a sound deep down in his throat, a sort of animal sound, full of a mindless energy. She had wanted to hear it again. She had wondered what could be so funny to make him bray like that. She'd have to ask him, she'd thought, threading a red velvet yarn through her crochet needle, but when she'd finally gotten up the courage to ask, he'd been annoyed. Angry even. When he was angry he forgot to talk like a Northerner and drew out his syllables into a soft Southern drawl.

"Laugh?" he'd repeated, pulling on his moustache. "You want to know what I was laughing about with Marie? Can't a man laugh in his own house?"

The night of his birthday came back to her. How she'd reached out for him and felt only cold emptiness on his side of the bed. How she'd gone down to look for him in the kitchen—thinking he was eating a second helping of the birthday cake she had made him, the one with his favorite frosting of raspberry jam and marzipan—and then she'd heard him in Marie's room laughing with her and feeding Lara. That still infuriated her. Debauching a child that way. She had a vivid image of Lara perched on Marie's lap eating cake from her father's hand, her face flushed and avid.

Agnes thought of confronting him, but what could she say? Eugene laughing or eating cake with the maid was supposed to be invisible. Those were the unspoken rules. It was only when she found the girl crying in her room in her slip, her stomach clearly swollen, that Agnes had been able to do something.

"I'm sorry, Marie," she said, conscious that she looked contained, regal, with not a hair out of place. "You'll have to go. I can't have you around the child in this state." The girl cried harder but Agnes was firm. She wanted her out by morning. Before Lara woke up.

"She'll think I deserted her," Marie wailed.

"You should have thought of that before sleeping with Mr. Kamener," Agnes spit at her. "Now get out." Her vehemence surprised her. She had meant to be gracious and icy cold.

Marie, still crying, began jumbling her things into an old grip, pulling them off hangers, stuffing them in any which way.

Agnes remembered with satisfaction that her cornflower eyes had turned an ugly red. Her nose was running and she wiped it with the back of her hand. Why she's only a child, she had thought, surprised. A child with a snotty nose. What is the point of terrorizing her? It isn't all her fault is it? Isn't it partly his?

That's when she got the idea of asking Marie how she had made Eugene laugh. Marie had looked at her bewildered. "I said, how? Tell me what you did." She took hold of the girl's shoulder, caressed it, told her not to be frightened. The skin was very soft. The shoulder was soft. She could see the flesh between her fingers as she pressed, and further down the soft rounds of the girl's breasts. Her own breasts felt dark and constrained under her corset.

"What was so funny about your butterfly pin, for instance? Why did he laugh when he saw you wearing it?"

"My pin?" Marie unconsciously fingered the spot between her breasts where she'd pinned it. "I don't remember. Maybe he thought butterflies belonged in gardens, not. . . ." She hesitated.

Agnes put her face so close to the girl that she could smell her breath. "If you tell me, I'll let you talk to Lara before you go."

The girl had touched the spot between her breasts again and glanced down, sniffing and, yes, smiling. It was hard to believe that in such a condition—thrown out of her job, with a bastard child to take care of—she could actually be smiling.

Following her glance, Agnes noticed the ruddy color of her nipples. They showed through the thin fabric of her slip, a frank deep red.

She'd suddenly understood the breasts, the nipples, the roses, the butterfly—it was a revelation of another world where men and women play with each other like children.

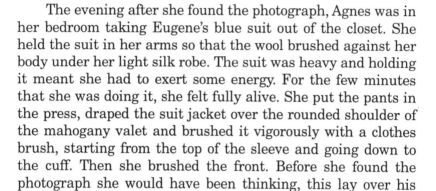

The evening after she found the photograph, Agnes was in her bedroom taking Eugene's blue suit out of the closet. She held the suit in her arms so that the wool brushed against her body under her light silk robe. The suit was heavy and holding it meant she had to exert some energy. For the few minutes that she was doing it, she felt fully alive. She put the pants in the press, draped the suit jacket over the rounded shoulder of the mahogany valet and brushed it vigorously with a clothes brush, starting from the top of the sleeve and going down to the cuff. Then she brushed the front. Before she found the photograph she would have been thinking, this lay over his heart, I am brushing the cloth that covered his heart, or his arm, or his wrist, or his thigh. And she would have cried a little. She'd done this every day since he died, brushed his clothes, inspecting them for buttons off, for tears, giving them to the maid to be mended. It made her feel connected to him. Made her feel she was doing him a service that somehow he would appreciate.

Her nerves still felt connected to him.

When the wind made the shutters of the farmhouse creak, she thought she heard him coughing in his room. When the maid let something drop upstairs, she thought he was banging on his nightstand calling for his medicine. The thought wasn't unpleasant, it kept her in the warm cocoon of his presence. But after she had seen the lock of hair and sat twisting it in her fingers, it was laughable. It was insincere. He was no longer alive in his pipe or his suit. They were simply dead pieces of wool or wood. And for her to keep on tending them as though they were his outer skin no longer made sense. She realized with a stabbing pain to her head that she wasn't going to take the clothes with her to the cottage on Friday. She was going to put them in boxes and give them to the poor.

But something made her keep on even though she guessed this was the last time she was going to do this. She finished the jacket and turned to his trousers, brushing harder than she had to. The brush was soft and the pressure she was exerting on the cloth felt good to her. Her hair, unbrushed, tumbled across her face. Her silk robe came undone and she tied it up carelessly. I am becoming a slattern, she thought, relishing the ugliness of the word. He's been dead only a month and here I am spending all day in my robe. Not caring what I look like.

She saw her daughter go by the door of her room dressed in a light, bright dress that despite her slenderness swelled slightly over her hips, and felt unaccountably angry. But I do care, she thought, I do. I want to put on my gayest dress and go dancing. Instead, she brushed the other leg of his suit. There was a small stain on the thigh. Wine he had spilled during a quarrel—she had wanted to go with him on his trip to Paris. She could have shopped, strolled by the Seine. She couldn't understand why he wouldn't let her. Or on any of the other trips either. She hadn't understood when she married him that practicing international law meant you were always on the other side of the Atlantic sending your wife letters from the best hotels. She thought of the embossed stationery engraved with pictures of what she was missing: the Grand Hotel de l'Arc Romain, the Grand Hotel de l'Athénée. She turned the leg so the stain didn't show and kept brushing.

Agnes wondered if this was how the nursemaid felt, always at the service of others, always scrubbing faces and necks and hands that weren't hers. Tying up shoes, tying sashes, tying hair bows. She raised her arm to take the jacket off the valet and felt her small breast lift against the silk of her robe. The nipple contracted as the silk rubbed it. I look like a girl, she thought, catching sight of her flushed face in the dresser mirror. She wondered if Eugene had come on Marie when she had her arm lifted and her breast pushed out against her starched uniform. Was she standing on a stool, reaching for something on the top shelf of Lara's closet, her legs showing? And did she jump and say, "Oh Mr. K., you startled me." And then did he say, in his most gallant tone, "Marie, you're not tall enough to reach that, you're such a little thing. Here, let me help you." And then when he tried to help, did Lara's straw hats come spinning, tumbling down covered with ribbons? And did Marie say, "Fine help you are, Sir," and clap her hand over her mouth pretending to be frightened because she'd been so bold? And then did he laugh?

I'm going mad, Agnes thought, and she did look strange to herself in the mirror with her red face and tumbled hair and her not perfectly clean robe showing her white neck. Even my room disapproves, she thought. The ornaments looked crookedly at her. The gold cupids and china dogs, even the brocade chairs seemed to draw themselves up more stiffly. Well she wouldn't have to see them reproaching her for long. Most of them wouldn't fit into her bedroom in the cottage. She had to put them into storage. The moving man was coming day after tomorrow. They would be piled up under clothes in the dark. She laughed and then sobbed. Lara heard her and looked into the room.

"Are you all right? Can I help?" she asked.

"Help me cry?" Agnes laughed again as her daughter came into the room. "Yes, cry, please. You can do all the crying if you like. All of it. I won't keep any of it." And then she fell on the bed and began to cry in earnest. Crying when she wanted to scream in rage. Keeping her face turned away.

Lara patted her back, then rubbed in a rhythmical, soothing motion, circles, round and round. The crying got softer. Lara rubbed more vigorously.

Agnes sobbed a word into the pillow.

"What? I can't hear you."

"It hurts. Need. . . ."

"Need what?"

"Oil."

"Oh, you want me to massage you the way they do at the spa? With that special oil you use after the bath?"

"Mm," Agnes murmured, not wanting to look at her daughter, just wanting the hands to keep on moving, to get softer and smoother and glide over her skin. While Lara went to get the oil from the bathroom, Agnes loosened her robe.

"If I could only relax enough to sleep," she said when Lara came back.

Agnes rolled over on her stomach languorously and let her gown off her shoulders. As she turned, Lara caught a glimpse of her mother's breasts. She had never seen her mother naked and was surprised at how firm her breasts were. Small and nicely shaped, like her own. And the same tiny waist too. Her mother extended her arms. Lara sat down gingerly on the edge of the bed—her feet didn't touch the floor.

"I can't seem to find a way to sit without bumping your arm."

Her mother sighed and put the arm across Lara's knees.

"Is that too heavy?"

"No," Lara said. She wished her father were here. She poured some of the thick oil into her palm and smoothed it on her mother's upper arm.

"See how loose it is underneath," her mother said, holding it up, "how it waggles."

"It's not so bad," Lara replied brightly. "If you'd exercise regularly you'd see it would tighten. If you like, I'll show you how." She determined to exercise every day herself to keep her flesh firm. She moved down her mother's arm to the wrist, held her hand for a minute then started gently to massage it, her thumb making deep circles on the palm, with its mysterious lines. She pulled off her mother's rings, massaging the red circles they left, and stretching out the beautiful long fingers. When she finished, she poured more oil onto her mother's shoulders, leaning over, working her fingers into the hollows. She could feel knots of muscle everywhere. The biggest one was farthest away from her, right above the collarbone. She reached across Agnes's back and tentatively pushed her thumb into the skin.

"The woman at the spa sat over me, straddled me," Agnes said.

"My dress is too tight."

"You can take it off."

"Take it off," Lara echoed. There was something about the tone of her mother's voice that bothered her.

"You'll only get oil on it and ruin it." Her mother turned her head on the side and watched while Lara pulled her dress over her head and hung it over the scrolled chair. "That's right," Agnes said.

Lara climbed up on the bed and squatted over her mother, holding her weight off her back.

"You can sit down, Lara. You won't hurt me. And really push hard." Lara dug her thumb into the tightness. Her mother grunted. Lara pushed and prodded, listening to the slight cracking sound.

"It hurts, but it's good." her mother said. "Don't stop."

Agnes felt the warmth and heaviness of Lara's thighs on her back and began to relax. It had been so long since anyone had touched her or soothed her. Eugene had been sick for years. Not that what he used to do was exactly pleasant, but afterwards she got to lie in his arms and he would rock her like a baby. She felt the faint trickle of oil between her shoulders and shuddered. Her skin was coming alive. It felt supple. Lara's hands made her vividly aware of her shoulders and back. As Lara stroked her with the oil, Agnes felt her shape swell and narrow as though she herself were molding a body out of warm clay.

The rhythmic motion of Lara's hands slackened. Twisting her neck, Agnes saw her staring at the gold enameled clock on the mantel. She wondered if Lara was planning to go out tonight and felt a surge of irritation. Why did she have to be distracted just now? Couldn't she pay attention for just an hour? Was that so much to ask? Couldn't she see how much pleasure she was giving? She thought of asking Lara to spend the night with her.

"Tell me about your young men," she said instead. "You haven't talked about anyone for awhile."

"That's because there isn't anyone."

"How about that Mortimer? The philosopher. The bony one." She giggled coquettishly.

Lara climbed carefully off her mother's back and knelt next to her, putting the top on the oil. "We broke up last year, Mother, before Daddy went on the new medicine. You know that. We're just friends." That wasn't quite true on Mortimer's side, but it was all Lara felt like telling.

"You don't have any trouble attracting beaux. You should give your brother lessons."

"If Johnnie wants lessons, Mother, he'll ask."

"Ohhh," Agnes moaned, "my leg got a cramp. Here, oh." She curled around and rubbed her calf. "Oh, it's bad."

Lara sighed. "Let me do it," she said, pushing her mother's hands away and taking the leg firmly in both hands. It was obvious she wasn't going to make the concert. "Better?"

"It's moving up." She paused. "You and Johnnie used to be so close. What happened?"

Lara pressed hard right below her mother's knee. "Here?"

"Up more." Agnes touched her thigh vaguely. "He used to say you were prettier than anyone."

"And you used to say he doted on me too much. That he'd never marry as long as I was single—as though it's my fault he's a misfit."

"You know I don't like name-calling," Agnes said. "I never allowed it when you were little. Could you use a little oil, sweetheart? I don't want my skin to get sore."

Lara poured some oil on the back of her mother's thigh and started to massage it. Her fingers sunk into the soft flesh. It was like kneading a sponge. A big soft white sponge.

Agnes wriggled with pleasure. "Mm. Thank you. That's lovely. The man that gets you will be lucky. I only hope when you find someone new he won't wear spectacles. You don't want to marry someone with a deformity."

"Mother, glasses aren't a deformity." Lara punched her mother's thigh with her knuckles.

"Not so hard. Yes, like that. I still can't believe you kept him waiting outside in a cab while you kissed his friend."

Lara started on the other leg, pinching and squeezing. "Mother, stop. That's over. It's past. There's no point talking about it. There's no fiancé. There's just you and me—and sometimes Johnnie."

"And next week we'll all be crammed together in the guest house," Agnes said unhappily. "I hate the idea of it. Only three bedrooms. One bathroom for all of us. I don't know what was in Eugene's mind."

"Oh Mother, if you'd think of it as a cottage—something picturesque out of Meredith— you'd like it better."

"It'll be horribly cramped," Agnes said, putting her forehead against the pillow and speaking in a muffled voice.

"We don't really need all this space. Three floors, front parlor, back parlor, dressing rooms big enough to sleep in. We were rattling around in it."

"I wasn't rattling. I liked walking from room to room, each one with its different mood. I liked having a sewing room and a room for music. It felt gracious . . . and it makes me feel awful to send all the servants away except Catherine and my little maid."

"People don't have hordes of servants these days. And with fewer things around, there will be less to take care of. It won't be so bad, you'll see. On the days that I go to the Art Students League, you'll have the whole place to yourself. I may even spend the night at my new studio."

Agnes sat up abruptly. The embroidered flowers on the sheet had imprinted parts of themselves on her breasts. She wants to leave me here alone, she thought. The little bitch. I might have known there was a man in it somewhere. "It's your teacher, isn't it? The one with red hair. That Englishman or whatever he is. I suppose you've set your cap for him now."

Lara looked angrily at her mother. "I've been painting seriously for years. Do you have to turn everything into a sexual adventure?" She felt like slapping her mother's dry cheek. "Besides, he's boring. Just repeats the same tired comments. I need to find someone else."

"Don't be fresh. You talk about your adventures incessantly."

"I only tell you things because you ask, you ask, do you know how much you ask? 'Did he kiss you, does he love you, what did he say?' Why do you ask me those things? Every time I go out you're waiting up for me wanting to know."

"I want to protect you, that's all."

"You don't, you want my life for yourself." Lara went pale, Agnes red. "You want to have a man."

"Stop," Agnes begged.

"You do. You envy me my freedom. You hate me."

Agnes covered her eyes. "I don't hate you," she moaned. "I hate being old, I hate being fat. I hate being . . . finished." She tugged on the loose skin under her jaw and started to cry.

"Don't cry, please. . . ."

"How could you?"

"I'm sorry, I don't know, but please don't." She kissed her mother's wet cheek. "You're beautiful. You can get a haircut, we'll be like sisters with our hair marcelled. We could even go on double dates."

Her mother gave a feeble laugh—she liked it, she liked the idea of going out with her daughter.

❧

"Did he make you happy? Were you happy?" Lara asked her later when they were lying in the big room in the dark.

Her mother didn't answer, but let Lara stroke her hair, nestling her head on her shoulder. It still amazed Lara how easily her mother could pull her back by some simple act of childlike trust. Just an hour before, Lara had been frantic to get away but now, with the curly head pressing against her shoulder, she was overwhelmed by the same urge to protect and possess that she'd felt as a child.

"I used to listen outside your door," Lara whispered to her. "I heard him making love to you. I thought he didn't know how to make you happy." I could have done better, was what she thought. I would have known how to hold you, be gentle with you. "I wanted to bang on the door and disturb you, to make him stop."

"You did disturb us. You had nightmares. Don't you remember?"

"No."

"You used to scream until we took you into bed with us." She'd been a funny child, intense, flushed.

"Did you like it?" Lara asked now. "Making love?"

"I liked being held," her mother whispered back. "Otherwise, what was there to like? I shut my eyes and tried not to notice."

"Poor Mother."

"We didn't do any of the things you do, when I was young. We didn't take our little hobbies seriously. Only loose women smoked and wore makeup. They even have petting parties in college now." Her voice sounded aggrieved. "I was reading about them in the *Ladies' Home Journal.*"

"I wasn't criticizing you," Lara said, "I just wanted to know how you felt." But the intimate moment had passed.

❧ 3 ❧

Johnnie was sitting under the arbor, reading his paper and smoking when he saw Lara walking toward the garage with the portfolio she used when she went to her art class. She was glancing impatiently at her watch.

He thought she looked very beautiful. She was wearing a short green dress that showed her legs to the knee and a little hat that hugged her head like a cap. Her stockings caught the sun and reflected it—gleaming like armor. Everything about her costume called attention to itself. He didn't like her going to the city alone, it was a dangerous place.

Last time he was there buying kite supplies, he'd only had small coins. When he'd tried to give them to the shopkeeper, he'd scattered them, pushed them back across the counter at him, and said, "You must be a Jew. Only a Jew would try something like this. Get your pennies offa here." He'd had to wander around looking for someone who would take them. But when he told Lara, she'd only shrugged. "Things like that never happen to me."

Now she was looking into the garage, then again at her watch. He folded his newspaper and walked quickly over to her.

"I wanted to show you something," he said, noticing she'd put something on her eyes to make them bigger. "There's been another piece in the *Frankfurter Zeitung*. See!" He held it out to her, folded to the page. "Another incident of antisemitism. Quite alarming."

She glanced down for a second and then looked back into the garage.

"What is Otis doing in there? Polishing the hood ornaments? Just when we're going to the station. Johnnie, look, I'm sorry I can't concentrate on that now. I've got to catch the 9:05 train or I'll be late to my class."

He rattled the paper. "A synagogue was defaced. It's almost sure it was the National Socialists—or their sympathizers." He lowered his voice, "They scrawled NDS on the front door."

She made a gesture of dismissal and for a minute he felt like shaking her the way he had when she was little and wouldn't play.

"Oh Johnnie, it's bad and I'm sorry about it, really. But that's Germany—we don't even have family there anymore—it's not New Jersey or New York."

"It could be," he said darkly. "I told you about the man in the kite store. He'd have liked to hit me in the face, I could feel it."

"He was angry because you gave him a handful of pennies. I would be too. Don't exaggerate." She touched his cheek lightly but he could tell she wasn't paying attention, was just thinking about getting away. "This is all out of proportion."

"He called me Jew. He would have liked to beat me up, the way they beat up Jews on the street in Frankfurt. What's exaggerated about that?" He slapped his open hand with the paper. "It's just a matter of time."

Otis backed the Chrysler out of the garage and Johnnie could see the relief on Lara's face. He'd have to find a better way of convincing her, he thought. She was a visual person. Maybe if he showed her the pictures. Distilled hatred that went right inside you. He imagined opening his book of cartoons and showing her page after page, watching her face pale as she finally understood.

But now Lara was turning her head restlessly with its green hat—like a bird about to take flight. Johnnie needed to make her pay attention. He had to draw her to him again by some gesture that she couldn't refuse. They were standing in front of a rough wood bench at the edge of the gravel path. He sat down, pulled Lara close to him and leaned his head against her breast. He heard her heart flutter. Yes, this was the way, he thought, his eyes filling with tears. Her hand rested an instant on his hair, then he could feel her tense. "Johnnie, no, you can't do that," she said, pulling away, "we're not children anymore." She straightened her dress, not looking him in the eyes, her face flushed. He stood up rubbing his cheek where it had rested against the silky fabric. His lips trembled. He felt as if she had struck him.

"Lara," he stammered, "I didn't. . . ."

"It's all right, John John," Lara said, her voice coming at him from some cold, distant place, "I'm not mad at you." She patted him lightly on the shoulder. Then she opened the car door, jumped in and let down her motoring scarf, wrapping it around her eyes and mouth. He could no longer see the blue vein beating in her throat.

Good, he thought grimly. That's how he'd keep her. Veiled. If the Jew-haters didn't see you, they couldn't hurt you. Though it was a warm clear day, he felt chilled. He drew his head down between his shoulders so as not to see Otis and Lara driving off.

❧4❧

Lara took the train from the Princeton station, settled down in her plush seat with Dorothy Parker's latest book on her lap—she didn't feel like reading—and tried to put Johnnie out of her mind. One good thing, maybe the best thing, about having a monthly allowance was that Lara could afford the little studio in New York. Even though it annoyed her mother, it gave Lara a space to be alone.

What she liked about the train was the succession of images framed by the large windows. But this time the dairy farms with red barns and cows standing at the salt licks failed to have their usual soothing effect. She felt restless and, since no one was sitting on the seat opposite her, she opened her portfolio and started to look through her latest sketches for her portrait of her father. She'd hoped that after a few days of not looking at them they'd seem better, but they didn't, and she still couldn't figure out what was wrong with them. The features—high brow, deepset eyes, patrician nose with high arching nostrils, thin mouth under the brush of moustache were all there, the proportions seemed right, it was carefully drawn, she'd gained technically in the past weeks, but somehow it failed to add up.

She shut her portfolio and after an indefinite space, neither country nor city, saw the industrial smokestacks and factories that signalled the approach to New York.

The train drew into Penn Station and she got down into the swarming mass of people. It felt good to be anonymous for a while, buoyed up by the murmur of voices under the great glass dome. She had tea in the station restaurant, then took a cab from under the covered ramp uptown to 57th Street, to her art class.

She got out of her cab across the street and looked at the building for a moment before going in. It had a handsome Renaissance façade with three arched windows gracefully set off by Corinthian columns over the main door. Above the highest set of windows, three decorative tablets were engraved with the words Painting, Architecture, and Sculpture.

"Note the Roman candelabrum," said someone behind her. She jumped. It was her life drawing teacher. He must have been at least fifty, had onion breath, and she was sure he dyed his hair. Besides, he was boring. She dutifully noted the candelabrum.

Inside, she took a place next to her friend Mina. The model, a young woman with bobbed hair, came out from behind a screen where she'd taken off her clothes, and sat down, twisting partially around, so they could draw the complicated curves. Lara wanted to get her engines started, energize herself, but the broken planes were hard to get and the woman's pretty, vapid face, smirking toward them over her shoulder, was annoying.

While she sketched the model's thighs—with red chalk— she kept seeing images of her father: reading his history books in the study, smoking, isolated. Even if I can't seem to finish his portrait, I should do something for him, she thought. He liked monuments. Maybe she could do a series of epic paintings— battles, cavorting horses. "Highly patriotic" the obituary had called him, noting with satisfaction the officer training class he had taken at Columbia to prepare "for any demand his country might make." She pictured her father walking admiringly past a succession of monumental canvases hung high on a white wall.

Her eyes moved up the woman's body, measuring the distance from shoulder to hip, and suddenly she imagined a frieze of women sitting waiting for their men's return from war, holding the dead bodies of their sons. The unasked-for images irritated her. She pressed her chalk so hard it broke and she had to take a fresh one. Why was it women were always waiting? Suffering? Why couldn't she think of anything else? She felt the life drain out of her lines. And in an attempt to recapture it, went over and over her drawing, changing the position of the arms until the woman looked like the goddess Kali with a hundred arms.

"You can do a lot better than this," the redheaded teacher told her, tapping with his pointer at the smudges and erasures.

She glared at him. "Don't you ever have bad days?"

"Start again. You've got another hour. Look!" He took out a sheaf of drawings from the portfolio he was carrying around with him. "This is what you should be doing. The line should be smoother, clear." His lines were clear all right. His woman looked like a vase or a still life of pears.

"I don't see her that way. Her body's really quite fluid. . . and then there's that imbecilic face."

"Imbecilic? She's a pretty girl." He stuck one of his sketches of the girl's face in front of her. "Pert nose, bowed mouth, good eyes, small chin. What's your difficulty?"

"The face is all makeup and pose. It isn't her." She saw the look of genuine bewilderment on his face and shrugged. "Forget it. Maybe I need glasses." Lara wanted to explore the contrast between the bored, empty face and the fluid, teasing lines of the body. It seemed to have an energy all its own that the face denied. Besides, it was sexy. Arm touching breast. The enticement of the red-brown nipple was honest in a way the bowed mouth wasn't. When the teacher had moved on she took another sheet of paper and started again. This time she drew a simple oval for the face and left it vacant, made the body more abstract. She wished she had her crayons. What it needed now was color. In her excitement she didn't even notice when the teacher came back until she felt his breath on her neck.

"We're trying to learn a craft, Miss Kamener. We're not surrealists, not modernists . . . not à la mode. I'm afraid, Miss

Kamener, you don't think learning how to draw correctly is worthy of your efforts."

Lara saw Mina looking at her sympathetically and grimaced. God, she hated him. She concentrated on the spot at the back of his head where the hair thinned. He had combed a long strand over to cover it. She longed to twitch it aside. Imagined him standing with it dangling ridiculously by his ear. The ironic part was she wanted so much to learn. She took her chalk and sketched in the woman's insipid features.

Mina leaned over to her. "I have a new teacher," she whispered. "I had my first lesson last week. He'd be perfect for you."

"He couldn't be worse than Red Wig," Lara whispered back. "pompous ass."

"Well, Gorky isn't pompous, he's wonderful. . . ." She hesitated. "Though he's hard."

"Who cares, if I learn something. This. . . ."

"Shh." Mina scrawled Gorky's name and number on a piece of paper and slipped it to her.

Before Lara left she crumpled up the sketch she had made and threw it into the big bin by the door.

Mortimer picked her up after class and drove her off to Coney Island to have one of their discussions. He was an enthusiast of the Socratic method, felt, in fact, it was the only way to teach. He made Lara into a seminar of one.

He was as ill-favored as Socrates, she thought, with those thick lips, but she liked the passion he put into education and was intrigued by the sheer number of things he knew. She had never succeeded in finding a subject he hadn't thought about. When he was only a college student he had gotten unlikely candidates through their doctoral exams by anticipating the key questions. And it wasn't just what he knew; it was the way he managed to hold all the disparate chunks of knowledge in his mind and find out how they related. His aim—if she understood it rightly—was to organize everything we know into a graspable (and therefore teachable) whole. It seemed a heroic undertaking.

"You would have enjoyed my honors seminar today," he said as they wove their way out of the city. "We were discussing the morality of a modern art form—the movies—and whether society was justified in restricting it. My students couldn't seem to grasp the fact that the principles for making prudent judgments about censorship have been around since Plato. If you just add Aquinas for the Christian dimension and Rousseau for the democratic, you have all the tools you need to deal with the problem."

"Didn't Plato banish poets from his Republic?"

"And painters." Mortimer gave her a shy look. "He thought of them as corrupters of the young. Societies have always banned things. The Christians banished the pagans, the Puritans banished Restoration comedy. Well, today there are people who want to restrict the movies." They were passing over the Brooklyn Bridge and with a wave of his hand he drew her attention to the masses of steel mesh and gave a brief history of the engineering feats involved in its construction. While she was still considering this, he returned to describing his seminar. "One of my students took the Sophist position that all ethical systems are based on shifting mores—there are no absolutes. He got quite passionate about it and ended up by defending pornography. I thought there was going to be a riot. Then another student took Plato's position that moral relativism is a denial of reason. They went back and forth with the utmost engagement. It was really quite a perfect example of how the Socratic method works."

"What was the upshot?" Lara asked. "Will your prudent man shut the movies down? I hope not. I like the visual effects."

"We reached a compromise on what is basically an insoluble problem. The prudent man shouldn't interfere with content or technique—but though he can't tamper with the artist's soul, he can regulate the product for the good of society."

"No obscene movies for underage children?"

"Exactly."

"Shall we discuss the aesthetics of the movies?" he asked her when they had changed, set down their bags and were spreading out their towels. "That's a whole other topic. Or are you in the mood for something more outré? Brancusi's goldfish? Goya as a satirist? African sculpture?"

Lara, narrowing her eyes so the sea and sand made a pleasing blur, thought of asking him where intuition and relaxed attention fit in his scheme of things. But she didn't feel like making the effort.

"You did bring our notebook, didn't you?" He looked at her big bag and smiled when he saw the top of her leather folio. "Of course you did." It was a large folio made of Florentine leather that she used to keep track of all the conversations she had with Mortimer, by name and number. She was up to fifty. He reached over and caressed the leather lightly for a moment, running his fingers over the embossed fleur-de-lys and the stitching around the edges. It gave him an immense feeling of power to have her recording what they said.

"You know, Mortimer, I don't think I'm up to a Socratic dialogue today. I'm feeling like hell, in fact. At the rate I'm going, I'll never have enough paintings to show by next year. No direction. . . ." She waffled her hand, tacking to and fro.

Mortimer was struggling to set up the umbrella against a stiff breeze. "Why get into this competitive stuff? Let *us*"—he meant the men—"have the ulcers. You have a beautiful place to paint. Enjoy it."

He might be a genius but he was so stupid sometimes. "Mortimer. I'm 25 years old. I'm invisible. I need to be seen."

He ducked out from under the umbrella and squinted at her. "You're an art work, yourself, in that black swimming costume. Who else would wear black with white . . . what are they, thunderbolts? It's bold, it's beautiful." Mortimer was conscious of her swelling hips and full round bottom, her small breasts pressing gently against the fabric. The contrast between breasts and hips excited him. It reminded him of the mysterious statue of a hermaphrodite in the Villa Borghese museum. "I can't take my eyes off you," he continued fervidly. "Honestly, I can't stop thinking about you."

"Well, stop for just a few hours, can you? I love your muscular brain, but sometimes a woman needs something else." Suddenly she got up, ran to the water that was foaming softly against the sand and filled her bathing cap with water, ran back with it spilling over the edges and poured it next to her towel.

"What on earth are you doing? Have you gone bonkers?"

"We're going to do sand sculptures. Go fill your cap. Go on." His legs weren't badly shaped, she thought as he scurried off and she followed with her cap. Pale and too thin from under-use but not bad. Carrying his own cap, even he seemed to loosen up a little. It's hard to be serious when you're running in the hot sun with water splashing on your legs. She dumped out her water and ran back to the foaming edge, scooped, went back faster. She heard him beginning to puff. She laughed.

"That's it. You've got some pink in your face."

"It's the heat. I'm bushed." He collapsed next to the moistened sand. "If it weren't for you I'd never exert myself at all, you know."

"And I probably wouldn't read philosophy."

"So we're good for each other?"

"That doesn't logically follow." She drew an oval in the damp sand with two fingers, loving its slightly gritty squeaking resistance. "Come on, help me. This isn't a time to go blah." She dropped her hands and let her shoulders sag, showing him how he looked.

"I haven't the least idea where to start."

"Here at the most important point." She mounded up the center and made two round holes at the bottom, so it looked like a fleshy broad nose. "It's yours."

"Not very flattering."

She sketched two lips with her finger, keeping her eyes on his face. He put his hand up, covering his lips which were large and bluish. "Hey!" he said behind his hand.

"Alright. You don't like being looked at any more than I do." She rubbed it out and started again, made a dog's head in half relief and a paw. "If you don't want to sit there and model you've got to work, make the back legs."

"I feel silly."

"Try." She took his hand and guided it, pressed it around the sand. His fingers resisted fastidiously.

"What's the matter?"

"It's wet . . . I don't know . . . I don't like it."

She sketched a jaunty tubular shape under her dog's belly where it joined his leg. Made two round shapes next to it. Setting it off. Then grinned at him.

"Have I got the scale wrong?"

He shrugged, turning violently red.

She made it three-dimensional, piling on sand. "Since you don't know, let's give him an immense one."

"Oh, really!" He looked around nervously to see if anyone was watching.

"It is quite convincing, isn't it? If I had a funnel I could rig up a spout."

Mortimer turned away from her and lay down on his towel. "Spoilsport." She turned him over and patted warm sand onto his thigh. "If you won't help me you're going to be punished. I'm going to bury you alive."

He brushed the sand off weakly but she kept scooping, covering him with warm sand, patting and smoothing. After a while he got an erection, pulled her down and kissed her and she thought this time it was going to work. But though she felt his erection pressed against her, his mouth was nervous and dry. He wouldn't open his lips to let in her tongue. She took him by the shoulders and shook him lightly, willing him to loosen up but it was no use. He couldn't get the grace notes. Trills and complex harmonies were just not there. After a few more awkward moments of pressings and pushings, as though sheer will would make some epiphany, he got up and went down to the water to wash off the sand.

❧5❧

The next day, Lara came on Muriel strolling around the lawns with the little patient—at least that was who she assumed the child was. The girl was slender, with pale, almost translucent, skin and blond hair that rippled down over the shoulders of her blue dress ending in a mass of almost white curls. Baby curls, Lara thought. She looked more like an elfin escapee from a Celtic fairy tale than a disturbed child, an enchanted princess waiting to be released. The mysterious child skittered off when Lara approached then came back—hopped rather—and leaned against Muriel's hip.

"Why don't you join Robin and me?" Muriel said. "We're just ambling around, then maybe we'll take a swim."

"Would you like to see the far pastures? I'd be glad to show you the path. The wildflowers are better than they've been in years because of all the rain. Or the apple orchard?"

"It's probably better to work from the center out," Muriel said, meaning it's too much for Robin, "for now anyway." So they kept to the perimeter of the house. They saw the vegetable garden in the back, with its freshly sprouting rows of corn and peas just beginning to stretch out spidery tentacles to their poles. They investigated the potting shed that smelled of moss and clay and had always comforted Lara as a child. When they reached the old maple on the side of the house by the roses, Lara clambered up the wood steps nailed to the trunk and disappeared into the leafy branches shielding the platform.

"This used to be mine," she called down. "It was a perfect station for spying." She parted the leaves. "Would you like to come see?" she asked Robin. Didn't all children love secret places? The child didn't respond. Her blue eyes slipped past Lara's shoulder, seemingly caught by a sunbeam that brightened the leaves when the breeze moved them. Chastened, Lara climbed down.

They went on walking slowly, covering the grounds. Muriel pointed out interesting looking things as they went: bugs that puffed out when you touched them, a caterpillar with gold fur, a butterfly that resembled a leaf. Lara didn't see how she could keep doing it with such cheerful naturalness when Robin never gave any sign that she noticed. Lara tried to imagine having Robin as a child. A nerve started twitching under her eye. She'd probably lose her temper the way her father used to with Johnnie. Shake Robin until her teeth rattled.

Now the child put her head under Muriel's cotton sweater— it was long and loose—and seemed to be trying to burrow her way in. Muriel didn't seem upset or embarrassed. She simply undid the bottom buttons and draped one edge around Robin's head like a cape.

Robin started softly patting Muriel's breasts. Muriel let her. No, really, that's too much, Lara thought. There has to be some privacy. It was as embarrassing as watching someone having sex. But it wasn't really sexual, she decided. It was more the way a baby would pat, kneading and stroking his mother's skin.

"I think it's pool time," Muriel said, putting her arm around Robin. "How about it, my fine bird?" Lara thought for a moment of excusing herself—she could see her mother on the other side of the garden—but she was inexplicably curious.

The pool was set at the top of a little rise with a small bathhouse at the back and looked over the wheat fields surrounding the carefully trimmed lawns to blue hills.

Muriel dug into her canvas sack and pulled out suits, along with a cap, ear plugs and the snack she'd apparently brought for afterwards. Then she took Robin over to the bath-house. But the child crouched by the door and started to whimper in alarm.

"I'll go first, then," Muriel said calmly. "Can you stay with her for a minute?" Lara nodded though she wasn't at all sure she wanted to. What if the child took a flying leap into the pool or decided to run away? She could see herself bounding after her over the plowed field. Muriel went into the bathhouse and left the door ajar so Robin could see her. Then she took off her sandals, her slacks, her shirt. The child stood a little way off and pretended to be studying a broken flagstone, but Lara could see she was watching Muriel intently. When Muriel's hands began tugging up her suit over her thickening belly, Robin lifted her head and frankly stared. Her lips were pulled back in a sort of grimace. Odd the way she kept her mouth open, Lara thought, as though she were afraid to bite someone. Mr. New Baby would be Lara's guess. Or didn't her thinking go that far?

"You can pat my belly, if you want," Muriel announced as she came into the sun. "There's a baby growing in there." Robin reached forward, as though she were going to touch, and then shrank back, whimpering. Lara felt her own muscles tense. Watch out, don't let her punch you in the stomach.

But nothing happened. After a minute, Robin turned her back, squatted down and picked up a handkerchief with a big tear down the front of it. Lara recognized it as the smudge rag for her charcoal. It must have fallen out of her overalls. Robin was pulling at the torn place. She looked at Muriel questioningly.

"It's alright," Lara said. "She can tear it. I need a new one." She gestured to the child, miming something ripping, "Go on, go ahead." Robin didn't show that she'd heard her, but she tore a little way and then stopped, frightened of her own daring.

"That's the first thing besides my belly she's shown any interest in," Muriel said.

"I have some extra pieces, from a cloth collage I was mak-ing, some squares in different patterns and textures. They'd be a lot more pleasant to handle than a dirty rag."

"Perfect. I have a huge basket. We'll put it in her room."

Muriel tried, again, to take off Robin's dress and this time the child let her. "I'll have to get her some play clothes," she said, half to herself, "shorts and polo shirts." Lara looked at the beautifully ironed dress. Robin's mother had probably sent a suitcase full of them, to go with Robin's perfect hair. She reached out spontaneously and helped Muriel pull on the bright blue wool trunks over Robin's slim hips. The child made no move to help them, just let her body be manipulated as though it were a dead lump. Muriel fingered the halter and put it aside.

They sat together on a step in the shallow end. Muriel cupped her hands and splashed water gently over Robin's legs. Lara took off her sandals and sat on the rim cattycorner and splashed too. It was nice having everything slowed down, restful. She liked having to sit still and repeat a simple motion. The sun was warm on her shoulders and the smell of newly mown grass came to her from the pool edge. Idly she noticed the gentle swell of Muriel's stomach, the way it rocked back and forward changing position as she bent and how the curve of her cupped hand echoed it. Both curves contrasted with the angular stick of the child's leg. The motion of the lapping water brought them together.

Robin reached over and began patting Muriel's thigh and belly. She did it the way a blind person would. Trying to learn the language of another body. Robin moved her own arms and legs, as though they were sticks attached by glue rather than live parts of a single creature. Lara wondered whether the child had the concept of a single body at all, or just of mysterious fragments: knee, thigh, belly. The hand continued its tentative patting.

Muriel scooped up Robin and slowly walked into the water. The child gasped as they went in deeper. Muriel stopped and spoke soothingly to her, rocking her back and forth. Robin reached up, put her arms around Muriel's neck and held on. It looked like the spontaneous gesture of a normal child, Lara thought. But then she looked at her face and saw how frightened she was. It was a reflex gesture. Somehow it reminded Lara of Mortimer. Scared stiff. Lara didn't want a child. She'd be too afraid it would be deformed, a monster with two heads or some vital organ missing. Or the Kamener specialty, a skewed mind. Muriel bobbed slowly up and down.

At first Robin hung on tightly, giving small worried squeals. But then she seemed to relax a little and Muriel laid her down gently in the water, supporting her with her arms.

"The water holds you up, if you trust it. Do you want to learn to swim?"

Robin clutched her again, like a monkey. She's no fool, Lara thought, she knows the water could just as easily drown her.

Muriel sat down on the steps again with Robin in her lap and moved her pale legs in a kicking motion. "The water feels nice on your skin," she said. "It's warm, almost like a bath." She clearly hoped Robin would start kicking by herself, but her legs were stubbornly inert. Lara began to feel restless. She needed to stand and stretch, get back to her drawing. She eyed her sandals on the pool edge.

Just before Lara got out, she noticed Robin give what could be interpreted as a kick, pressing one small foot with a barely perceptible movement against the water. Lara had such large expectations for herself, but maybe with children like Robin hope took on entirely different proportions. Muriel looked as if Robin had flown the Atlantic single-handed.

That night, Lara woke up from a dream of bats skittering in her mother's closet, making horrible scratchy sounds with their claws. It was so real that she was tempted to go into her mother's room to look. She went into the big bathroom that separated her room from Agnes's and Johnnie's bedrooms, peed and washed her face and neck with cool water. By that time, she'd gotten out of the terror of the dream and contented herself with standing outside her mother's door and listening to her light snoring. Then she went back through the bathroom to her room, which she'd painted a strong yellow the day they moved, and down the funny twisted stairs to the dining room with its graceful polished table and breakfront. Agnes had wanted to duplicate the big house in miniature but Lara had begged her to take only the less fussy pieces, and except for her bedroom, Agnes had agreed. Grieving made her more pliable, Lara thought with a twinge of guilt.

It was actually pleasant to wander through the rooms. The living room—which would have fit in a corner of the old one—had a nice sofa with a cherrywood frame, comfortable chairs, and a small mahogany desk at the window that looked out at the kitchen garden. Lara passed back into the dining room and veered off into the small kitchen where she sat on what Catherine called her cookery stool and ate a piece of her chocolate cake. Afterwards, feeling much better, she went back up the crooked stairs to bed. When she woke up again in the morning, the maple tree outside her window was flailing it with its branches—a sound that she half recognized from sleep—and rain was streaming down the panes.

Later, Lara sat with her mother in her bedroom while they ate breakfast from identical wicker trays. Every time she came into this room, Lara thought, it depressed her. Though Agnes's bedroom was half the size of the old one, she'd kept the big fourposter and as much of her furniture as she could stuff in. The effect was as if the walls were gradually squeezing shut. She pictured them closing with a vicious snap on the bed.

Lara was asking for a small loan so she could get a daybed and a cheerful rug for her New York studio. Her mother wouldn't see why she needed them: "There'll be lovely things left over from our move."

"You're quibbling," Lara said, squeezing the juice angrily from her grapefruit half and popping the cherry into her mouth. "It doesn't seem fair when I'm so careful about money and you never even ask the cost of things." She didn't even keep her household records straight. Eugene had done all that.

"I don't have a head for figures."

"I don't either but you can learn. You don't even try. Look, Mother, please, I'm going into New York tomorrow, I could drop into Bonwit's and order the fabric." The wicker sides of the tray constraining her legs made her feel as if she were in a cage.

Agnes fingered one of her crochet squares in the basket between them, purple velvet curled round a vibrant orange center.

"I've always given you what you needed for your work," Agnes said, looking bewildered, "French crayons, oils—not the cheapest either—but this seems frivolous."

"I want something with clean lines and a Sonia Delaunay fabric. Is that so strange? You have all sorts of risky color combinations in your afghans. That purple and orange for example. It's pure Matisse."

"But the sofa I offered you is a museum piece."

"I don't want it," Lara said. The thought of its heavy curlicues made her skin itch as if she were going to break out in hives. She had barely convinced her mother not to install it in the cottage. "I want something modern. Why is that impossible for you to understand? I don't want my studio to look like Queen Victoria's drawing room."

"What do you have against Queen Victoria?"

"Mother! Everything!"

Agnes pursed her lips. "Besides, you've already gotten Sol to advance you I don't know how many months' allowance for a car."

"I need that, Mother. I can't be dependent on Otis driving me around. What do I do if he's busy and I have a train to catch? This way I can drive myself in for my lessons."

Johnnie opened the door a crack and peered in, looking like a ruffled bird. His hair flopped damply over his forehead and a button was coming loose on his jacket.

"You're arguing. I hate it when you argue," Johnnie said, his face drawn. "I'll go outside."

"It's nothing. We're done. It's finished. Really, sweetheart," Agnes said. Then, flapping her hand, "Go to my purse, Lara, it's on my vanity, and take what you want."

Lara removed her tray, swung down and found her mother's bag among the clutter of perfume bottles, silver-backed mirror and brushes, and bowls of potpourri. As she slipped the money into the pocket of her silk dressing gown, she saw Johnnie's eyes skimming over her hips.

"Did I spill? What are you staring at?" She looked down at herself.

"Nothing," he mumbled.

"Come in, love," his mother called in her siren voice, patting the bed. Her fingers made a little indentation in the quilt, a coffee-colored nest.

Lara gave him an inquiring glance. She was never sure what mood he was going to be in. Yesterday he'd been beside himself about some political murders committed by the National Socialists in Vienna and she'd spent nearly an hour letting him talk to her. But this morning he didn't have the brooding look he had when he was obsessing; he looked slightly apologetic. He sat down obediently on the quilt.

"Have some steak, Johnnie dear," Agnes said, "I can't finish mine and it's really delicious."

He toyed with the fringe of his mother's robe, tapping it so that it swung back and forth under her arm as she tried to cut the meat. "I've eaten already."

Agnes pouted. "I asked Catherine for steak because I knew you were coming for breakfast. And she thought of giving you Father's ale. Taste the steak at least, to please me. Mmmmm." She pursed her lips, offering him a morsel on her fork. He took it, chewing it slowly so as not to take another and looking at the place where Lara's dressing gown had opened slightly showing the faint swell of her breasts.

Lara drew her gown shut and sat rigid.

She felt waves of heat behind her eyes. "You did always need to be coaxed, John," she said, whacking the top off her boiled egg with the blade of her knife.

"That's right." Agnes smiled as though this petting and spoiling were a neutral topic.

Lara made a feint at her mother with her fingers splayed like claws, "grr," then scooped out the egg white from the severed top, salted it and reached over her mother's lap to poke it at Johnnie. "Have some nice eggie, John John."

"Hey, quit that. You know eggs make me sick. That white stuff particularly."

"It's not really slimy and it's very good for you." Lara wiggled the spoon and a little viscous drop hung over the edge.

"Lara," Agnes took her by the wrist and pushed her hand back, "stop it."

Lara sucked the egg off her spoon with a slurping sound. "Well, go ahead. Feed him yourself." Then she caught a glimpse of herself in the bedroom mirror, cheeks flushed, lips curled back. God, what am I doing, she thought, disgusted by her look of childish petulance. I'm as bizarre as Johnnie. This room is getting me down. For every hour I spend with Mother I lose a year. She pictured herself steadily shrinking until she floated in a sea of amniotic fluid, and choked on a laugh.

"Enough nonsense," she said, putting the spoon down and pushing the hair off her face. "I don't know about you, Johnnie, but I think this family needs a little outside entertainment. What do you think of having the new tenants over to tea next week?" It would relieve the claustrophobia.

"Why? They seem to have settled in alright without our attention. Besides I don't much like strangers."

"Well, then, we won't do it," Agnes said quickly. "You're right, darling, there's absolutely no need."

"Don't be so quick to defer to him, Mother," Lara said, putting her hand on Johnnie's arm. "Most friends were strangers once. You miss a lot if you won't even give people a chance."

"I don't like their clinic idea," Johnnie said. "Who knows what odd experiments they'll do? Inject monkey hormones into people—things like that. God knows what they're already doing to that child."

"From what I've seen, Muriel is doing nothing more malevolent than taking her swimming," Lara said. "They're analysts, not Frankensteins. Come on, Johnnie. They're nice people."

He furrowed his brow. "Oh, psyching is all the rage in the Village now. Freuding parties where you tell each other your dreams and analyze the way a man holds his cigar. I wouldn't go near an alienist myself."

"It might do you some good," she said.

"What do you mean by that crack?" he asked, reaching out and running his finger along the piping on her gown, near the throat.

She brushed his hand away. "They help people with mental blocks. It might make you more productive. That's all I meant."

"Johnnie is working on his formulas," Agnes said primly. "It's very taxing and he needs understanding, not criticism."

"Let them come to tea if it would please you, Lara," he said, raising his eyes slowly to her face. "But I still think analyzing how a man holds his cigar is a lot of bull. . . ."

"Johnnie!"

"I'm sorry, Mother. Baloney. Is baloney better?"

"Not much. At least it's not nasty but it's still slang."

"They're fascinating people," Lara went on, ignoring her. "You know Muriel comes from one of the big Chicago meat-packing families. Well, she told me that when she was in college she decided she hated material possessions and gave her things away."

"That sounds remarkably foolish," Agnes said.

"Everything?" Johnnie asked, beginning to sound interested. "Like a saint?"

"Just her furs and jewels, things like that. She wanted to burn her books but at the last minute she couldn't, so she sold them to a library and sent the proceeds to starving Austrian students."

"It sounds like your cousin George." Agnes put the breakfast tray to one side. "Preaching socialism and living on an inherited income. She's still rich enough to afford to take over our house."

"She decided it wouldn't do anyone any good if she lived in a hut with no water," Lara said defensively. "She's really an extraordinary woman, Mother. And it will be fun when she has the baby."

"Is she Jewish?" Johnnie asked.

"Dammit, John, do you have to bring everything back to that? Just because we are." Lara saw a look of horror on her mother's face. She made a point of never mentioning their Jewishness.

"We're not Jewish, Lara, not anymore. You know that. We go to church like everyone else now." She motioned fiercely toward Johnnie, meaning don't talk, you see how it disturbs him.

"It's not me that's making him worry about it," Lara said. "If anything, it's your pretending. . . ."

"Well, is she?" John repeated.

"I think not, but David is," Lara said, then added, looking defiantly at her mother, "his father ran a kosher deli in Chicago."

"That's nice," Johnnie smiled, "a love match between Jew and gentile. Mixing races, mixing people—classes too—is the only way we're going to get rid of all the hatred that's building up in the world."

He looked as if he were having an ecstatic vision. Maybe he was imagining some wild purifying rite to make the world less brutal. Lara thought of the frightening cartoon images he'd showed her of hooknosed, hideous Jews. Maybe he was imagining a giant bonfire. Or the birth of a Savior. A little mixed-blood Christ. She looked at him with a kind of despair. Why couldn't they have five minutes of normal conversation together? With a start she realized that she wasn't even sure what ordinary people talked about in private.

6

Lara went to Gorky's studio on Sullivan Street and climbed the little staircase with her canvas under her arm.

When she saw him again, she was just as impressed as she'd been when she met him at Mina's. Foreign, dark, huge, vital, he was like an explosion of everything other. But above all, he could paint.

"Is that yours?" she stammered, setting her painting down by the door. Some paintings looked like the Cézannes she'd seen in Paris, others like the Matisses. She couldn't believe that she was seeing this in New York.

"All is mine here," he said simply. She looked closely at a drawing etched in bold sharp lines, crosshatched—a still life with a Greek head. It seemed uncanny that he was working in this way when most Americans hadn't even heard of Picasso. "Did you see Picasso in Paris?"

"No. In magazines." He looked bemused. "And prints do come to 57th Street galleries, sometimes." His teeth were very white under his black moustache.

So he did what she did—walked through the galleries seeing everything, searching for the one work that would speak to him. He copied but not slavishly. His copies weren't imitations.

He was learning to speak Picasso's language. "I'd like to see more," she said, dizzy with what she'd seen already, "but it looks as though you have them stored." The entryway to the studio was crammed with paintings stacked against the walls three or four deep.

"That's alright. I know just where they all are. If I want to work on something, I can get it like that." He snapped his fingers.

He's not like a bohemian, Lara thought. The studio itself was scrubbed clean. The floor had the bleached quality of drift-wood. The palette on a table by the window had a low-lustered sheen. The brushes, flat, round, worn or new, were clean. Everything suggested a care for his materials.

While he searched for the canvases he wanted to show her, she studied him. What dramatic looks he had—that great height, the long black hair, the moustache, the soulful eyes. She imagined him modelling for her, wearing the velour hat hanging on a peg near the door—she'd pull the hat down low to emphasize his black eyes—and the long black overcoat.

He lifted out a canvas from the back. "This is a portrait of myself with my imaginary wife."

The man's dark face was tilted down. He had blue-black hair like Gorky, the same long, low-bridged nose and sensuous mouth. The woman's face was ivory. "She has inscrutable eyes," Lara said, wondering what had made him draw the two figures so isolated. Their heads were touching but each seemed preoccupied.

"She sees through things," he said cryptically, turning over another canvas. "This is a study for a portrait of a young boy with his mother."

"You?" The boy was wearing a coat that came to his knees, dark, close-fitting trousers and slippers.

He nodded soberly. "The red slippers were my father's gift to me when he left for America."

The mother, her head and neck covered in Middle Eastern fashion, had the staring masklike face of a Picasso *saltimb-anque.* "She appears to be looking backward into the space behind the canvas. Your women seem to be seers."

"I wanted her to be solid in the midst of things that are flowing. I wanted both permanence and change."

"Is that why you've painted the hands like that? To give them weight?" They were white and circular, without fingers. He nodded gravely. "I think I see now," she said with increasing excitement.

"Early work," he said with sudden impatience. "Too soft. What I am doing now"—he gestured at the boldly etched still life—"has more clarity, more form."

Lara swallowed hard—she loved the rich evocativeness of the early pieces, and her own new work was intensely colored—but he cut her off. "I think we shall be able to work together, that is the important thing. Now let me see what you have brought me."

Lara retrieved her canvas from where she had set it near the door. She had thought of bringing him the preliminary sketch of her father's head but decided that she didn't like it enough to show him. Instead, she'd brought him a painting of her father's chair and footstool with his pipe lying on the chair. She'd painted it impressionistically with clearly defined brush strokes and heavily laid-on paint. When she was finished she was pleased. The slightly electric colors she had chosen gave a sense of something eerily absent from the scene—as though her father were both there and not there. But now, setting it on the easel, she was suddenly afraid he'd say it was overdone.

"Good, you've chosen something simple," Gorky said, standing back from it, "but you're relying too much on color to give you a sense of form. And you've placed your chair in the space without thinking what impact it would have. What does it do to the curtain, or here?"

He squeezed some gray-green paint out onto his palette and started painting over her chair in quick strokes, changing the contours, painting out most of her light effects and toning down the color.

"Do you have to do that?" she sputtered. "Couldn't you just tell me what's wrong and let me do it?"

"No, I can't. Words are confusing. This is easier, faster. If you're too sensitive for my method. . . ." He paused and shrugged his shoulders.

"Don't worry, I can take it," she said, wondering if it was worth it. Mina had said he was 'hard' but that was scarcely the right word for him. The man wasn't just patronizing, he was pushy.

"Then. . . ."

She saw that he was making the drapes swell out, echoing the curve of the chair back, which he had made more pronounced and distorted slightly so you seemed to be looking at it from two angles at once. The background was now a complex hourglass shape, as interesting as the chair itself. What's more, the whole composition had a unity it hadn't had before.

By the end of the hour she was exhausted, as much by her conflicting feelings as by the effort of absorbing what he was teaching her. Going back on the train, she went over his comments on her defects, grimacing and biting her lip. What made him think his complex shapes were more important than her light effects? She'd been overwhelmed by his dexterity, that's all.

"I think we can work together," he'd said in that patronizing way, as if he were a prince and she was . . . she couldn't think what. Well, what if *she* didn't think they could work together?

Her head was beginning to ache. She closed her eyes and lay back against the seat listening to the clackity clack of the wheels. Behind her eyelids she saw him shifting the outlines of the shapes. Painting with a sureness she couldn't begin to imagine. He's amazing, she thought. Be honest. Don't be a fool. Let yourself learn something. Suddenly she saw a new image of her father's face. For the first time she sensed the possibilities offered by the curve made by her father's close-cropped hair against his skin. It swept away from a slight peak in the center in a rich half circle then came to another little peak and curved back toward his ear. I've been too literal, she thought, tried too hard to copy him literally like a photograph. She opened her eyes and stretched, feeling her muscles relax.

As soon as she got back to the farm, she called to arrange for another lesson.

7

Agnes was feeling well this morning. For the first time since Eugene died two months ago, she'd opened her eyes with a sense of energy. The rippling curtain blown by the breeze at her window reminded her of the folds of the dress Lara had worn to the opera last night, one of those new ones that were short in front and had diaphanous trains in back. She had a sudden urge to take Lara's picture.

"Did you have a good time?" Agnes asked, when Lara finally came downstairs and had had her coffee—she could be cranky in the morning if things hadn't gone as she planned. "Was *Tristan* wonderful?" Lara and Mina and a group of their artist friends had taken standing room only.

"It was alright." Lara stretched and yawned. "The soprano's over the hill though."

Agnes looked at her to see if she meant to be insulting. Probably not. It was just her unconsciousness of anything but her own ambitions. Lara's face always wore a slightly pouting expression. Despite that, Agnes couldn't stop looking at her. She'd taken a marvelous photo of her last year naked in the bathtub and another in her coat with a fur collar and that turban, looking up from under her lids, her lips half smiling.

"Will you let me take your photograph?" she asked. "I'll call it The Young Artist."

"Well, if it'll get you to use your camera," Lara said, putting her cup in the sink. She pretended not to like posing but Agnes had seen her looking raptly at the results. She liked the way her mother saw her. Agnes went to the closet under the crooked stairs, got out her old bellows camera with a tripod and brought it into the center of the living room.

"Could you put on your green brocade, dear?" she said as she set up her camera and checked the light. "You know, the one that's cut like Isadora Duncan's tunics."

"I'd hardly paint in that, Mother. Why not my smock?"

"It doesn't need to be literal. It's just a study—the brocade has such beautiful texture. You stay right there." Lara had plumped down on the sofa with a bored expression. "I'll get it." She went upstairs to Lara's room and came back with the dress over her arm.

"How was the lesson with your new teacher?" she asked nonchalantly as Lara slipped out of her painting overalls and pulled the dress over her head. Agnes restrained herself from referring to him as 'the Armenian giant with the black moustache.' That would be sure to annoy her, make her think Agnes wanted to know if she was attracted. People didn't understand how hard it was to have a daughter.

"Do you really want to know?"

"Of course I do."

Lara narrowed her eyes at her. "You don't just want to find out if he went with us to the opera? If we're having an affair?"

"I'm always curious. You know that. But I'm not snooping. I really want to hear. Now put your arm up a little more." Agnes liked the sight of the dark, curling hair caught in the hollow between the brocade and the white white flesh of the arm. "Close your eyes until they're almost shut. As though you're dreaming. Good."

"It's exciting to be taught by someone who knows what he's doing," Lara said, giving herself to the pose. "And he loved my new work."

Agnes just wanted Lara to keep that expression. It was perfect. "The landscape with the pond?"

"No, a still life . . . you haven't seen it. I've been playing more with planes and surfaces."

Agnes thought of the sketches she'd seen everywhere in Lara's room, faces done in cubes and squares, eyes and noses at all angles. If this was how she was planning to do her father's portrait, it wasn't going to be recognizable. She moved away from the camera and pushed back Lara's hair to expose her ear. It was amazing how perfectly shaped it was, small, like a shell. "Hold your wrist with your other hand so your bracelet shows." Agnes bent and peered at the upside down image of Lara.

"And close your eyes again. You've lost that dreamy expression. Stay perfectly still. There!" She clicked the shutter. "I've got it. Why shouldn't he like your work?" she said finally. "You have the prettiest colors. So feminine." To her surprise she saw Lara flinch. Now what?

"Please, Mother. Feminine isn't an adjective of praise in painting these days. He liked the forms, they had elegance and energy. He said my painting was strong."

"Sorry," Agnes said. "I always seem to say the wrong thing, don't I? What can I do to atone?"

"Forget it, it's not important."

"It obviously is."

Lara dropped her arm and rubbed it. Then she got up and took a few steps toward the door.

"Lara, where are you going? Don't just walk off like that. I said I was sorry. If you took the time to explain things to me I'd understand them better."

Lara walked back slowly and sat down.

"I don't know why I never have this sort of misunderstanding with John."

"You don't say things to annoy him. You make an effort."

Agnes knew she shouldn't talk about John when Lara was irritated but she felt suddenly anxious, something clawing at her heart. "There's some girl in the city, isn't there? Is she at all suitable?"

Lara gave a short laugh, "Probably not. I haven't seen her."

"I asked him to bring her for tea but he didn't want to."

"Maybe he's afraid you'll stand on your head the way you did when I brought Mortimer over."

"I was showing him my yoga posture."

"And your bloomers."

"Why are you so mean?" Agnes felt her hands shaking against the camera.

Lara looked away. "You irritate me . . . on purpose."

Agnes pulled down a fold in the tunic so it hung like a dark banner, a triangle of black under the white arm. She knew she shouldn't let Lara get away with this sort of thing but she felt that there was some justice to what she was saying. Maybe she had spoiled her.

"Close your eyes."

"I don't want to. I'll look dead."

"Not dead," Agnes said, "sleeping." She thought of walking through a minefield where every step was dangerous. There was no point in saying, I really don't mean to irritate you. There was no point in saying anything more. She shouldn't have mentioned Johnnie.

8

Lara was sitting in the garden with her sketch pad and watercolors. She'd been trying some more abstract sketches of her father's face, concentrating on the curves and planes, but she was too tense, too conscious of doing something different for it to really work. Maybe if she turned her attention to the birch tree in front of her, and left her imagination free to improvise, she'd go back to her portrait refreshed.

Picking out a small brush, she dipped it in the container of water at her feet, rubbed it over a block of soft brown. Working quickly, she made the broken clods next to the silver birch with its chameleon leaves. She always thought she was going to remember what colors she had used but she didn't, so she labelled every part of the sketch. Madder, ochre, pearl gray.

When she looked up, she saw Robin watching her with fascination. Muriel had told her that when Robin grimaced she thought she was smiling, and that Lara could ignore her or talk to her if she felt like it. The girl was wearing another blue dress and Lara was struck again by her startlingly white skin and delicate features. She was twirling a piece of her hair around her finger. The illusion of ethereal charm lasted until she started to walk. She moved in short hopping steps as though she were some kind of wind-up toy. When Lara looked up, she moved away and stood with her finger in her mouth.

Lara sensed it would be better if she didn't look at the girl. "You can watch me if you want," she said in a low voice. "I like having an audience." She thought how she would tell Mortimer, "Art's best audience these days is in insane asylums." Later she'd tell him. There was something frightening about seeing a person who had all the attributes she had—body, face, hair, even beauty—but who couldn't get comfortable with them. The girl threw her arms up as though she were surprised to find these appendages hanging from her shoulders. Still the eyes, when she caught them accidentally, were—Lara kept searching for the word—the only word to describe them was hungry.

Moving very slowly so as not to startle the girl, Lara began to sharpen a pencil. Yellow no. 2. Then she tore a sheet of paper off her pad and put it on the ground. Then she turned her back and pretended not to notice when the girl crept up and looked at them.

"This is for you." Lara sharpened another pencil with her knife. "Come on, you don't need to be afraid." She held it out but Robin only whimpered. Lara stroked her pad with the flat side of the point and made a thick line, then she made a thinner one. Just that, thinner and thicker. The girl watched, then hesitantly put her hand on Lara's wrist. As though she were reading braille, she let her hand feel the movement Lara was making, softer than a bird's wing. She stood with her eyes closed as if she were blind or hearing music, with an ecstatic look on her face. There was something infinitely touching about it. The girl made soft guttural sounds in her throat.

Without thinking, Lara drew an oval for a face.

The girl suddenly snatched the other pencil and jabbed awkwardly at the center, making a small dot. An eye? Do you want to make another? No? The girl was shaking her head frantically. Lara didn't have the slightest idea of what was going on but it seemed that they were communicating.

Lara looked at the paper again, letting her mind move freely. "Oh, I see," she said, excited, "it's this." She rapidly sketched thighs and legs under the oval, making it a belly.

"Or maybe this?" She drew another quick sketch (with her soft pencil on the creamy paper), this time of two big breasts. Robin drew back her lips, showing her teeth like a cornered animal, then began scribbling frantically over one of the breasts.

"Good," Lara encouraged her, "you're helping to color it in." She could hear the child's breath and feel the tenseness of her body as she leaned over, pressing against her shoulder. Robin kept scrubbing at the paper with her pencil, holding it in her fist.

"That's nice, you're filling in all the space, you don't want any white to show." The girl didn't respond. She kept on grinding the pencil to and fro almost as if she were in a trance. The paper was wearing thin in spots, in a few seconds it might tear. Lara felt an uncomfortable sensation in her stomach. "It looks good. Very strong, Robin. I think maybe you're finished. What do you think?"

The child was gasping as though she couldn't breathe. Raising her arm, she brought the point of her pencil down, making a round hole right in the center of the blackened breast. She stabbed it a second time. When Lara tried to stop her, she began to scream a sort of high thin wail, more like a dog howling than a person. Lara jumped up, the pad fell from her lap. I can't run away, she thought, but god, what can I do? She was afraid to touch Robin, who still had the pencil clutched in her fist. Just then David and Muriel opened the gate to the yard and ran toward her. In a moment, Muriel had her arms around Robin. The child collapsed like a pricked blowfish and lay limply against her. Muriel had no trouble taking the pencil away.

David steered Lara back to the folding chair, his arm around her shoulder. "Are you alright? Did she hurt you?" he asked. "You look as if you've seen a ghost. Here, sit down." He half pushed, half lowered her into the chair. "Do you want a glass of water?"

"Please, don't worry about me. Is she," she gestured at Robin, "having some sort of crisis?"

He glanced over at the girl, who had hidden her face against Muriel's shoulder. Muriel was rocking her gently and crooning to her. "Looks like she's retreated again," he said. "She disassociates when things get too much for her." As he watched, Muriel picked Robin up.

David got to his feet to help, but Muriel motioned him back. "You stay with Lara and find out what happened. I want to take her back to the house and see if I can feed her some chocolate. She let me put some in her mouth the other day. I don't want her to think she's done anything bad or that I'm angry with her."

"I hope I didn't make her worse," Lara said, looking at Muriel swaying slightly as she walked slowly toward the house. "She seemed so interested in the shapes I was drawing, I gave her a pencil. I felt as though we were doing it together." She bent to retrieve her pad and held it out to him.

"She did this?" David asked, his face intent.

"I drew the outline. She did the black."

"That's fantastic. A black breast."

"What does it mean?"

"You really want to talk about it now? You've had quite a scare. Sure you don't just want to rest?"

"I'm used to unbalanced people, there are a lot of them in my family. Suicides. An uncle in an institution." She stopped herself from saying, my brother. "I thought he was disgusting. But I don't feel that way about Robin. I understood the effort it was costing her to come near me and I relaxed my skin."

"You what?"

"Relaxed. People are so closed, they are always sending out messages: don't touch, don't disturb. I didn't want to shut her out, that's the only way I can describe it, I wanted to invite her closer. When she took the pencil, I could see her trembling."

"She was taking a risk—you too. I'm impressed by what you did."

"So you see, I want to know what she was trying to tell me. Why she made the breast so black. She scribbled so hard she tore the paper."

"Well, Muriel would say the black means something harmful or hurtful to her. She was showing you that this is a bad breast. It doesn't give good milk." He made a wry face. "It's almost too perfectly Freudian, really. Just the sort of thing you'd find in the textbooks. Then, of course, because the breast isn't satisfying the child stabs it with her pencil."

"But she didn't look angry exactly. She looked terrified," Lara said.

"The standard explanation would be that children like Robin can't distinguish between words—or drawings—and real things. So when she was stabbing the drawing, she thought she was hurting her mother's breast."

"What a strange idea! Though it makes a certain poetic sense. Did her mother treat her badly?"

"She was sick when Robin was born and had to stop breast-feeding." He stopped, glanced down at his knees, then up at her. "Look, I could go on all day with this but to me the only thing that's certain is that Robin has a terrific rage that needs to be discharged. And you've helped enormously in getting her to express it. If you hadn't been here with your drawing pad, it might have taken her weeks to let out this much." He smiled at her. "I have a more practical approach than Muriel. Oversimplified, she'd say. But I like results."

Lara noticed he was looking at her mouth. She rubbed her lips, not liking him to see they were quivering. "I wouldn't mind letting Robin come sometimes and watch me paint if you think it might do some good."

"Are you sure? After what just happened, I wouldn't want you to get hurt."

"If Muriel is nearby, I'd feel fine."

He lit a cigarette and blew the smoke out of the corner of his mouth, away from her. "Think it over. You can always change your mind."

"I should read some more Freud," she said abruptly, "know more about what the theory is. I've dipped into his lectures." She paused, remembering what she'd read about childhood sexuality. Maybe symbols could be overinterpreted, but that seemed real enough. "Those lectures gave me almost a physical sensation, as though I were being blown open by a high wind."

He looked at her curiously. "I can lend you some books if you like. The *Interpretation of Dreams*?"

"My artist friends are always talking about his dream book."

"They'll be on your doorstep tomorrow. Now I should go and see if Muriel needs any help."

Lara got up quickly. "Sorry. I should have thought."

"And you should probably go lie down for a while."

"I've got too much going on in my head. You know, when Robin was scribbling, I felt something so fierce about her—as though she was defending some last internal stronghold. As if, if that goes, everything is lost and she'd have to die."

He nodded. She noticed that he had patches of gray hair on both sides of his temples.

"I have an image for it," Lara said, "no words, or rather, a color, a core of silver. Just that, all the rest dark."

"A spiritual x-ray," he said, touching her lightly on the throat. It struck her that he was taking a reading. What would an x-ray see in him, she wondered, besides his restlessness and his differences with Muriel.

9

Johnnie thought over the things he had done for Merle since he'd met her in the Old Turk coffeehouse on MacDougal Street. He'd brought her a cord of wood for the small stove in her Greenwich Village apartment. Stacked it outside the door so she would find it when she woke up in the morning. He'd gotten her some amber beads she'd liked in a window, taken her kite-flying, and now he was going to buy her a bird.

The shop was hot and steamy as a jungle, filled with the smell of sawdust and seed, rank. Cages were stacked one on top of another to the ceiling, each filled with birds clamoring for attention, making a constant blur of wings and color.

He stayed in there for an hour staring first at one bird then another, unable to make up his mind what to get for her. In the center of the store, a multicolored parrot walked to and fro on a small platform, rattling its chains and calling out cheerful greetings, "Hello Matey. Pretty Polly." Johnnie was caught by the idea of teaching him to say "Love you, Merle."

He imagined Merle's sleek dancer's head thrown back in surprise when she heard the bird speak, her eyes wide. Then would she smile? She'd been smiling less and less lately. Saying she had to rehearse and couldn't meet him anymore for coffee.

He thought of her thin lips—so like Lara's—and suddenly felt anxious. What would those words mean to her, coming from such a strident creature? The curved yellow beak looked cruel. It looked as though it wanted to bite.

But maybe Merle would like that, find it fascinating the way she had the lion at the zoo. She'd paced up and down outside his cage, imitating his soft stride, wanting to dance it. He'd told Lara about it.

"Just what you need, a primitivist," she'd said, and made a face. Tried to find out "how far he had gone."

"She looks a little like you," he'd told her, thinking that would please her. He didn't tell her that they'd never even kissed.

The parrot gave a squawk and he imagined him flying to Merle's shoulder, digging in his claws, biting her white flesh. No, he could never rest with that bird near her. Even thinking about it made him break out in a cold sweat.

Their first meetings had been so nice. She'd flirted with him, said he was cute. "Isn't he a sweet boy?" she'd asked her roommate.

"I don't have a sweet tooth," the roommate had said. She was a tall dark-haired woman with slanted green eyes.

He moved away over the sawdust-covered floor between the rows of cages to where a troop of tiny finches twittered on their perches, flicking seed with nervous beaks. He thought they were exquisite, but the blood red of their breasts made them look as though they'd been wounded. He closed his eyes, stroked the soft fur of the rabbit's foot in his pocket and concentrated on Merle's image.

Merle was a little smaller than Lara, more slender in the hips, and had a cap of smooth black hair. He wished that Merle had Lara's soft lustrous brown hair with its auburn highlights and the faint smell of perfume that came from underneath. Merle didn't wear perfume and, unless she was dancing, didn't wear makeup. Ordinarily he had trouble deciding in the morning what to wear or whether he needed a haircut. But this choice was infinitely more important. If he chose wrong, it could ruin everything. Set up the wrong vibrations. The bird was like a message. It was a message. It had to tell his love without words, to show they were still in tune. Johnnie wondered how people could make choices so cheerfully, saying almost without thinking, "Yes, I'll take the green scarf." Or, "No, I must have the red." Every time he made a choice, it was as if he were choosing among three caskets and one was death.

He loved Merle so much that he stuck it out even though his head hurt. Let himself hear the emanations each bird was putting out, looked into those bright black eyes. Finally he chose the canary because of its song that kept going higher and its pure yellow color like the buttercups that he used to hold under Lara's chin when they were children. Buttercups were Lara's favorite flower.

He tried to call Merle from the store but the line was busy so he decided to walk over to her place. She'd always discouraged him from picking her up at the apartment. He hoped she wouldn't mind. He walked over slowly, delaying the pleasure of the surprise, holding the cage carefully under its thin paper wrap. He passed a pushcart seller in a white apron offering ice-cold lemonade and hot franks for five cents apiece. He could hear the bird scuffing and pecking at his seed tray under the paper. The sun was getting hot—it was one of those days with hardly any breeze. He walked under a gunsmith's sign. The huge revolver swinging out over the street reminded him of the National Socialists. Maybe later in the afternoon he'd go over to the 42nd Street Library and see what new magazines had come in from Germany.

He stopped at a barbershop to call her again but the line was still busy. When he finally got to her apartment, in one of the few small houses between lofts, the door was opened by her roommate. She seemed annoyed to see him.

"Whatever it is, we don't want it," she said with a flash of white teeth. She had a deep husky voice that reminded him of Marlene Dietrich.

"It's for Merle," he stammered. He saw Merle's triangular face peering from the bedroom door.

"I tried to call," he said. The walk-up was very small but neat, and the walls were decorated with paintings and photographs of the tall woman with slanted eyes.

"Merle's always talking to someone," the tall woman said.

"Are you slandering me, Raquel?" Merle's voice was mocking.

"Not at all. First it was Martha about the show, then the upholsterer, now your new friend with the mysterious parcel in brown paper."

He held it out to Merle, his hands trembling. Merle took it, looking all the time not at Johnnie but at Raquel.

"Merle, thank the man for his gift." Raquel's voice had an ironic tone that Johnnie didn't understand. "Honestly, sometimes I think this girl didn't have a mother."

"I have one now," Merle said. "A double whammy swinging mother." That seemed to be a private joke and they both laughed. Johnnie was glad to see the tension go out of Merle's face. Now maybe she would look at him and smile.

She undid the paper slowly. The minute the bird saw light he began to hop on his perch and chirp. "How lovely, but why?"

"Because you are like buttercups," he thought but couldn't say, so he hung his head. A few minutes later, he excused himself and left.

∽10∾

Lara was sorting through her childhood books, looking for bright pictures to show to Robin. Despite herself, she'd become painting teacher for a wild child who wouldn't even pick up a brush. Muriel brought her over for a half-hour every morning simply to watch her paint. It was slightly bizarre, but Lara found it actually helped her get started. She smiled, thinking of how Robin would stand transfixed, watching the paint ooze out of the tube onto the palette. Her attraction to bright colors was encouraging Lara to use a more vivid palette even though Gorky would often urge her to tone it down.

Lara finally selected a child's history of Alsace, a book of famous paintings of cats, some colorful geographies, *Babar* with its playful exuberant figures, Barrie's *Peter Pan*, *Grimm's Fairy Tales* and several beautifully illustrated books for younger children. She imagined Robin taking the picture books to bed with her. Soaking in healing influences. Excited, she put them in a twine bag and set out to look for Muriel. David was standing on the path in front of the big house in work-overalls, smoking. "Muriel's over at the pool with Robin," he told her.

"I wanted to give these to her for Robin." She held the books out for him to see. "Even if Robin only pats the pictures, I thought she'd get something out of them. I'm convinced she notices outline and color."

"Really?" He blew out a curl of bluish smoke.

"I painted a bright red chair yesterday, with a strong black outline, and she got very excited. It was the first time she really paid attention. Usually she just twiddles. I have the feeling that pictures are more real to her than the real things."

Lara noticed David looking at her through the faint haze of smoke. She was all in white—white slacks and a linen shirt.

"That's a fascinating thought," he said. "Do you think you can get her to paint? She has the manual dexterity. She's done some simple block building and a lot of tearing things to bits," he said, making a wry face, "but painting would be a real means of communication."

"I want to. I tried giving her a pencil but she only bites it or moves it back and forth in front of her face. Maybe the pictures in the books will stimulate her."

David dropped the butt of his cigarette on the gravel path and ground it out with his heel. "I've got to get back to the craft room, now that I've had my smoke. Why don't you walk me over? It would be a nice place for you to paint when it's finished."

Otis was mowing the lawn in front of the water tower. They waved and went on to the game room; Lara hadn't gotten used to calling it the craft room yet. When they went inside, Lara saw that David had broken holes in the pine-knotted wall to thread new wiring. The small openings made the familiar room look unfinished, like a room in a dream. There was a ladder positioned under a gray steel box on the ceiling. Lara put the books on the table next to his open tool box.

"I loved these books," she said, spreading them out in a fan, "they saved my life when I was a child. I didn't go to school until I was nine because my mother thought crowded rooms weren't healthy. It was my people substitute."

He followed her to the table and looked over her shoulder for a moment. She was staring at the flyleaf dedication to *Les Gourmandises de Charlotte*—"from Mother to her Lara, Christmas 1908."

"Well, you're no child now," he said, taking out his screwdriver and a roll of tape and putting it in his overall pocket. "You're a woman of the world."

"I probably was a spoiled brat, anyway," she said.

"Probably." He gave her a quick mischievous smile.

"That's not very nice. I was going to tell you how my mother read me about Charlotte being thrown out and attacked by rats just because she wouldn't drink her soup." She thumbed through the book, and stopped at a picture of a little girl lying on the floor in a tantrum, kicking her feet. The next page showed her mother getting a bundle of switches from the family doctor.

"And what was I going to tell you?"

"Oh I don't know. Just sympathize and tell me it was a marvel that children trust their impulses at all, when they're threatened with punishments like that."

He smiled and she noticed how his eyes changed color from gray to brilliant blue. "Well, there! You did it for me. Now can we forget about nursery tales for awhile? I'm sure you don't spend time telling your other friends about Charlotte and Babar."

"I thought analysts liked talking about people's childhoods."

"Nope. No special penchant. Not on off-hours anyway."

"Really?" she asked, surprised. "But there's Robin and . . . you're having your own child soon."

"Having a baby doesn't make me more inclined to talk about childhood. It makes me hungry for adult life. Soon Muriel will be up at all hours, feeding, changing diapers. I'll be hearing about nothing but teething and formula. People aren't born parents, you know. They're born pleasure-seeking mammals."

"You can still go out and have fun," she said.

"But you have to plan. It kills spontaneity. Anyway, changing diapers is one thing; I'll get used to that." He screwed up his face in a way that suggested he wasn't looking forward to it, "Probably even get to love the little bugger, but I'd rather talk about electric circuits. Negative and positive poles. Live wires." He reached over and picked up the white globe at the end of the table.

"How about helping me for a minute? I'm just at the point where I could use another pair of hands."

"Sure," Lara said, "What do I do?"

"Take this," he said as he gave her the globe, then quickly clambered up the ladder, "and hand it up to me. You'll have to come up the ladder. Are you afraid of heights?"

"Me?" she said mockingly, "I'm half bird. When I was two, my nurse caught me just as I was going to jump out a ten-story window."

"Did you think you could fly? In that white get-up you look more like a snow leopard than a bird."

"I was sure of it." She moved her arms rapidly like a bird taking off. "I was flapping my wings."

"I wanted to fly an orange crate in the war," he said, following her with his eyes while she climbed the ladder below him and held up the glass. "But somehow I ended up in the trenches."

She noticed a muscle jump in his cheek, then another under his eye. "What was it like?"

He didn't answer for a minute. "It wasn't romantic, wasn't pretty like a Rupert Brooke poem. A lot of mud, constant shelling. The inaction was the hardest part. I liked it better when we had some action. Even hand-to-hand combat is better than squatting in a trench, waiting. Can you hold it while I attach the wires? Is it too heavy?" She shook her head and watched while he quickly stripped the insulation from the ends of the wires in the box, then reached down to her and stripped the ones inside the fixture. He motioned to her to hold the globe higher and she moved up another step, leaning against him slightly to keep her balance. She could feel the warmth of his legs. He smelled slightly of sawdust and paint thinner.

"Did you kill anyone?" she asked, straining to lift the globe over her head so he could join the wires.

"Two or three that I'm sure of, probably more. It's funny, you get used to death after a while." While she watched, he tied the bare ends together, took the roll of tape out of his pocket and taped them together. "At one point we even used corpses as sandbags to shore up the trenches." He put the fixture against the ceiling and started screwing it in.

She backed down the ladder. "I can't imagine getting over being afraid."

"Everyone's afraid, except for a few kids who read too many cowboy stories. They were the first to get hit. Being a little afraid can actually help you. It sharpens your senses. Every time I crossed the enemy lines to reconnoiter, I expected a bullet. . . ." He shrugged.

"Were you a scout?" she asked, imagining him crawling belly down under barbed wire.

"We took turns."

"You were lucky you weren't wounded." Hadn't Muriel told her he'd been in a war hospital? And was writing a book about shell shock?

His face darkened. "Actually I was, but it was just a surface wound. A grenade exploded near me. My best friend was blown up. After the explosion, I thought I was wounded, I felt all this wet stuff on my face. I kept touching it and looking at my fingers before I realized that it hadn't come from me. It was him, literally splattered all over me, blood and bits of bone. I spent hours picking bits of him off my gas cape."

He coughed. "Sorry, I didn't mean to get into the gory details. . . . I had a touch of shell shock, trouble seeing. They put me in the hospital for a while . . . warm bed, clean sheets, three meals a day. Before I could get out and go back to the front, the war was over."

Lara had a feeling there was a lot he wasn't telling her. "Johnnie had a friend with shell shock. He lay curled in a ball with his hands over his ears for weeks."

"It was rough going, at first. I couldn't remember anything, but I woke up screaming from dreams of being torn apart. I hallucinated corpses walking around my room. It didn't matter to me that the doctors were telling me I was safe. I was in a state of terror. A psychiatrist who'd been trained in London came in every day and talked to me, tried to convince me that the only way I'd get my sight back was by remembering what happened, that not being able to see was a reaction to an intolerable situation. I hated him at first. Every time I heard him coming, I'd turn my face to the wall. But somehow the doctor got through to me. He was a very decent man. I remembered and got better. Muriel thinks that's why I decided to be a psychiatrist."

"It seems paradoxical, getting men well only to send them back to die. Usually you think of getting people well so they can function—like Robin."

"I'm glad I'm not working in wartime. I don't think I could have persuaded men that they were able to fight again. After all, losing vision was a protective device, even if it was unconscious. I didn't want to die. Having that experience made me understand anxiety neurosis the way nothing else could have. When I saw my first patient, a girl with hysterical paralysis, I had a shock. I saw myself. I knew firsthand that emotions can be as lethal as chemical poisons. I'd become blind because I couldn't stand what I was seeing. It was the same with her. "

"You could have gotten mean and bitter. You could have had contempt for anyone who hadn't suffered the way you did."

"Well, I did. I had to work very hard to change it in myself." He grabbed her by the wrist, pulled her toward the door.

"What are you doing?"

He laughed and put her hand on the new light switch. His voice reverted to its ordinary charming, bantering tone. "I want you to turn it on."

"You do it, you did all the work."

"Come on, to make up for my not looking at your books. For my talking too much about myself."

"I wanted to hear."

"What else could you say? You were a captive audience. I meant to impress you and I ended up telling you my war story."

"That's OK. Hemingway gets boring."

"Good." He pressed her hand slightly, guiding her fingers, and she flipped the switch.

❧11❧

Johnnie was on the top of the pool hill adjusting a kite strut when he saw Muriel and Robin walking in the field below. After a while, in which they seemed to be looking for crickets in the long grass, they came up and Robin edged toward him, twiddling her fingers together. Then she squatted down next to him, observing him intently, still twiddling.

"Hey," he said softly. "What if I do that? And give you a chance to help me with the kite?" He began to twiddle his own fingers in front of her face. She slowed down and stopped. Tentatively she reached out a hand and touched the kite strut.

"That's it," he told Robin, as she touched the formulae he'd written along the struts in red paint. "Now that your hands are free you can fly it. Pick it up. Go on."

Robin slowly raised the kite. She held it awkwardly, her arms didn't seem to move easily, but still she held it and he could have almost sworn she smiled at him. He kept twiddling, bent over a little toward her while he told her how to lift it up.

A gust of wind took the kite right up out of Robin's hands and Johnnie gave a shout.

"Don't be scared," he said as Robin jumped back. He took the spool and pressed her hand around it, then started backward, letting the string unreel as the wind took it and the kite bucked and plunged.

"She's got a natural talent," he said to Muriel. "I'd let her do it alone but I don't want to take the risk of a crash. You don't mind me helping you?" he asked the child who was nestled against him like a cat.

"Look at it," Johnnie whispered to her, as the kite tugged against their fingers, "it's dancing. All the particles that make up its body are shimmering and melting into the air. Do you see? The air is opening and closing. Everyone should learn kite flying," he said, turning his face slightly toward Muriel.

"It's certainly exhilarating to see it swooping and soaring."

"It's more than that. It's a sign that a free existence is possible. Despite what I read about today." He suddenly wondered if it would be possible to make Muriel see it. Wasn't it her job to understand things other people couldn't?

"If you just look at the facts, you see how it's starting to add up," he said, holding her eyes. "Acquitting the Nazi murderers in Vienna, Dolfus. Now the elections in Germany. Terrible!"

If Lara had been there, she would have shushed him. She hated him to bring up his theories in front of other people. But Muriel didn't seem shocked, she seemed interested. She looked at him steadily with her eyes that were like gray pools.

"Your reading of the German elections seems quite sensible to me," she said. "David and I were talking about Germany's move to the right this morning at breakfast. There was an allusion to it in this morning's *Times*."

Well, at least she read it, he thought. Though it clearly wasn't as important to her as it was to him, she had taken note of it. He smiled at her. It was a beginning. He musn't alienate her by telling her everything too soon. That was the mistake he'd made with Lara. This time, he'd be more discreet.

"My sister thinks I exaggerate," he said, pausing to uncurl Robin's fingers enough to let the string out as the kite gained altitude, "but it's just that I pay attention to things that are happening outside and Lara doesn't. Yesterday when I was coming here on the train I sat behind two businessmen and I could hear them talking all the way between Penn Station and Princeton Junction."

Lara would have been thinking about her painting or looking out the window but he made himself listen because he sensed it was important. "Do you want to know what they said?"

Muriel gave Robin a brief happy glance, then turned back to him and nodded.

"They said, whenever there's a cover-up on the Street, you can be sure a sheenie's behind it." He paused. He hadn't meant to go on but he couldn't stop himself. "Anyone can see the destruction that's coming."

When he'd said this to Lara she'd told him it was absurd.

"Encounters with bigots are always disagreeable," Muriel said mildly, "but just because someone says a Jew cheated on a business deal doesn't mean there's going to be a wholesale slaughter."

"It's happened before," he said and then he made himself stop. He didn't want to see her eyes narrow with disgust the way Lara's had.

"If everyone flew kites," he said, helping Robin play out more line, "it would dissipate some of the hatred that tugs our souls down." Maybe if he was patient, Johnnie thought, he could bring Muriel around.

~12~

Moonlight was flooding through the window of Lara's room when she woke. She tried to get back to sleep, counting pebbles, feathers on a bird, but the light making everything look different excited her and finally she got up, pulled on her clothes and crept quietly down the stairs and out the back door. The lawn looked like a shimmering lake, the great trees islands of darkness. She made her way slowly over to the pool, wanting to see the moon on the water. As she got near, she heard the murmur of voices. After a minute she recognized David's voice, rough—and Muriel's, more clipped. "It was wonderful," she heard Muriel say in a tone that could only refer to lovemaking. Lara felt goose bumps on her arms despite the warmth of the night. I shouldn't be listening, she thought, but she slipped around behind the bathhouse and stood in a shadow where she could see them.

Muriel was lolling on her back totally nude, the swell of her stomach boldly outlined in the moonlight.

"I want a round house someday," Muriel said, "no straight lines, all curves and round windows like portholes."

Lara looked around for David, then she saw a match flare and made him out sitting on the other side of the pool. His knees were drawn up but Lara could see by the band of white flesh on his thigh that he was also suitless. He was smoking his usual cigarette.

"I need more of your time," David said in a voice Lara didn't recognize, full of yearning. "This isn't turning out the way I planned."

Muriel said something that was covered by the sound of the water slapping.

"Why are you always so reasonable?"

Muriel swam toward him. Lara could feel his discomfort and Muriel's almost palpable tenderness.

"David, love," Muriel said, and Lara saw her reach up and stroke his leg, then pull gently at his foot. "Don't be glum. The night's too beautiful. If you didn't want the clinic, you should have told me. . . ."

David gave an exasperated sigh, twisted away from her and dove to the bottom.

Lara walked out of the shadows. "Muriel?" she said, hesitatingly.

Muriel swam over to the edge. "Are you a night owl too?"

"I couldn't sleep so I thought I'd see what the moonlight made of the flowers. I found one I'd never seen before that opens at night."

"They're almost like ghost flowers, aren't they?" Muriel asked, looking at David who had surfaced under the board at the other end of the pool. "So papery white."

Lara felt awkward. It was hard to act natural after hearing the secret fragments of their talk. "I could never get that white in a painting, it's almost translucent." She crouched down at the edge of the pool next to Muriel. "How's the water?"

Muriel hesitated for a fraction of a second. "Try it for yourself. It's glorious. Still warm."

"It's more fun without suits," David called. He grabbed the diving board and hung under it doing pull-ups.

"If you come in, I'll teach you the correct form." His voice was assured again.

"I don't like calisthenics," she said, watching the play of muscles in his shoulders. The hair on his chest seemed to have incandescent tips, outlining him in silver. The water seemed to suck his body in. She felt a twinge of excitement.

"What do you like?" he asked, his arms taut before he went up again.

He was showing off, but his boyishness cleared the air. Made her feel more at ease. She smiled and crouched down, stirring the water with her hand and watching him covertly. The pull-ups were getting harder for him and he gave little grunts as his arms tensed.

"Things with rhythm, dancing, jazz."

"We should all go to a club sometime," he panted, "it would be fun. Twenty. That's it." He collapsed with a groan.

"Well, are you coming in?" Muriel asked. "Now that David's exhausted himself performing for you."

"It was for both of you," David corrected her. "What more could a man ask than an audience of beautiful women?"

Lara was intrigued by their teasing tone. It implied a sort of tolerance she wasn't used to. Not in married people, anyway. Certainly not in her parents. There was something so free about them—whatever their differences—swimming naked, inviting a near stranger to join them. She could see why David might want her to join him. But why did Muriel? Wasn't she jealous?

"If my mother wakes up and looks out the window, she'll have a fit." Lara waited. David didn't urge her again.

"All the more reason to do it," Muriel laughed. "If everyone went naked, there'd be a lot less trouble in the world."

Lara laughed too. Muriel was more daring than she'd have been. "All right. Why not?"

She turned her back to them and quickly slipped out of her slacks and shirt. She could sense David watching from under the shadow of the diving board. She could almost feel his eyes straining to see her softly blurred contours. She turned, holding one arm in front of her breasts, and jumped in.

She gasped as she felt the shock of the water and swam slowly over to Muriel, who had turned on her back again and was floating in the center. David stayed in the shadows looking out at them, somehow apart. He stayed, treading water. Lara thought she could make out his penis bobbing against his thighs. She imagined the three of them caressing one another.

"I think the baby is swimming inside me," Muriel said into the electric space between Lara and David. "I feel it."

"Mmm," David grunted.

Lara understood that Muriel wanted David to revel in it as much as she did, but that he couldn't. She swam slow circles around Muriel, fascinated by her bulging belly.

"Can you really feel what it's doing?" she asked. "That's amazing." The shape was beautiful. The curve. She thought of painting it in red like a huge red flower. She'd paint the baby inside like an exotic glimmering fish.

"If I get tense, or angry, he kicks or makes fists and hits. Right now I think he's quiet. I think he's sucking his thumb."

David grunted again.

"Next we'll be hearing what he does when we make love," he said. "Play with his little cock." He dove down and swam along the bottom, scissoring his legs. When he came under Muriel, she screamed and went under.

Lara had a moment of terror when she didn't know what was happening. Then she saw Muriel emerge spluttering, her long hair plastered against her head. David was treading water and smiling broadly. He had dunked her, that was all. He hadn't hurt her or the baby.

"You devil!" Muriel started to splash him, hitting the water hard with the heel of her hand, sending up great sprays into his face. "Lara, help me."

Lara splashed too. It was exhilarating. She liked ganging up on him. He was like an angry boy now, splashing first one of them and then the other, furiously. But they kept on laughing and splashing. Muriel dared him to dunk her again but he made feints at Lara, pushing off from the side, as if he were going to throw himself on her, but always falling short. Then he turned over on his back and kicked his legs, deluging them with spray. Finally Muriel attacked him, grabbing him around the middle, and tried to pull him under. He resisted.

Lara joined Muriel, pushing on his shoulders with both hands. She was startled by the warmth of his body under the slippery skin. Suddenly he stopped fighting and she could feel him let go. She watched him take a deep breath and sink, staying down, holding his breath, until she thought he would burst.

❧13❧

When Agnes saw the small knot of people clustered on the lawn to celebrate the 4th of July, life suddenly seemed normal again—people, croquet, straw hats. And Muriel was there in the middle, naturally. She was the kind of person who would have been wonderful at organizing charity suppers, or symphony benefits. Too bad all that energy was going to be wasted on one disturbed child. She really should have that girl intern come in more often to help, Agnes thought, as Muriel strode toward her, still in those shocking pants, and pulled her over to meet her friend Gordon.

Agnes wondered if this was a man Muriel thought would be good for her. Someone to be relied on. If she did, she was wrong. He seemed frightfully old. Agnes hoped she didn't look like that to Muriel. She touched her hair under her hat and wondered whether to color the gray. This Gordon had let himself get stout—always a mistake, it aged men ten years. Eugene had been so trim and dapper. While Gordon wrung her hand, his ruddy face creased into a smile, Agnes wondered about the nattily dressed young man standing behind him.

"Gordon," Muriel asked, linking her arm through his affectionately, "why didn't you bring your son?"

"A country outing is too wholesome for him, I suppose. He's busy hanging out with bolshies and bohemians in the city."

"Gordon, if you weren't such a dear friend, I'd be very cross with you," Muriel said. "I'm more of a Red than Robbie will ever be, and Mrs. Kamener's daughter is a painter."

"That's all right," he said cheerfully, "it's not fatal. She's a woman, she'll probably give it up when she marries."

The young man with Gordon gave a snort of laughter quickly suppressed and Agnes looked at him again. He was strikingly handsome. "Allow me to apologize for Mr. Scott," he said with a slight bow. He spoke in softly accented English, somewhere between French and German. "In my opinion, businessmen should support artists, not denigrate them." He looked at Gordon slyly. "I think we call them names out of secret envy. The artists are living in ways we would like to, living out our fantasies of freedom and beauty. We should be grateful to them. Particularly the women, they risk so much more."

"Bravo," Agnes said. This man not only knew how to dress but he had the right opinions. He had class. She took in his large dark eyes, his perfect classic profile. "You're right, artistic women risk their reputations, their marriages. . . ." Lara was getting a reputation already. Who knows if she'd ever find a husband.

"I don't know how you come up with these things," Gordon said to the young man, "but you seem to have gotten me off the hook brilliantly." He turned to Agnes, "Let me introduce Baron von Hesse."

"Just Walter," the young man interrupted, with a graceful self-deprecating gesture.

"Sorry, I forgot he doesn't like the title—though I admit I enjoy using it."

"Americans still love titles," the young man said softly. "It's amazing in a democratic society."

"Walter is the stepson of a good friend of mine who lives in Austria. He's here to learn my import business." Gordon put his arm on the young man's shoulder, obviously charmed by him. "But he seems more interested in finding new enterprises to invest in."

"America has the advantage over Europe now in that respect," Walter said with a smile that flicked over them all, resting longest, Agnes noticed, on Lara.

"This country is caught in an escalating spiral of greed," David said, with a grimace of obvious distaste. "But be careful. If you make it fast, you can lose it faster."

"I'm not out for a fast buck, as you put it here. I'm looking for investments that have sound value, but with something peculiarly American about them." Walter lit a cigarette with a graceful movement of his hand. "That's why I'm thinking of buying land in Florida. It's the new frontier, absolutely virgin."

"Personally, I think he should have gone into the market," Gordon said. "The Investment Trust has done wonders for me."

"Is Florida as beautiful as they say?" Agnes asked, trying to remember what she'd heard recently from her friend Ruth. "Isn't it full of swamps?"

"They're draining them. It's magnificent. Miles of lagoons edged by gnarled mangrove trees that look like primitive sculptures. Huge birds, alligators. Have you ever seen a baby alligator? They're quite sweet, actually. It's what I imagine the cradle of civilization to have been like. Watery, steamy, filled with color and texture and strange noises. You could buy your own piece of paradise for very little." He smiled at her. "I'm going to go down next week. They are offering free bus tours throughout the state to anyone who will come and look." He laughed. "The food will be free, too. Probably not very good. And the opportunity is priceless. When I get back I'll bring you some literature, if you'd like to see it."

"Yes," Agnes said, "I would." Real estate wasn't something she knew anything about, but she was almost sure her horoscope this month had mentioned heat and exotic places.

They formed croquet teams by drawing partners out of a cap. Muriel drew Gordon, Lara drew David, and Agnes Walter. Agnes slammed vigorously into Muriel's ball and sent it off toward Gordon. She had thought she would feel miserable playing—Eugene had bought the croquet set for her as a present—but she felt more energetic than she had since his death.

His gift was supposed to mean he'd spend more time with her. But of course she knew he wouldn't. Agnes contemplated hitting Lara's ball—the angle was right, she could imagine the satisfying crack as it hit, but at the last minute she decided to go through the wicket instead. She rolled to a stop next to Walter.

"What do you think of that fellow?" David asked his partner, motioning toward Walter.

"Attractive but too sure of himself, too cocky."

"Slick, I'd say."

"I think he's just naturally seductive. He certainly made an impression on Mother. She has a history of being attracted to people with excessive confidence—faith healers, psychics, salesmen. Walter's charm appeals to her."

"And not to you?"

Lara was about to admit to liking Walter's diamond-patterned knickers and matching cap when she caught the look on David's face. "I've got too much of a tendency in that direction myself," she said instead. "I know its drawbacks."

"Good. I was worried about you. He looks like a real womanizer."

"I don't need a guardian. I've been taking care of myself for years."

"Sorry, being paternal is almost an occupational hazard. At least it was when I had a regular practice."

"I can't imagine it would be good for your patients, either."

"Are you having any chance to amuse yourself?" Agnes asked Walter gaily as they started off through the next wicket. Gordon had failed to get back in place after a huge effort, and they were clearly winning.

"I have a boundless appetite for pleasure," he said after his ball came to a stop. He had a way of looking directly into her eyes that suggested complete absorption. "I want to eat in all your restaurants, visit your galleries, see all the best theater." He lowered his voice and took on a softer, boyish tone. "It's not always easy being in a foreign country. I feel I make mistakes, not understanding the culture. Will you advise me, tell me what I should do next?"

Agnes felt flattered and reassured at the same time. He was only a boy, after all. "There's so much—where do you want to start?" She thought of the galleries she had visited lately, the concerts, the lecture series on spiritual phenomena.

"Anywhere. You have such a cultivated life. Your daughter's an artist. Maybe she would . . . ?"

"I don't know if this would interest you," Agnes said quickly, "but I have two tickets to a lecture—my friend couldn't go—by a man who has started a center for Yoga. They meditate in complicated postures. I've heard it's really special, very"— she paused, choosing a word that would appeal to a sophisticated man of the world—"aesthetic. He learned his technique from an Indian holy man, and he's going to lecture on it next Thursday at the country club in Nyack." She could feel her heart racing. "But perhaps you'd rather go to the theater— though of course we can do that too. Or do you think it's silly?"

"Not at all. I'm very interested in subconscious forces of all kinds. They show us things about ourselves that we're missing in our Positivist society. Spiritual fervor, spontaneous passion." He looked into her eyes. "I'd love to go. You're a generous woman, I can see that, besides being very lovely."

"I'm afraid he may not look very prepossessing." She picked at the rim of her straw hat, torn between pleasure that Walter shared her interest—Lara was always accusing her of being an escapist—and fear that the lecture would disappoint him. "I'm told he wears a baseball cap on the back of his head and chews on a big cigar." She looked at him anxiously to see if he'd sneer. Good. He didn't. "But I've heard he can do amazing things. When he meditates he doesn't feel pain. They can stick pins into his arms and he doesn't feel them." She gave a little shiver.

"Like this?" Walter pinched her arm lightly, making her shiver again. "How wonderful you Americans are, bringing together baseball and Indian mysteries. I love it."

She laughed.

"I like your laugh," he said. "I have the feeling you don't laugh enough."

Agnes and Walter won the game. Afterwards everyone changed into bathing costumes except Agnes, who had never gotten used to bathing in public. Especially now when they'd given up covering their legs and had those skimpy one-piece suits that showed every fold and bulge. She sat by the pool nibbling on nuts and watercress sandwiches. Muriel was floating peacefully on a rubber mat—Agnes couldn't see how she could expose herself that way—and David and Lara were taking turns going off the board. Walter scooped up a rubber ball of Robin's and started bouncing it restlessly in front of the table where Agnes was sitting.

"Go swim," she told him, uncomfortably aware of the muscles in his thighs and calves.

"I wanted to be a professional soccer player when I was a child," he told her, throwing the ball in back of him and bouncing it on his heel. "It was all I cared about."

"It's like juggling," Agnes said, wishing she could take her eyes off his body, that he would stop moving it around in front of her. His chest was covered, of course, but there were cut out places on the sides of his suit that made her more aware of the nakedness underneath. "It's so graceful."

"I thought all artists and intellectuals despised sports." He bounced the ball on his head, threw it back again, kicked it up.

She smiled nervously. Her lips felt oddly stretched. "On the contrary, I always wanted my son to be more active—you know, *mens sana in corpore sano*." The Latin had a protective, soothing sound. So did the mention of Johnnie. She felt safely motherly.

Walter bounced the ball around her in a circle. She tore her eyes away from his legs to his waist. It was amazingly slender, she thought, like a young boy's.

"If you like, I'll show you how," he was saying.

"I can't see myself doing that," she stammered, "but I'd love you to show Johnnie, my son. It would be so good for him."

"I'd be delighted."

"Mother," Lara called out from the edge of the pool where she was resting, "you know John hasn't touched a ball for years. Not since he was sixteen and broke his arm."

Agnes got up and walked over to her. "Don't be negative, darling," she said, looking down at her.

"Really, Mother," Lara whispered, fiercely. "You'll only embarrass him. Don't say anything."

"Why, there he is!" Agnes waved vigorously at a figure who was ambling slowly toward them up the rise. "Johnnie."

"Catch!" Walter shouted suddenly and threw the ball toward him. Johnnie put his hands up feebly in an attempt to catch it but the ball hit him in the face.

Lara pulled herself out of the pool, but before she could get to him, David had run over and was mopping Johnnie's face with his handkerchief.

"It's only a bloody nose, John," David was saying reassuringly. "I don't think the bone is broken. Does it hurt?" He was touching Johnnie gently, and it seemed to calm him.

"Not much." Johnnie leaned his head against David's hand for a moment.

David got up. "I'll get some ice."

"That's sweet of you, but it's all right. I'll get it." Lara gave him a quick smile, then turned angrily to her mother. "You and your bright ideas about healthy sports, Mother." She knew that blaming her wasn't exactly just, but she felt this was part of her mother's pattern of unawareness that, in some deep way, left her children exposed to danger.

"I'm terribly sorry," Walter said into the handkerchief-covered face. "I had no idea you wouldn't catch the ball."

"Your mother really seems to take to Walter," David said to Lara, "even after he bloodied your brother's nose." They were back at the croquet course on the big lawn outside the screened porches. He'd seen she wanted to get away from Walter and her mother after the disaster with the ball and he'd offered to help her put away the croquet things.

"I don't think he was a bit sorry, either. He had the kind of supercilious smile I dislike. And, of course, Mother, with her infallible judgement, picks him to play ball with Johnnie." Lara blew a wisp of hair out of her face and gathered up the mallets. "It's so ridiculous. When he was little she never encouraged him to play with other children. Kept him hanging around her skirts."

"Maybe she realizes it was a mistake."

"I doubt it. She likes Walter, that's all. It's odd. Usually she can't see anyone but John."

"Who knows, it might be a relief for him to get a little less of her attention." David pulled out the last of the croquet posts and they walked slowly toward the front of the big house. Lara had a ball in each hand and was swinging them back and forth like a clock pendulum. Red, blue.

David smiled at her over his armful of posts and mallets.

"I certainly felt that way about my mother. She was obsessed with everything I did, no matter how trivial. If I'd let her, she would have looked in the toilet to see if my bowels were moving right. The war was a godsend. It got me away."

They passed the bare place where the jockey statue had been and strolled east along the gravel drive. Lara shrugged. "The proverbial Jewish mother."

"Sorry," he said, looking hurt. "I forget you're in a privileged class. The comfortably assimilated."

"I didn't mean that." She'd have to remember he was sensitive about being the son of a Jewish shopkeeper—probably Orthodox too. She paused, wondering if it was worth the effort to explain.

"It's not just that Mother cared so much. She did, of course, but that's not why she concentrated on him. From the time he was small, she had a kind of selective blindness. She didn't want to have to compare him to other boys. To admit he was different."

"And is he?"

Lara wondered, not for the first time, if David could be a friend. Help her figure out her family's entanglements, fault lines, blood bonds. "You're the alienist, what do you think?"

"He seems shy. A little awkward, but kind." He nodded at the far pasture where Johnnie was silhouetted against the sky with Robin and the young intern, holding a kite to the wind. "Robin seems to have taken quite a liking to him."

"But look at the way she is." Lara cracked her knuckles, liking the definitiveness of the crick, crick.

"Disturbed people have sensitive antennae." He leaned his armful of posts to one side and put his hand briefly over hers, quieting the grating bones. "They can detect fakes better than anyone I know. Maybe Robin notices something we don't, some basic kindness." He opened the craft-room door, walked over to the rack and inserted the mallets one by one in their holes. "And he certainly loves you. His eyes shine whenever he looks at you."

"Oh, that." She felt herself reddening—yes, I guess you could call that love, that crazy whispering in the dark—and bent to put her balls in the bin.

He straightened and looked into her face. "It obviously means a great deal to you. Otherwise, why would you worry so much about him?"

"I'm tired, that's all," she said. She knew she'd never be able to tell him. It was unthinkable. "Most people's love is a pleasure."

"And his is a burden?"

"Exactly," she said. She couldn't describe how it weighed on her. How every time she looked at Johnnie, she felt as though a hand was squeezing her insides.

They wandered out and around the back, past the greenhouse and laundry to the orchard—a grove of old apple trees with gnarled trunks and branches that later in the summer would be bent to the ground with ripe fruit. She snapped off a branch with a still green apple at the tip.

"You're disappearing," he said, moving his hand back and forth in front of her face, "come back."

"What's analyzing people like?" she asked him suddenly. "Does it make you feel you're scooping out the inside of a turtle? Make you feel powerful?" She bit her lip. "I guess what I want to know is, does it do any good? Can you help people who don't even know they need help? Sometimes I feel as if I'm Johnnie's motor," she went on quickly, "as if he can't run without me. It almost makes me hate him."

David let out a low whistle.

"I hate waiting for him to do something crazy, get hurt, crack up." She snapped the apple from its twig and threw it hard against a tree. It splattered, the juice running down the bark between the crevices.

He picked another and handed it to her. "Maybe he's not so fragile as you think." He paused. "Maybe you like to feel he needs you."

"I suppose that's one of your Freudian ideas. But it's wrong. My brother needs a translator to follow a conversation. He can't even catch a ball. Of course I'm worried."

"Lots of mathematicians aren't good at practical things—like daily life," he said.

She gave a weak smile. "If it were only that."

"What else? Some dreadful secret? Tell me. It's probably not half so bad as you think."

"Look at Walter," she said. "The guy isn't nearly as bright as John but that doesn't stop him from knowing what he wants. He's proud of himself, of his looks, of his natty clothes, of his accent. He feels entitled." She took a breath. "Johnnie is inert inside. He doesn't feel he should get what he wants. He doesn't expect it, can't even try anymore. I mean, most people throw themselves into things. . . ." She felt her voice trail off.

"Was he always like this?" They were walking side by side and she felt his shoulder bump hers.

What was she going to say? Look, from the time I was eight until I was ten I let my brother sleep with me. Enjoyed it. Let him snuggle close and whisper sweet words into my ear. It was bad for both of us. Maybe worse for him, it broke his heart.

"He fractured his arm when he was sixteen. It was very bad and he had to stay home from school. Every day when I came home, I'd sit with him and talk, bring him things—a leaf, a bird's egg. That's when I started noticing. Most boys would have been dying to get up, get moving, play baseball. But he didn't mind lying in bed." And she'd been pleased because he was weak now and couldn't bother her, just lay there looking at her with big eyes. What she felt then with a shock was the extent of her power over him and, with it, a sense that she had to take care of him.

"I was looking at some photos of him as a baby," she said. "He was beautiful. Eyes alert, smiling, reaching out his hand. What happened?"

"Look. Paint twelve hours a day, take up fencing in your spare moments, but stop thinking so much about Johnnie."

"Why shouldn't I?" she asked. "He's my brother, isn't he?"

"Your brother has an advanced degree in engineering. Did you go to school with him? Do his homework?"

"No . . . he was always good at that. He's brilliant. But it's what he does with his mind in his off-hours." She gave a little laugh. "He thinks the Jews are going to be persecuted."

He smiled. "So do my parents."

"You don't think it's crazy?"

"Half my relatives in Poland were wiped out in pogroms. Maybe he's been reading about them. He's a sensitive man."

"He has been reading but it's not like that. Things aren't things to him, they're signs of something else." It suddenly occurred to her that she didn't have any real friends. She kept them all at arm's length. "Okay, one of our cousins did bring him a novel about a nouveau riche Jewish banker who gets hanged."

"Ha, see. . . ." He was triumphant. Let him be, she thought. He'd listened. Just that was some comfort.

"Look at that," he said, pointing to the sky, "he's got his kite up and it's a beauty. Don't worry so much," he added with a self-satisfied look, "people grow."

The kite swooped and soared. Streaks of yellow-gold motion against a cloudless blue. Lara suddenly pictured how he saw her. Little Miss Innocent Dark-eyes. Maiden in distress. Well, the distress was real enough. But they were talking at different levels. He was on the street floor and she was in some nightmare basement with no exit.

✌14✌

Mortimer picked Lara up at her studio on 64th Street. They were going to meet David and Muriel at a jazz club in Harlem.

They got into his old Model T and headed uptown on Park through the soft black punctuated by winking night lights.

At an intersection, the car stopped suddenly and he put out his arm to keep her from lurching forward. Then, as the neighborhood became more convivial and the brownstones gave way to tenements, he pushed down the door locks.

"There's no point in taking risks."

Lara looked out at the house stoops where groups of black men were sitting, talking and laughing.

"It's a warm summer night. They're having a good time," she said. "You're as much a worrier as my brother."

Mortimer looked hurt and stammered something vague. I'm not being nice, she thought. I'm being cruel. After all, she had liked him for his mastery of Nietzsche, not because he was a carefree cricket.

She reached over and patted his knee. "Maybe worry goes with a ferocious intelligence." Mortimer beamed. He was wearing his best suit, but it needed pressing and looked no better than his usual outfit of rumpled tweeds and a crooked tie. The light from the lamppost made a diagonal streak across his jacket.

He shifted into gear as the Model T lurched past a window advertising bail bonds and lawyers who spoke Italian.

"I had the most amazing lesson today," Lara said, smiling sideways at him. "Remember I told you about Gorky, my new teacher?"

He nodded.

"Well, I had no idea what it would be like to be taught by someone who's really good. The difference is tremendous. It's like night and day." She looked out the window at the houses with their long rectangular brown stoops, imagining them as a flat arrangement of planes. "I've been doing some cubist studies. Thinking of doing my father's portrait in a different style. What I'm doing doesn't feel quite right to me yet, but I've started changing and I'm not sure where I'm going to stop." She paused, head turned toward him, waiting for a response.

Mortimer compressed his thick lips, which turned a surreal reddish blue at the next stoplight. "Why do you need a painting teacher?" he asked her. "Why not learn by trial and error?"

"You don't mind my learning from you," she said. "All the great painters had masters or worked as apprentices."

"Van Gogh didn't. If he had, he probably wouldn't have developed that tremendously original style. Art isn't like geometry or history, you can't really learn it. It could short-circuit your own process."

She had worried about this herself. She leaned over and adjusted her pump strap.

"Maybe it's a matter of timing. Right now, there *are* things he can show me about composition, things I need to know. You should have seen him, Mortimer. He drew a black line in the corner of my painting and it brought the whole thing into focus. The way he did it was brilliant. Even if he just inspires me to work harder, it'll be worth it."

They were ushered into the club through a heavy brocade curtain and Lara felt a moment's embarrassment at being with such a rumpled specimen when most of the men were in tuxedos. They'll think he's an anarchist, she thought and smiled at the idea. She noticed that all the faces in the huge mural to their left had fat lips like his but they were obviously not Jews—the colors of the stylized faces ranged from reddish brown through gray to black—all with large white eyes dotted with jet. It was a stereotype, she thought, but not a hostile one.

The waiter—in a short white jacket with brass buttons—showed them to a table toward the front where they could see the stage. Six black men sat on a raised platform in shirt-sleeves and vests and sweated over their instruments, their outlines blurred in the light haze of smoke that drifted everywhere.

Lara watched while they plucked the strings, drummed, strummed, rippled the keys, blew their horns, and the beat came alive, was taken up by the dancing couples. She loved the saxophone best, she thought—looking out at the crowded tables ringing the dance floor—the golden curve of it as well as the sound.

"I think I'm jealous," Mortimer half shouted over a clarinet riff while they waited for Muriel and David. "You know I respect your art. But I thought I was enough of a teacher for you."

"You're a wonderful teacher. You've given me a college education in the year I've known you and I'm grateful." She touched his arm. "But I'm an artist, not a philosopher. If I don't take myself seriously, no one else will."

"I do," he said gravely. "Remember our deal. I was going to give you everything I give my postgrad students at Columbia and you were going to show me the world of art and sensuous beauty. I'm as grateful to you for our trips to museums, for your explaining Michelangelo's plasticity, as you are to me"—he hesitated—"but you're no closer to me than you were when I met you. When you sat in on my lecture at Columbia. I'm not making any progress with you."

A woman with a tight-fitting hat and brilliant yellow dress shimmied by in the arms of a man who looked suspiciously like a mobster.

"Progress—I hate the word. Why does everything have to go forward? Why can't we just keep on the way we are? Now shush and listen to the music."

When the music turned to a slow blues song Mortimer asked her to dance.

She didn't really want to. Dancing with him wasn't really dancing, but she was restless, still excited by her class.

"Do you know how much time I've spent trying to figure you out?" he said as they danced slowly around under the richly colored circular canopy that made Lara feel as if she were dancing in a sheik's tent. "My seminar has turned into a Lara discussion group."

It really was amazing how he could manage to ignore his physical surroundings. He might as well have been in a lecture hall. The image of a brain on a toothpick came to her mind. Uncharitable, she thought.

"Mortimer, you're sweet, but I just don't feel that way about you."

"You don't like me to touch you," he said mournfully, his feet on the verge of tangling with hers. "I know I'm not very good at it. But I think I'm learning." She winced. If she had to grade his kissing at the beach she'd give it a C–. "I want to. Won't you give me a chance?"

"You'd get tied to me. The last man I slept with—I think he was a virgin"—she lifted her eyebrows—"followed me all the way to Europe. It was a terrible nuisance." She laughed. "My poor Suzy."

"Don't call me that. You know I hate it."

"A little lighthearted experience is what you need. Are you still a virgin, Mortimer? You are, aren't you?" She swung away from him gracefully, turned and came back to his arm. "No, really. Don't scowl. I want to know."

"Lovemaking isn't just a sport or an entertainment, Lara. There are plenty of arguments for a moderate and temperate use of the body—starting with the Greeks. Excess is harmful."

"Listen to the rhythm, Mortimer. One, two"—she pumped his hand in time.

He counted under his breath, gravely, seriously, breathing hard. In his concentration, they almost collided with the woman in yellow, and her partner gave him a dirty look.

"Mortimer, you aren't pressing, you're clutching me like a drowning man."

"But you said harder."

"I meant firmer. You have to have confidence in your hands. Leave it to them. Look at this"—she shook his arm—"you are tight tight tight"—she shook it again. "Let it go. That's a little better. Now put it against the small of my back. Close your eyes and feel the rhythm through your fingertips."

"Better?"

"A little."

"Was your first time very special?"

"No, it wasn't. It hurt and it was dull. Look, besides, what difference does it make? You forget, after so many."

"Won't you ever settle down? I don't mean with me, though I want that very much. But ever? There's something so restless about you."

"I need to be in love. I like to have different kinds of love with different people—spiritual, friendly, sexual. And I can't stay in love very long. It's very simple, really."

"Not to me."

"Poor Suzy"—she couldn't stop herself this time—"poor, poor dear. Let's go sit down. I see David and Muriel waving to us."

Lara felt a surge of relief at seeing them. Maybe now there'd be some life in the party. After their greetings, Lara took out her cigarette case and flipped it open. "Anyone want some marijuana? I know Mortimer doesn't."

"I rather like the idea of getting the baby potted." Muriel reached out her hand. It was the first time since she had arrived that Lara had seen her in a dress. The gauzy purple fabric billowed over her breasts and stomach making her look like a fertility goddess. True to Muriel's style, she hadn't worn heels or makeup. Just her tan.

"I'm not so sure I like that idea," David said, frowning, and Muriel stopped, her hand suspended. "But go ahead. I'm a postwar modern man. I do what my wife wants." His wry tone reminded Lara of the fragment of conversation she'd overheard at the pool.

"Don't worry. It won't hurt him." Muriel laughed, taking a marijuana cigarette from Lara. "He'll be a life-lover, that's all. A jiving baby."

Lara took out a long cigarette holder and stuck the joint in it. David immediately whipped out his lighter, lit hers and Muriel's, then took one himself and leaned back. Lara inhaled and let the sweet taste into her throat. The excitement of the lesson with Gorky modulated into something else. She wanted to get back into the mood of that time in the pool where they were swimming together, distinctions blurred. Playing.

Mortimer was looking at the saxophone player, then covering his eyes. He listened, then covered them again.

"What's this?" David asked, "some sort of exotic ritual special to jazz clubs?"

"Hide and seek?" Muriel offered, amused.

Mortimer reached over and held his hand up in front of Lara's eyes. "Listen . . . now look." He took them away. Do you think there's a correspondence?" he asked. Lara took a puff, leaning forward over her hand. Congruence of sound and sight was number twenty-four on their list of conversations.

"Correspondence?" David echoed, beginning to move his body to the beat.

"In nature things seem to fit," Mortimer explained, "like the roar of waves and the way they look when they break." He glanced hopefully at Lara.

"Well, there's no fit here," Lara said. "That man's face is too intelligent to be making that sexy wail."

Mortimer's face fell. "There's no reason intelligent people can't be sexual, is there?" he asked Muriel. "I mean, theoretically?"

Muriel gave him a sympathetic look. "Of course not. Any animal can have sex, but to be truly erotic you have to have imagination."

"Imagination and intellect aren't the same thing," Lara said shortly. "Look at that couple in the corner—that's imagination."

They were kissing, arms wrapped around each other's necks while their feet kept up a shuffling rhythm.

Mortimer opened his mouth to say something and then shut it.

"Here's to the animal mind," Lara said. "I'm in the mood for the bear strut, isn't that what the new one's called?" She rolled her shoulders with the beat.

A young man with dark Mediterranean looks had started to dance by himself in the center of the floor. Lara watched him, mesmerized. Next to her she heard the faint buzz of Muriel talking to Mortimer about suppressed feelings, mind as an instrument of defense, mind tricks—attack, parry, hide. Lara let it drift in and out. Talk wasn't what she was here for tonight.

The young man was loose-limbed with an aquiline face, high forehead and soft, brilliant eyes.

"Sometimes feelings are in a pretty rudimentary state," she heard David say, laughing.

She watched the young man. Energy rippled from his hips and shoulders. On an impulse, she went over and started to dance opposite him, moving by herself to the beat. He grinned at her, accepting it, making moves for her to echo. She let the rhythm take her, keeping her eyes on him, dancing around him.

Once she'd taken a negro drummer out to Central Park and made love under a tree by moonlight. He'd been all invisible smooth muscles like a cat. That had been crazy, though, she thought, dancing faster now, picking up the pace. He'd called her a "love addict." She smiled at the young dancer. Sweat was glistening on his forehead. "I'm not a collectible, honey," the drummer had told her, "I'm a man."

David touched her shoulder and she started, then smiled at him.

"You're going to get that man in trouble," he said, edging her away from the young man.

Lara laughed.

The saxophone player put down his horn and started to sing in a husky voice about a pretty momma with nasty attitudes. "You doin' things I can't stand," he sang.

David and Lara slow-danced past their table and Mortimer looked up at them with a pained expression. He was fiddling with the shade on the elegant small lamp in the middle of the white cloth and Lara thought he was going to knock it over in a minute.

"Your suitor's pretty miserable," David said.

She laughed. "So now you're on a mercy mission?"

"Just mentioning it."

"He can't dance," Lara said, as David put his arm around her waist.

"Why did you bring him, then?" he asked. She could feel his body shiver when it swung against hers. The music was clear as crystal. "You must have scores of men wanting to dance with you."

"He's too full of himself. I like to tease him about his deficiencies."

A thin black woman with a powerful voice began to sing, "Take it easy, Daddy, don't shake my orange tree," punctuated by saxophone. David swung Lara away then pulled her back. She could feel him looking at her bare shoulders and the long pearl necklace that swayed between her breasts. She felt as if she were dancing underwater.

"Is it fun to tease him?"

"It peps me up," she said. "Especially when I've botched a sketch."

"Why not do another one? He can't help it that he's brainy."

"Don't be so logical. Tormenting people is more fun than learning how to do things. You know that, don't cha?" She put her mouth close to his ear and started to sing along. "Just relax and rock me like a Daddy."

She could feel him shivering as her breath touched his ear. As she swung out and away from him, she noticed Muriel, still talking patiently to Mortimer. She didn't seem to mind David flirting a little. That was nice. Maybe she knew he loved her. Lara tried to imagine trusting someone.

The music stopped before she was aware and couples smiled at each other. "Bum da dum dum," Lara said, echoing the ending beat. "I'm stoned."

"You're especially beautiful tonight," he said.

"Ain't I always?" she asked in a mocking voice. "That's what the proper coquette would ask. Oh what a bore!" She gave a little snort of impatience. "Have you any idea how hard it is being a woman. . . ." She heard her words beginning to slur. "And trying to do anything serious? Being attractive only makes it worse. No, don't smile. It does."

"It's hard being handsome, too," he said with mock gravity.

"You wouldn't like being looked at as if you were a series of curves."

"If they were good curves, I'd probably love it. I love to be admired for my body. You do too. Admit it."

She was suddenly aware of the voluptuous way her beaded dress clung to her thighs. "It's bad for me. It's distracting. I can't work. I pose." She glanced in the burnished mirror next to the mural and saw herself, gold beads reflecting the light, red lips like a shout, long slender legs ending in new shoes with that sexy strap over the ankles.

"Look. What you have to do," his voice was getting slurred too, "is get up every morning and put on white clothes. That part's important. Then work like a tiger . . . through lunch if you want, 'til three or four. I don't care. Then take a shower, put that fabulous coal dust on your eyes, and go out and have fun. Simple."

"Simple," she leaned toward him smiling, then suddenly she caught sight of Johnnie coming in through the curtain at the end of the room. She recognized one of the women. It was Merle, she'd seen her picture in a dance program. The other woman was a tall, handsome woman in a black tuxedo with short hair slicked down and parted in the center like a man's. She carried herself in a haughty way, a slight sneer on her face. They went over to one of the few remaining tables and sat down. The tall woman put her arm around Merle.

"Johnnie said his girlfriend had a roommate, but I certainly never imagined anyone like that," Lara said, feeling suddenly queasy. "I wouldn't like to get into a brawl with that one." She strained to see better.

"Want to take a closer look?" David said, changing direction. "I'll take you over."

He two-stepped her through the crowd. They were almost at the edge of the floor when a drunken man, trying to execute a tricky step, slipped and kicked Lara in the shin. "Merde!" She buckled. "Kicked me right on the bone."

David took her arm and held her while she rubbed her shin. Then when he saw she was steady he knelt and ran his hand up her leg.

"Hey, no need for that!" she said, suddenly aware that he wasn't just having a good time, that he wanted to make love to her. She limped over to the table, David following behind her, and flopped into a chair. "Hello, Johnnie. Some creep just ruined my new stockings—not to speak of my shin."

Johnnie looked confused. "Lara? What are you doing here? Did we have a date?"

"No, silly! I'm here with David and Muriel. Mortimer's here, too." David reached out his hand and Johnnie shook it dubiously. Lara was painfully aware that the white shirt cuffs protruding from straight sleeves were slightly soiled and the crease was out of his striped trousers.

"How'd you know I'd be here?"

"I told you, I didn't. Pure chance."

"There is no such thing! Everything's connected." He looked at her intently. "What music they play when I walk in! Whether there's been a thunderstorm. You know there was a thunderstorm as I was walking over to Merle's. I got soaking wet—had to go over to your studio to change. You can't tell me that doesn't mean something." His voice got more excited. "I almost changed my plans, it was so ominous."

Lara thought she could see wheels clicking behind David's eyes.

"I'd like to meet your friends, John," he said in his cheerful doctor manner. But right now his solicitude grated.

"Sorry, that was rude of me." Johnnie passed his hand over his eyes. "Dr. Gluck, Lara, this is Merle." He spoke in a hushed voice. "And Raquel." Lara saw Raquel looking her over with frank interest. She had insolent, bold eyes. David gave a little bow.

"David, Muriel's been sending you SOS signals for the last five minutes," Lara said. "There's probably a limit to how much philosophy she can take in an evening." He gave Lara a parting squeeze and excused himself.

As soon as he was gone, Raquel held out her hand to Merle. "Let's dance."

"Oh stay for a bit," Lara said to Merle, "it's not every night I get to talk to my brother's dearest friend." She caught a look of pity from Merle. If the woman had been interested in Johnnie, she wasn't anymore, or only mildly.

"Ah, sisterly solicitude," Raquel said with heavy irony. "I'd think you'd want to be alone with your big brother to give him your opinion. I'm sure you've already arrived at one." She made an elaborate show of adjusting her cufflink and Lara saw her fingernails, cut short but painted red.

"Lara's not a gossip," Johnnie said.

"Oh, I'm sure she's not"—again the irony and a purr of foreign accent—"but I can see it in her face. She's got a lot on her mind. Come on, Merle."

Merle glanced sideways at Johnnie then got up with an exquisitely graceful gesture.

Johnnie looked agonized. "I don't know why Raquel said that. Did you really have something to tell me?"

"She was just being catty. Dance with me, John John. That way we can be near them. You won't have to miss looking at your Merle. And I can talk to you, too."

As they were moving slowly around the floor, Lara winced. "You got my toe. Ouch!" She looked down at her shoe ruefully. "You're as bad as Mortimer. And that's the leg that got kicked."

"Maybe that's what the thunderstorm meant. Bodies colliding."

"Johnnie, never mind about that, okay? Just pay attention and you'll be fine. One, two, three. Got it? That-a-boy."

"Look at how lightly Merle dances," he said wistfully, after a moment of trying to attend to his own steps. "Her feet barely touch the ground."

Lara decided to get into the subject obliquely. "Her friend's not a bad dancer either. Is she in Martha Graham's company too?"

"I think she's a singer," Johnnie said indifferently. "Isn't Merle's neck pretty?"

"How long have they been roommates?"

"See that little chain with the charm on it? I gave it to her."

"I'm surprised Raquel lets her wear it," Lara muttered, watching the two women dance together. She saw Raquel lean over and kiss Merle on the cheek, on the eyes. "Johnnie, doesn't it bother you that they're so close?"

"Should it? They're friends. They've been living together for two years."

"What if they were more than friends?"

"I don't understand you."

"What if they were lovers?"

"Merle and Raquel? That's impossible. Disgusting. Why are you saying that? You just don't want me to have any happiness—like Mother. She doesn't want me to have anything she hasn't picked for me." He was blurting it out. "This is my choice, my love. I haven't even brought her home. I didn't want Mother to get her fingers into it."

"Some people love both men and women. It's not such a bad thing, really. It doesn't need to upset you. I just thought you'd want to know if you had a rival, if things weren't working out. I'm trying to help you. If she's your choice, you'll have to fight for her." As she said it, she knew he wouldn't do it. Even this conversation had been too much for him. His face was closing down. She could almost see him moving off into the familiar landscape of his obsessions.

❧ 15 ❧

Agnes wished she had dared tell Lara how far things had gone. Since Lara had been staying in the city at her studio two nights a week, Agnes had been letting Walter stay in her room, not all night—somehow she had qualms about that—but until after midnight.

Tonight, though Walter was only a few minutes late, she was restless. She put down the illustrated French novel she was reading and paced around her bedroom. Though he wasn't coming until 8:30, she'd been anticipating his visit since tea, rubbing lotions on her skin, looking at herself in the mirror, trying on her new undergarments. How did some women get their self-confidence and poise? They weren't ashamed.

Agnes felt ashamed of everything, always. Where did it come from, feeling you were worth something? Worth being loved? She laughed. Maybe it was simply a matter of practice. Some women knew the worth of their bodies the way Agnes knew the price of stockings or eggs. She moved to the dressing table and looked, unsure if the image she saw was pretty or plain. Dark, too dark, Jewish gypsy, she thought. She tried a smile, baring her white teeth. Play, pretend it's play, she told herself. You're a courtesan, you know how it's done. You arrange the folds of your robe to show the curve of your shoulders. Just enough to tantalize. She smiled again, more naturally, admiring the effect she'd created.

Walter slipped into her room while she was sitting at her dressing table. She saw him in her mirror but pretended not to, rolling her head to the side with what she hoped was a voluptuous motion under the stroking brush until he came up behind her and put his hands on her shoulders. Then she gave a little cry of mock surprise.

"You are a funny one," he said, kissing her under the ear. "You're pretending you're a romantic heroine, aren't you?" She stopped brushing her hair and looked up startled. "How did you know?"

"There's a book open on your bed with the picture of a woman at her dressing table. You've slipped your robe off one shoulder. . . ." He ran over to the bed, snatched it up laughing, and brought it to her. "See—though I think you should show a little more breast." She pushed his hand away, embarrassed to be caught being silly.

"I wanted to please you."

"You do please me, just as yourself. You're beautiful." He held her chin and made her look at herself in the mirror. "Look at yourself." She smiled tentatively. "That sultry mouth, those eyebrows."

"My hair is too curly. I can't do anything with it." She decided that at least she could dye it blond.

"That's the wonder of it, it's natural—like a mane or some animal's pelt. Here, let me do it." He pulled the brush away from her and began to brush.

"You're doing it too hard," she complained, but for the first time in her life, she was aware she was beautiful.

"Sorry, I'll be gentler. Look at the electricity you generate. Even your hair gives off sparks. Don't grimace at me. Enjoy it. Pretend you're someone else if it helps. Call me darling, you can do it in French if you like." He gave himself a quick glance in the mirror. "Go on, pretend you're in a play."

"Mon chéri," she said weakly, turning her head to kiss his hand.

"You could have been an actress. You have such expressive eyes, but you have to speak up. Say it as if you meant it, mon chéri, chéri, darling"—he used his deepest bass, rolling his r's—"how I love you! I want to make passionate love with you." He kissed her neck. "Go on. If you want to be my mistress, you have to get that guttural note, choking with passion."

"I do love you," she said, "but. . . ." She pursed her lips. She had a sudden image of Eugene in the doorway, a pained expression on his face, and felt a pang of guilt.

"But what?" He ran the brush lightly over her shoulders, and she shuddered. "You wish I'd be more romantic? Is that it?" She nodded. "I don't feel like it now. I'm in a different mood." He leaned over and kissed her neck. "Say you want me to show you what I have," he whispered in her ear, "my little man."

"I can't say that, Walter. Don't tease me." She bent her head to one side, wanting him to go back to kissing her neck, making her feel beautiful. But he was rubbing himself against her back now with a look of intent concentration.

"You never even look."

"I've spent a lifetime trying not to think about what men have down there," she said lightly.

"Down where?" He took her hand and put it where he wanted it. "You can't even say 'between their legs,' can you? You're like a virgin. It's like seducing a virgin. Can you say penis?"

"Penis," she said, hating the sound of it, "penis, penis."

He laughed, "That's better. Now come to bed." He guided her over to the big four-poster, his hand on the back of her neck. "Don't be angry with me," he said, stroking her neck and back, gentling her, she thought, the way he would a horse. "It was all in fun." He kissed her shoulders. "Let yourself relax now, go soft. Don't think." He pulled her down beside him on the bed.

She felt a moment of panic. Why did it always have to end this way? "Not too fast—I can't."

"Don't worry—very slow." He ran his hand gently over her breasts. "I can go on like this for hours, just touching your skin. I love the curve where your hips meet your waist, right here." He ran his fingers down the sinuous shape.

Do you love me? she wanted to ask, but couldn't.

"You like this, don't you?" he asked, stroking her thighs, "though you'd rather die than say it. You even like this"—he slipped part way in—"if I go very slowly, don't you? If you keep your eyes closed and can't see what I'm doing."

"Mm," she said, lids pressed close together. She imagined herself enclosing him warmly. She was finding a way to like this, falling into a sort of trance with images of water rolling on white beaches, rolling and then drawing back, and she could see the green underside of the waves and felt herself floating in the green fluid.

"Do you still like it?" he asked suddenly, right against her ear. His voice shocked her. It made her aware that she was naked, sweaty, open legged. Her pleasure evaporated. She was too embarrassed to talk or open her eyes. She tried to imagine herself saying, "I like it, keep on. I like it, but don't talk to me, let me forget." She tried to whisper, "I love you," but only a faint hum came out of her throat.

"You're tightening against me," he said angrily, "closing yourself." His body was covered with sweat, hers too. But he kept on.

"It's enough," she whispered finally.

"Damn," he said. In a moment he came and rolled off her. "I've never known a woman so hard to please. Why won't you relax? Why won't you open up to me? Why are you so cold?" He wasn't teasing now, he was sulky, angry. "Nothing works with you. It's fine up to a point and then you just aren't there anymore."

"How can I relax," she said defensively, "when I've got to get up in a few hours and send you away?"

"So what if I have to go? I'm here now. Besides, it's not that, is it? You're tense because you think you're dirty. It's something like that, isn't it? Some idea that a romantic heroine shouldn't have private parts. She makes water through a rose bud, not a. . . ."

Agnes gasped.

"Don't worry, I'm not going to say anything more to offend you. But I wish you could see how bizarre it is, to be so afraid of knowing what you're doing, of saying it. That's what's keeping you tight."

"I feel like a hired creature."

"That's ridiculous, Agnes. People don't even use words like that anymore, they're archaic. The whole way you think is twenty years out of date."

"Maybe my language is old-fashioned but what I'm saying isn't. I'm new to this, I haven't had years of practice. I want to be caught up in it as much as you want me to, but I need you to reassure me. Tell me you love me, that I'm safe with you. Women don't get to make as many mistakes as men."

Eugene told her she was "indispensable . . . his best part," called her his "dearest, darling Agnes," said he felt "dismembered" when she went away. And no matter what he did on his little jaunts, he always came home again. Oh why had he left her?

Walter gave a huge yawn. "You're safe enough," he mumbled, and fell into a profound sleep.

The next morning Agnes wrote David a note. "If you could just give me an hour, I think you could help me."

She had dressed carefully. At three, she came into his office wearing a green coatdress—a cool lime color—and carrying a volume of *Psychology* by André Tridon.

"So you read psychology too," David said in a voice she imagined was designed to put her at her ease. He was studying her surreptitiously.

"Did you hear Tridon lecture at the Harmonie Club?" he asked. "The women's division, wasn't it? I read about it in the *Times*. It sounded like quite an event."

"It was very . . . provocative," Agnes said, remembering how the chairwoman had hailed the spirit of the unclad flapper and urged members to throw off their corsets. She wondered if David shared Lara's view that Tridon was a vulgar popularizer.

David motioned her to the chair across from him.

She sat, smoothing her skirt. "I hate bothering you this way. I know how much you have to do, but I have a problem that's obsessing me. I can't get it out of my mind. I can't seem to concentrate on anything else. I wake up in the middle of the night thinking about it. I couldn't think of who else to ask."

He nodded, not speaking. It gave her a feeling that what happened in this room was intensely private, different from anything outside.

She hugged her volume against her, comforted by its bulk. "I know this is going to sound silly, but I'm worried about Walter. I think he has a mother complex."

"Walter, Gordon's friend's stepson?" David asked and she saw a faint flicker of amusement. What was there to be amused about? She considered explaining that they'd been going to cultural events together. Telling David about their late suppers. Slowly leading up to her real fear.

"Sometimes a mother complex can be a good thing," David said, putting the tips of his fingers together. "If a man worships his mother, he'll worship other women too."

"It's not like that. He never says a good thing about her. She fell into some sort of melancholy when his younger brother was born and he was left to bring himself up. I understood how he felt. My mother ignored me too. I never had a proper child-hood." Agnes could hear herself sounding agitated.

"I see," he said, "so there are things you have in common, powerful things."

"Yes, I really sympathized. He's a charming young man. I felt as if I could make it up to him a little."

"That's perfectly understandable."

"And, at first, he seemed grateful to me, but then, I don't know what happened. He started to get angry and resentful. He acts as if I'm his mother."

"It seems to be causing you a lot of discomfort."

She bit her lip. "It is."

"Then why not simply stop seeing him?" She saw that he was watching her face intently. "You've done the friendly thing. If he can't appreciate it, well, so much the worse for him."

"I can't," she blurted out. "The truth is, I've become very fond of him."

"Oh," David leaned forward, urging her on by his posture. "Has it gotten very"—he paused—"involved?"

She felt herself flush and looked down. "Very."

"Please excuse my directness, but are you lovers?"

She hugged her volume against her. "You won't be shocked?"

She saw David start. He couldn't hide it. Oh dear, maybe this had all been a mistake. For one thing, she'd forgotten about David and Muriel's friendship with Gordon. Mightn't David feel compromised? She waited for him to chastise her, but he just lowered his eyelids slightly.

"Nothing you can possibly tell me would shock me," he said slowly, "but if you want me to be of any help, you have to tell me what's really bothering you. I promise you, I'm used to listening."

Agnes considered this for a moment. She wanted to say Walter had accused her of being frigid. Not just cold, frigid. It had an awful sound, unnatural, unwomanly. It was driving her crazy. She had no idea what she was supposed to be feeling.

"I'm so frightened," she said. "I love him as much as I've ever loved anyone. And he's so young—I'm afraid he's going to leave me." She thought of the young women who wore dresses that showed their legs, their garters, danced the shimmy and the shag. They wouldn't have this awful trouble with their bodies. "It's so confusing," she went on, near to tears. "He says different things. Sometimes he says I'm . . . insatiable." She gave an agitated survey of the room. "That it would take a Hercules to satisfy me. Could that be true?" Could you be both insatiable and frigid? Tridon said that the frigid woman was either a cripple or a neurotic. That she had poorly developed genitals. Agnes realized she had never really looked at her own body. Had no idea of what a woman should look like.

"Maybe he feels your passion as a demand he can't meet. Some men are afraid of intensity."

"He certainly doesn't look like Hercules, lying there with his mouth open, snoring. He looks dissipated or"—she hesitated—"debauched."

"You suspect him of having other women?" David asked suddenly alert.

"Not really," she said, "but he goes to speakeasies, stays out late, doesn't always tell me where he's going."

"And you think he should?"

"This is pointless," she pushed back her chair. "This doesn't help me. Please"—am I frigid? she wanted to ask him. Is it my fault? What can I do? But she couldn't seem to get the words out. Instead, she thrust the book at him—"just read these places I've marked," she said with as much dignity as she could muster, "and tell me whether I'm like this woman."

He handed it back to her gently. "I don't think I can do that. First of all, I don't know you. How can I possibly tell you if you're like Tridon's case? That's not how I work. Second, what good would it do you?"

"I need to know. If there is something wrong with me, maybe I could have it corrected. A spa cure to relax my nerves. Or if that didn't work, I've heard there are operations. Princess Bonaparte had one." Clitoridectomy they called it.

"What makes you think a painful operation would make you feel better? What if there's nothing physically wrong with you? You say you're frightened he'll leave you. You suspect things. Maybe what you have to do is talk to him honestly about the things that worry you."

"I've never done anything like this before." She hesitated, wondering if she should admit her total ignorance about love-making, ask David to give her some sort of instruction manual. "I'm afraid Walter doesn't respect me."

"Why shouldn't he? You're a widow. Your children are grown. You have every right to some pleasure for yourself."

"I know the modern views," she said. "I can act like a modern woman but inside I don't feel that way. I feel like a— you'll laugh—a scarlet woman. I feel as though I should embroider an A on my breast."

"Have you told him?"

"I've tried. At first he just laughed but now he's gotten mean. He lashes out at me, tells me I'm a nasty hypocritical little puritan like his mother. He acts as though I am her. And the trouble is that even though he says he hates her, I think when he comes to marry, he'll marry a virgin."

"The unconscious is a mass of contradictory impulses." David settled back in his chair. "But you've got to take the path of reason. Talk to him. Remind him of the loving things you do for him. Tell him right out that you think he's confusing you with his mother, if that's what you think. Unfortunately it's one of the commonest things in the world."

"It seems so unfair," Agnes said, thinking she'd put herself through this ordeal for nothing. She still didn't know if she was frigid. She imagined her lovely lime suit coated in ice and shivered, feeling cold even in the warm air. What if she couldn't manage to thaw?

∽16∾

Lara had been working feverishly on her painting. She felt if she could just push a little more, she would be in a different space. But now she was almost late for her lesson with Gorky. She put her canvas under her arm, grabbed her notebook, flung open the door to the front porch and almost hit Walter in the face.

He jumped back, startled. "Careful, you could ruin my most precious asset."

She started to move around him toward the steps.

"You're always gone when I arrive," he said, moving with her. "I'm beginning to think you don't like me."

She studied his self-assured face. "I don't. Not much."

That seemed to amuse him. He threw back his head and laughed. God, how she despised this fellow! She wished she could talk to Johnnie. Maybe they could make a concerted effort to drive him off, even talk to Gordon. But Johnnie had been spending more and more time at his place in the city. He was almost never around. She glanced at her watch. She'd think about it on the way.

Walter followed her to her car and gallantly opened the door. She jerked it away from him angrily, shutting it herself.

She could hear him laughing as she gunned the engine of her new roundabout.

Before the lesson she met Mina for coffee at the little place on Ninth Street where Gorky always went.

"I've some juicy gossip," Mina said.

"It'll have to be to distract me. I'm feeling wretchedly cranky."

Mina leaned forward. "Marni is in love with Gorky," she said triumphantly, "and she thinks he's falling for her." Marni was one of the students at the League, a girl from the midwest who wanted to learn something about fashion art.

"She's a simp. Not his type at all."

Mina looked hurt. "Well, he wrote her a poem."

The lesson didn't go well. Lara had trouble concentrating. She kept thinking about her mother and Walter. The man was such an obvious Don Juan. How could her mother not see what he was up to? She felt irritated rather than stimulated by Gorky's corrections. She didn't feel like muted colors and angular, self-contained forms. Her whole impulse today was to paint violently in reds and purples.

"Put away your brushes," Gorky said finally. "Today is not a good day for you. What you are painting is too raw. You need something to put your mind back in control."

They walked over to Union Square and strolled through the outside art show. That's how I'm going to end up, she thought, looking at a watery sketch of two chess players, sitting on a stool beside paintings nobody wants. She almost bought it, just to see the man smile. As they wandered from stand to stand—cityscapes, portraits, pictures of large floppy-eared dogs—she began to see that some of the canvases were good. Even though the artists were unsophisticated, certain paintings had originality. The unexpectedness of it gave her hope.

"Enough of this," Gorky said, after a while, leading her down the street toward the bus stop. "Now that you're calmed down, I'm going to take you to the Stuart Davis show. It'll be just the thing for you."

Calmed down, she thought, irritated again. I wasn't calm, I was stimulated.

"In the last six centuries, there hasn't been any better art than cubism," he announced dramatically, as they walked into the gallery on 57th Street. "See how he disciplines emotion"— he pressed his hands against the edges of an imagined rectangle—"how he subdues it to a higher order."

Lara imagined him compressing her into a gray wedge. "It's almost too cerebral, too cool."

"To me, his logic is beautiful. All clumsiness is dead. Don't you see, he's found new rules to discipline his feelings. He gives a fresh shape to his experience with new sequences"—he moved up excitedly and pointed to the painting, willing her to see what he saw—"brown, chalk-like white, metallic grays, dull blacks." He towered above the crowd, and people were staring at him curiously. "Whether he paints eggbeaters or streets or geometric organizations, he expresses his constructive attitude. He gives us symbols of tangible spaces with gravity and physical laws."

"It has a brilliant surface," she said grudgingly, "but I miss the organic. Living with it would be like living with an icebox." She could see from his eyes that he thought she was being illogical, womanish.

"Most people who say they don't like cubism simply don't understand it," he said more gently. "They can't even conceive of the elements that go into making art. But I will never insist on your agreeing with me. You will have your own taste."

"In practice," she said with lifted eyebrows, "I know you're not quite so tolerant." Hadn't he gone over her canvases not once but almost every time? What was that if not a way of insisting?

∿17∿

Lara and Muriel were sitting by the pool in the sun talking while Robin dozed under a towel, a plate of chocolate-chip cookies and a box of raisins on the little table nearby. Muriel had been hand-feeding her. She explained the metal spoon was too harsh for a child so alienated from her body.

There were some gains to being horribly sick, Lara thought while the pool motor chugged, dispensing a load of purifying chlorine. You had people at your beck and call day and night, hovering over you. Maybe if Johnnie looked more peculiar, Muriel would pay more attention to him. She wondered what it would take to get Muriel's attention.

"She looks exhausted," Lara said, glancing over at Robin who was lying in a small, damp heap. "But you seemed to be making progress with swimming."

"Some. . . ." Muriel put her hand on her belly and Lara could see it lurch. "I took a hint from your brother's twiddling for her. She puts up a kind of barrier. If you break it, distract her, sometimes you can get her to try something new. She actually paddled a little. But then she collapsed and shut me out again." She sighed. "It's slow work."

"Even though I see her every day, I can't imagine what she feels like." What did Eliot say? "Each in his prison/Thinking of the key." She tried to imagine but mostly Robin seemed like a small, frightened animal—a gopher darting back inside its burrow at the first sign of danger. Somehow Muriel managed to see something more.

Lara looked into Muriel's gray eyes. She gave off her usual sense of sureness. But wasn't there a kind of hubris in thinking you could break into the prison and rescue someone? Maybe Robin was right to be terrified. Maybe she'd already taken enough risks for a lifetime.

On the other side of the garden, Lara saw her mother walking with a book—probably by that quack she was fixated on, Tridon. She'd been carrying his book around for days. Her mother sat down on the white bench under a maple. It was a nice composition, she thought ruefully. The perfect combination of verticals and horizontals, *Woman Waiting to be Rescued.*

"I thought it would be nice if Mother shared my interests," she said, shading her eyes and looking at her mother, "but she manages to do it in a way I can't enjoy. I read Freud and she reads Tridon."

Muriel stretched her legs in the sun. "He may not have the best taste but he brings up a lot of important questions—marriage, sex, fidelity."

"But he's such a fop with his beard, his French accent and his painted toenails. There was an article about him in the *Atlantic.*"

Muriel laughed. "It wouldn't hurt some of our colleagues to brighten up. A little talk about instant gratification isn't going to kill the psychoanalytic movement."

"It might kill my mother," Lara said.

"It takes a lot more than one book to change a Victorian into a flapper," Muriel answered, smiling. "I don't think you need to worry."

Lara felt a surge of resentment. Sure, it was easy for Muriel to be calm and confident and optimistic. It wasn't her family and apparently her scheme of things didn't allow for tragedy. Lara had wanted to ask her what she knew about Walter but she didn't want to hear about his rotten childhood or that maybe he and Agnes would do each other good. She had a sudden image of Muriel and David sitting in their bedroom discussing her mother and Walter, laughing and making bets on how things would turn out.

Robin started to wake up and Muriel went over and held the box of raisins near Robin's face. "Food helps with transitions," she explained. Robin stared past it, her mouth slackly open as though the jaw had no muscles to hold it shut.

"Robin?" She shook the box but the child seemed not even to see it. "Just yesterday she ate a whole plate of chocolate chips by herself." Muriel took a raisin and gently put it into the child's mouth. Robin swallowed it.

Muriel took another and put it in Robin's mouth. Looking blankly into space, she swallowed it, then gave an odd rusty sound that resembled a laugh. That seemed like a good sign. Muriel dropped in another and the child ate it, still without closing her lips.

Lara tried to imagine how this sort of eating felt. The closest she could get was when she'd been given a local anesthesia that deadened her gums and lips. But even then she had known they were her mouth and lips, and she'd been careful not to bite herself. This child acted as if her mouth didn't belong to her, as if it were just the opening of a tube stuck into her face. Food went into it, travelled through her body and passed out the other end without her awareness. She tensed the muscles in her own jaw, newly conscious of the sensations that she took for granted.

Muriel kept on slowly feeding the raisins and bits of the chocolate-chip cookies. Lara could see Robin's wet tongue inert against Muriel's fingers, smeared now with melted chocolate. How could Robin keep from licking them, Lara wondered. It seemed as if she enjoyed the contact. A raisin fell on the spread and Robin picked it up and put it in her mouth, then gave that strange laughing sound. Muriel looked triumphantly at Lara.

For a moment Lara felt as if she understood the appeal of this work. Watching Robin move her hand and take the raisin had sent shivers of excitement up her spine.

Muriel took a candy bar out of her bag, unwrapped it eagerly and put a piece of dark chocolate into Robin's mouth. A minute later, she gave a cry of pain. What is it? At first Lara thought it was the baby, then she saw that Robin had bitten down on Muriel's finger. She put her hands out instinctively but Muriel motioned her back.

"Robin, open your mouth," she said quietly, the way you might to a dog you were trying to make give up a bone. "Come on, that's a good girl. I need to take my finger out." The child only clenched her teeth. Muriel's face went white with pain, and Lara took a step forward. This was impossible. Enough was enough. She gripped Robin's chin with the palm of her hand and slowly pushed her fingers hard into the sides of Robin's jaws and pried them apart.

Muriel drew out her finger. Lara could see purple indentations where the teeth had gripped but the skin didn't seem to be broken. If it was, she'd need a shot. Robin wasn't looking at them, but Lara could see her body was shaking.

"I've got some iodine and bandages in the bathhouse."

"Thanks," Muriel said.

When Lara came back from the bathhouse, Muriel was stroking Robin's hair. "I guess you didn't want me feeding you when you had been doing it so well yourself," she was saying quietly to Robin. "It makes sense."

It didn't make sense to Lara. She could understand the child wanting to do some things for herself but she didn't have to bite Muriel's hand off. Weren't there any limits? Shouldn't Muriel at least be trying to talk to her, explaining it was wrong to hurt people? It couldn't be good for her, could it, to think she could do that anytime she wanted. She watched aghast while Muriel took another chocolate bar and put it on the table. Still not looking at her, Robin took it and peeled off the wrapping.

☙18☙

Agnes was overcome with jealousy. She couldn't control it. Ever since Walter told her the girl had sent him three photographs of herself, Agnes spent much of her time with him asking about the girl and then brooding over what he told her. These photographs were a sign of moral depravity. How could she throw herself at him that way? Agnes invoked the rules governing the behavior of debutantes. Nice girls don't send photographs to a man unless they are engaged—and then only one. Not three. Three, the number itself obsessed her. Threefold power to destroy and torment. Her heart seethed. She became desperate.

Sick with jealousy, she went over what she knew. In her diary, she described the girl's childish handwriting, "copy-book hand", her childlike wish for silk stockings her mother would approve of, and her wish for more hugs and kisses. I'm cold and she's warm, that's what he is telling me, showing me those ridiculous, naive letters. But the more hurt she was, the more she yearned for him.

On the Thursday after he told her about the girl, whose name was Posie, Walter came to dinner as usual. He was slightly drunk, but he was affectionate, warm and charming. She saw he still desired her. The next night she asked him for supper again—Lara was staying over an extra night in the city—determined to make him want her even when he wasn't drunk. She herself made his favorite dishes. Engagingly grateful for the food, he thanked her, kissed her hands. He sat on the bed with her in the dark. She got him to say he loved her and then told him he had to leave. It was past ten. She had just wanted these few minutes holding his hand in the dark.

"You shouldn't start things if you're not going to finish them," he whispered against her neck.

"What do you want?"

"I have to talk to you about that," he said. "There's more than one way of helping me."

"How?"

He gently pushed her over into his lap, stroked her head, then opened his pants and took out his penis, rubbing it against her face, her mouth.

"Kiss it," he said, "take it into your mouth."

She had never been so close to it. Never really looked at it, always tried not to see it red and swollen, standing up. Now she couldn't see, thank god, but she felt the silky tip of it, opened her lips hesitantly and kissed it. It was soft as a baby's cheek.

"Not like that," he said, "take it into your mouth, suck it." His voice was hoarse, greedy. He took her head in his hands and pushed it down on him. She felt as if she was going to gag but she couldn't resist—something about his forcing her seemed right to her. Besides, as he was moving her head, pulling on her hair, she imagined the girl having to watch this, suffering with jealousy.

❧19❧

"Don't write him, Mother. What are you doing? You're just making excuses for him, trying to explain his acts to him. Believe me, there's nothing so maddening." Agnes and Walter had already had one dramatic quarrel and reconciliation this week. Ever since Lara's return from the city, Agnes had talked of nothing else.

Agnes threw down the pen and looked over her shoulder at Lara who was curled up on the living room sofa, reading. "He broke our theater date. After everything I've done for him. How could he?"

"What did you expect? Just because you've been generous. You can't buy people."

"That's nasty, Lara!" Agnes pushed her chair back dramatically, got up and started to pace. "Of course I know I can't. But I thought he loved me."

"I'm sure half a dozen other women think so too. Didn't you tell me just last week that he had a girlfriend in Boston he was thinking of marrying? So don't carry on this way. There's nothing wrong with enjoying his company—but for heaven's sake, don't make such a melodrama out of it."

"What if he'd made advances?" Agnes asked, stopping in front of her.

Lara put down the art magazine Gorky had lent her and stared at her mother. "Did he?"

Agnes stared back. "Yes."

"Are you sure you're not misinterpreting? Men are freer these days. Compliments don't mean what they used to."

"Lara, I'm not so stupid I can't tell an advance from a bit of gallantry." She bit the back of her hand.

Lara looked sharply into her mother's face. "What happened? You'd better tell me the whole thing."

"I can't," Agnes said, plumping down with a sigh.

"Come on, you know you can't resist," Lara said with a touch of bitterness. "You never could resist telling me things." She'd long ago decided that if she had children, she'd never tell them anything. There were things a nine- or ten-year-old didn't want to know.

When Agnes finally told Lara, sitting uncomfortably close to her on the sofa, she stressed the fact that it was her fault. "Walter was oblivious to everything but his own satisfaction, but I knew it was wrong. I knew. . . ."

"Nothing is wrong with wanting satisfaction, if he loves you." She said it because it was true. But she couldn't help feeling a mixture of pity and, to her surprise, disgust. So much for her being a modern woman.

"But it wasn't nice," Agnes said weakly, thinking of his hands holding down her head.

Lara could feel the warmth of her mother's body through her dressing gown. "Just name it, can't you," Lara said, as impatient with her own discomfort as she was with her mother's Victorian rhetoric. "You don't need to be so ashamed." She moved slightly away. "There's nothing wrong with the body. It's your mind that is making you miserable."

"What must you think of me?" Agnes leaned against her shyly.

"Oh, Mother, for God's sake." Lara pushed her gently upright, resisting her mother's signals. "I thought you were a sentimental idiot before, when you were mooning after him and catering to him. I thought the whole thing was in your mind. But if he's been making love to you, telling you he loves you. . . ."

"A friend once told me about a pervert who did the same thing to an innocent young girl," Agnes persisted. "I wish she hadn't told me. Why do you think nice women tell each other such things?"

"Mother, if you didn't want to do it, whatever it was, why did you?"

"I know, I know. I could have hit him, screamed." Agnes turned and put her face against the back of the sofa in an attitude of distress.

"You didn't even need histrionics," Lara said, not responding to the bent neck. "You could have just told him no, you didn't want to, and left the room. I don't think he would have stopped you. He's not that kind."

"I didn't want him going to that girl." She turned back with surprising fierceness. "I can't stand her to have him. Even if she is in society. She's just a schoolgirl. I think he wants to marry her."

"You did it just to keep him." Lara couldn't conceal her disapproval. "Jesus, Mother! There are some things you shouldn't do. Have some respect for yourself."

Agnes's eyes filled and she was soft again, pleading. "I'm not your age. I'll never see forty again. If I lose a lover, I may not find another. I had to try to keep him. Try to understand."

"I do. But I hate it. I can't bear your being so desperate. What's so necessary about having a man? You're not old. You're still beautiful. You know three languages. You're a wonderful photographer. You do miracles with your crochet hook. And if that isn't enough, you have plenty of money to live comfortably and two children who love you." Lara touched her mother's shoulder and caught a glint of satisfaction in her eye.

"That's it. Now rub my neck," Agnes said.

I'm about to do it again, Lara thought, offer myself as a stopgap man, the loving daughter who gives massages to her bereaved mother. And then, when Mother feels better, she'll be off without another thought. Stop it, she told herself, biting her tongue. Enough baby nonsense, stop all of it. She sat upright and straightened her shoulders.

Agnes looked suddenly alarmed. "You must never tell Johnnie. I don't know what he'd do."

"Of course I won't tell him, though he's likely to sense something. He's sensitive where you're concerned."

"But you won't tell him. Promise!" She moved her shoulder against Lara's hand, eyes closed, giving the illusion that she was totally in her daughter's power.

Lara deliberately removed her hand. "I said I wouldn't."

Agnes looked at Lara, unhappy for a second, then fell back into her memory of the event. "Afterwards, I felt so abused. So"—she hesitated—"vile. He wouldn't even look at me, just muttered 'Oh my God.' And the horrible part is, I think I make him abuse me. I like it. I love him most when he treats me worst."

"If you know that, why don't you make an effort to stop?" Lara wondered whether the psychology her mother was reading wasn't making her more hysterical. Instead of insight, Agnes seemed to have found a titillating new model for her own obsessions.

"I can't stop," Agnes said dramatically. "In my foolish way, I love him. He's brought vitality into my life. He's so real. Besides, ever since I was a child, I've felt I deserved punishment."

"Mother, I'm not a psychiatrist."

Agnes had a vivid image of his hand tangled in her hair, forcing her down. Something about the posture of her body, the discomfort, the strain of all her muscles, the ache in her mouth was right. "It wasn't just what I deserved, it was familiar. Can you understand what I mean? It was more like love."

Lara felt herself beginning to panic. She had ideas like this too—fantasies of being raped or beaten—and they scared her to death. Sometimes she thought she tormented Mortimer just so she wouldn't have to think about them. "Mother, please! This upsets me. I can't do it anymore. Maybe you should talk to David."

"I already have."

❧

"You're right to worry about Mother," John said to Lara who had come out of her room and was washing her brushes in the sink. "I went to an auction at Christie's with a friend— there was a German collection that I'd read included some anti-semitic prints—and there she was with Walter, standing up in public bidding for a painting."

Was she buying paintings for Walter now? Lara hadn't seen anything new in the cottage. "Did she buy it?" she asked, looking up at him, the soap in one hand, a brush in the other.

Johnnie didn't answer. He seemed intent on recapturing some image. "You should have seen her, Lara. She had on her amber earrings, a choker. She was glowing like a huge moon. All that amber and silver."

"But did she buy the painting?"

"She was sparkling in her jewelry. Too visible, much too visible."

"Johnnie," Lara said carefully, rinsing the brush and starting on another one. "I'm not following you. You seem more concerned about Mother's lack of taste"—(was that it?)—"than about Walter and Mother's extravagances. Do you realize how much she's seeing him?"

Johnnie started to tremble. "No, I didn't."

"Of course not, you've been spending so much time in the city," she said and stopped herself. She couldn't really blame him for trying to escape. As the brush bled darkly into the water, he came close to her, watching it.

"She's in more trouble than I thought, then," he said solemnly. "You know what happened to Jude Süss for going out with Christian women?"

"Who?" Lara squeezed the bristles gently. "Oh, that book you're reading. For heaven's sake, Johnnie, the problem isn't that Walter's Christian and Mother's Jewish. It's that he's not a nice person. He's rotten. And I'm afraid Mother's taken in by him"—addicted was more like it—"and that she can't resist his pressure." Lara didn't dare tell Johnnie that she'd already given in to his demands for sex.

"Lara"—he brought his face close to hers—"they hung Süss."

She moved away nervously. "Don't take everything so personally, Johnnie." He related everything to himself except what was really personal and *that* he made into myths and symbols. It was enough to drive her crazy. "It's only a story in a book."

"He's our cousin," Johnnie said with more vigor than usual, "our blood. I've researched it. So it does matter to me. And it should matter to you. He was an Oppenheimer. It's all true."

So that's what he'd been doing in New York. Digging around in the library. And collecting piles of those German newspapers he was always reading. She vaguely recollected hearing her mother talk about this Oppenheimer. He was a big financier, backed the Kaiser's wars.

"They hung him in a cage and killed him in front of a crowd just because he collected fine art and was loved by Christian women. What kind of a world is it that permits things like that to happen to an innocent man?"

"Maybe there were other reasons," she said, shutting off the water. "I think Mother said he was mixed up in politics. Maybe he was embezzling funds."

"He wasn't, Lara. He made money for the government, he didn't steal it. They hated him because he was too clever."

She looked at him hard. He sounded so rational sometimes. Seeing he had her attention, his voice got more desperate. "Lara, there's a reason for this book's being written now, in 1929, by a Jew. It's a warning. Danger is right under our noses and we don't see it. That's the trouble with Mother, she denies things. She took up Christian Science to hide what she is. Now she thinks she's hiding by dying her hair blond—don't think I didn't notice—and going out with a Christian. But really, she's drawing attention to herself."

He paused for a minute, frowning. "Be careful you don't do it too, Lara. I wouldn't show anyone your paintings if I were you, wouldn't tell anyone about them."

Lara felt a coldness in her fingers. She'd been punished, too, for showing off as a child. "Don't show them, Lara." His voice fell to a whisper. "Don't show yourself off. Believe me, it's a bad idea."

She felt like putting her fingers in her ears. His voice was sapping her energy. With an effort she shook off his spell. "Is that why you didn't go on with your engineering?" she asked suddenly, thinking she understood. "Because you were lying low? Because you were top student in your class and it scared you?" From the look in his eyes she could tell she was right.

"John, do you really think you attract less hatred by doing a disappearing act?"

"I was becoming what they saw," he muttered obscurely, "a loud, ambitious Jew."

"You weren't. You're nothing like that. Don't let yourself be taken over by a stereotype." She remembered having told David that Johnnie had never been discriminated against, that their family hardly knew they were Jewish.

"You know how Mother would say men don't like women who are too dark-skinned or who have kinky hair or who speak too loudly. You know what she meant. She was being dragged into the image too. And she was right to stay away from it, but now she's forgotten. She's flaunting just the things they hate. Here"—he ran to the side table and grabbed the book—"let me read you where Süss gets hung in the cage." His hands were shaking so he could hardly hold it. "They spit on him," he said, "They spit in his face. I don't want to live in this world."

Lara snatched the book away from him. "You have to," she said, more loudly than she intended. "It's the only world there is." Johnnie gave her the strangest look and all of a sudden she got the feeling that he really was crazy, as though this person she'd known all her life, played with and touched wasn't really there. Someone else had taken over and was looking out of his eyes with a sly, crazed look.

She took a long walk to calm herself. If he had been all one way or all the other it would have been easier. But this way he had of sounding fairly rational or at least not speaking gibberish and then babbling about hung men and not wanting to live anymore was intolerable. She couldn't imagine he'd really hurt himself—that was too awful—but he did seem worse.

She shouldn't even have tried to talk to him about Walter. She swung her arms, breathing deeply. And what was most frightening was that she understood him.

She kicked a stone along the dirt path. It was so beautiful here. The perfect place to live and create. She stopped and looked at a wisteria in full bloom. Put her face down to the blossoms and smelled them. Broke off some sprays to take back and paint.

It was true though, she and John were both open to things in ways other people weren't. When she looked at colors, she didn't just see them, they sizzled—like the purple of this wisteria—they leapt toward her, she felt them inside. Light went straight to her brain. John was the same way, except it was ideas with him. It was all right when they were benign, like the kite-flying and world harmony, but when he started sensing hatred, that's when it scared her.

She tripped over a fat, greenish slug next to the blaze of wisteria and shuddered. For a moment she felt as if its ugliness could get inside her and do dreadful damage. The next minute she thought of putting it in a painting. That's what's wrong with cubism, she thought. Not enough room for risk, for danger. Too much order, geometry. She had learned a lot from seeing things through its lens, but she wasn't satisfied with it any longer.

She thought of the studies she was working on—the ones of a cow and her calf that she was going to show Gorky next time. She'd been experimenting with patches of color in an almost symbolic way, letting herself go more, but it was frightening. She didn't know what would come of it. What if she were overwhelmed the way Johnnie was? She poked at the slug with a stick and forced herself to study the mottled shades of green and brown, the veil of moisture, its tiny horns. She thought of how she could represent it, even make it beautiful.

❧20❧

A few days later, Lara still felt unnerved by the conversation with Johnnie. She couldn't concentrate. If she kept on with what she was painting, she was sure she'd ruin it. Exasperated, she washed her brushes and headed toward the barn.

She walked up the ramp at the back, past the empty horse stalls, into the grain room with its huge bins of oats and corn. On impulse she opened one—a glossy full-bellied field mouse scooted off in alarm—and inhaled the musty smell. Then she took off her shoes and walked across the big open space flanked by haylofts, to the red and white cows munching placidly between their stanchions, tails swishing. Then she went back out.

"Where have you been?" David asked, catching up with her in front of the windmill. "I haven't seen you for days." She pushed a wisp of hair back under her cap but it poked out again and fell across her ear. "Are you alright?"

"I was visiting the cows," she said, guardedly, noting the tone of intimacy. She wished she hadn't gotten so high at the jazz club the month before, since he kept waiting for that mood to return. "They have such a comfortable, soothing smell—a mixture of hay and milk with faint undertones of dung. Now

I'm thinking of making butter. It's good exercise for the upper arms."

"Making butter?" He grinned at her. "You mean, it doesn't come in containers?"

"You really are a city boy," she said, stepping over the low stoop into the windmill. He followed her into the semi-dark interior. The light from the small windows fell in dusty beams, picking out churns and buckets.

"I was trying to make you smile. Usually it isn't so hard."

"Sorry, I shouldn't take my bad mood out on you." She wondered if she should tell him straight out she wouldn't sleep with him. She took off the top of one of the big containers that stood against the wall and started to skim off the cream with a cup into a bucket. It was a thick, creamy white.

She poured the cream slowly into the bucket.

"What's the matter? Or don't you feel like talking?"

She did, that was the problem. And he was such a good listener. She took off the top of the second container, put it down and dipped her cup into the cream. Flecks of it were getting on her hands. Fat droplets. She should have used a long-handled ladle.

She shook her head as if annoyed by a buzzing insect. "It's just Mother driving me crazy." She paused.

He reached out his hand and tucked the wisp of hair back under her cap. "Don't let her. You have some say in the matter, you know."

Lara screwed the shiny steel top back on. "I can't help it. She's learning the facts of life and she insists on telling me all about it." She carried her pail outside and poured the contents into a wooden churn set under an awning. "I suppose it shouldn't upset me so much."

"She's your mother," David said, watching her start to stir the cream with a pole stuck in the lid of the churn. "Mothers don't usually tell their daughters about their intimate life."

"She's always done it, complained about Daddy's drinking, told me how she hated it when he went on business trips. She thought he had other women. I wouldn't believe it, of course; I thought he was perfect." She gave an unhappy laugh.

"It's hard for a child to be a confidant."

Lara felt herself softening. What was it about his way of anticipating her feelings that was so seductive, that made her want to tell him more than she'd intended.

"When Daddy was gone, she always got into bed with me. She pretended it was for me. She sang me nursery rhymes, played One Little Piggy on my toes." Lara saw him listening intently. "But it always ended with her pretending that I was her mother. She called it The Game." Lara remembered her mother's heavy head against her chest, the way her mother clung to her. She felt a chill creep up her spine and then, inexplicably, a stirring at the pit of her stomach.

He whistled through his teeth. "That must have confused the hell out of you."

She fought off a feeling of panic, kept talking. "I had to look after her. She's so naive. I don't know how to explain it, it's as though part of her never grew up."

"You're explaining it perfectly." He paused, looking at her. "Here, give me a turn at that." He took off his jacket and started to stir.

"Sometimes, when I had boyfriends over, she would stand on her head. Right there in the hallway in her gym costume. She wanted to show off her ankles, that's what it was, but when I told her she was showing off and that I didn't like it, she got furious. She does things but she never admits what she's doing. Do you know what I mean?"

"She's the sort of woman who'd like to be ravished in her sleep."

Lara laughed. "Yes. Exactly. But why?" She reached out to take the churn and he put his arms around her, drew her quickly to him and kissed her hard.

She jerked away.

"Come back," he murmured. "Don't be afraid."

"What about Muriel?" she asked.

For a moment he looked embarrassed, standing there with his erection and his flushed face, breathing hard. "You get right down to it, don't you?"

"I like her."

"I do too. I love her. She doesn't mind. We have an open marriage."

"Open for you?" She bent away from him, scooping pale chunks of butter out of the churn into her pail.

"For both of us."

She straightened and gave him a skeptical look. "So she doesn't feel like exercising her option right now?"

"Why are you suddenly so interested in Muriel?"

Lara thought of trying to explain to him that the thought of Muriel had frozen her in mid-kiss, made her feel as if she were kissing a priest or her grandfather. "If she can't trust you, how do you expect me to?" she asked, instead, covering the butter with a cloth and picking up her bucket.

"Let's stop talking about Muriel, alright?" he said. "If she didn't exist, it wouldn't make any difference. You're so bound up with that family of yours—with your mother and Johnnie—there's just no room for anyone else. And besides, you're scared to really feel anything. You. . . ."

"Don't analyze me, David. I don't like it."

"You're beautiful even when you're frowning," he ran a finger lightly down her arm, "and you must know I love you. Have loved you from the first moment I saw you."

She shook off his hand. "I don't believe it for a minute. Besides, even if it were true, I don't want it."

"Don't you?" he asked with light sarcasm. "Then why did you lead me on, smiling, batting those long lashes at me?"

"Bad habit, I suppose," she said blowing a wisp of hair away from her mouth.

"Habit!" he repeated, provoked. "Well, how do you think that makes me feel?"

She shrugged her shoulders. "David, please don't ruin things. I like being with you, like talking to you. . . ."

"Want a Daddy to confide in," he broke in, "but you didn't think about how being your confidant would affect me, did you? People are all some sort of marionettes in your private daydreams."

"I didn't know how much I'd grow to like Muriel," she said weakly.

"Damn it, stop bringing her into it. Muriel this, Muriel that. Liking her rival never stopped a woman yet. It's not Muriel, it's something inside you. You have an Electra complex,

Lara. Do you know that? As long as I behave like Daddy, it's ok. But when I try to make love to you. . . ."

"Don't!" She held up her hand. He brought it sharply down to her side, held it there, glaring at her.

"Then," he said, his face close to hers, "you run back to your canvases, your little tubes of paint. You know what I think, Lara? I think this precious painting of yours is all sublimation. Clouds of displaced feelings." He made a sweeping gesture. "Red-hot, yellow, big black bulls, calves sucking teats, all the messy feelings you don't want to think about."

Lara gasped. "That's nasty," she said, finding it hard to think with his breath on her cheek. She pulled her hand free and moved back. "Do you really think your psychoanalytic theories have nothing personal in them? At least I know what I'm doing. Of course I put passion into my paintings. Sex too. But it's not a limited resource." She noticed that anger was turning his eyes a cool slate gray.

"But look," he said, "if you had real love in your life, you wouldn't spend all that time on something so frivolous. Illusions." He glanced up at the clouds forming shifting shapes above him.

"Illusions?" she said sharply. "To me they are more real than anything. My paintings are as full of life as I can make them. Making things brighter, sharper, bigger isn't an evasion, David. It enriches me." She was deadly serious now. "That's part of what's so exciting. It's not just making beauty. It's self-discovery." She looked at him standing with his feet apart, hands thrust into his pockets, his hair oblivious to his frustration, making delicious curves against the sky. "I would have thought you'd be for that. You were with Robin."

"Oh, with Robin . . . as a tool to help us get at what was going on. Yes. It did help. You helped." His tone softened for a moment. "But with you. . . . Can't you see the way it keeps you clinging to the past? Painting an Eden that doesn't exist. Doing those endless portraits of your dead father. What is that but being caught up in childhood? Refusing to grow up?"

"Preserving what you love isn't childish, David. Turning it this way and that, looking at it, even criticizing it. That's part of my growing, healing old hurts maybe. I admit I certainly had them with my father." She looked grim. Could David be right? Maybe her work was using up all her available energy. Maybe she was fooling herself when she thought she was open to love.

He saw her stop, rubbing her arms as though she felt a chill, and was suddenly contrite. "Lara, love, sorry. I shouldn't have said that about your father. It's my hurt pride, that's all. I'm not very good at being rejected. Maybe this isn't the best time to have this conversation." He came close again. "Though offering me a scrap of hope might go a long way toward softening my views. You can't slap a man in the face and then expect him to agree with you. Things just don't work that way."

She grimaced. "Poor David. I haven't treated you very well, have I?"

"No better than you treat anyone else," he said, smiling faintly. "But I never thought I'd hear you admit it. You're always so righteous."

"Am I? Well, it's not an attractive trait." She gave him a wry look, as she bent to retrieve the pail—the butter already melting a little. "You ought to know."

David laughed, and took the pail from her hand. "Touché. If you invite me in for bread with fresh butter, I promise not to exercise my righteousness even if you provoke me. But I warn you, whatever you do, I'm not ready to give up on you, Lara. Not by a long shot."

❧21❧

Lara was painting in Gorky's studio while he watched. She had brought her studies to work from—she was painting the cow with her calf, breaking up the shapes so the two rectangular forms seemed interlocked. She felt confident again. Even though she was worried at home, her painting seemed to be improving steadily. If I didn't have this, she thought, I'd be a wreck.

Gorky finally broke the silence. "I am starved for nature in this city. When I was a boy, I had an Arab horse, Astigy, and a sheep dog, Zongo. I used to ride up in the mountains facing Ararat and visit the shepherds." Dancing slowly, he broke into a high-pitched, mournful song. It made the back of Lara's throat tickle.

"You're making me want to cry," she said. "I can't concentrate."

"Sometimes you work better if you let your hand and eye go without too much interference."

"You're right. I seem to be concentrating from some deep point inside." It seemed to her that the cow's head she'd been painting echoed the calf's with great tenderness. The tongue was reaching for the udder.

He came close. "Be more daring. Break the forms even more. Remember, you don't have to stay outside on the surface skin. You can pierce it, open it up."

For the first time, Lara didn't want to do what he told her. It simply seemed wrong. Without saying a word, she squeezed out some cadmium yellow and laid a broad strip of color across the cow's legs and under her belly. She painted surges of strong orange red on both sides of the calf's tongue reaching for the teat. That's it, she thought—it marks the place of desire.

"Lara, it's too bright," he said, watching while she highlighted the curve of the cow's rump with the same color. "Too much pointing a direction."

"I can't help it. I want to bring your eye to it. Why don't you just ignore me for a while or tell me stories." She kept painting slowly, adding another cow's head, sketched lightly over yellow and green.

"I thought you wanted me to teach you."

"You have. But now I think I need to experiment a little, follow my instinct. Please don't get in a huff."

"In a huff?"

"It means angry, with ruffled feathers like a bird."

"Ah. . . ."

"I'm sure you had to find your way once too. What did Holger Cahill say about your first show? 'This Caucasian stranger, having just quenched his hunger and thirst, is ready to shoulder down the doors into a land of his own.' And you had the grit to do it!" She smiled at him. He was a powerfully sensual man. She liked him. She wished he had found a way to get more of that into his art, but it was all in his body, the way he moved, his burning eyes, his huge hands.

"What made your father leave Armenia?" she asked. "I want to know more about you."

He couldn't resist. "He didn't want to fight in the Turkish army. He would have had to fight his own people. I was too young to understand. I was so angry, I lost the power to speak." He was walking rapidly around the room, caught up in his story. She kept painting. "I didn't say another word until I was five."

She thought of this huge man mute, furious, small.

"You should paint that."

"What?" he asked, shocked. "That is nothing to paint. That is a story. My painting has nothing to do with my life."

"It could."

"No, it couldn't. It has to do with the relation of objects in space."

"Why limit it to that?"

"Cubism isn't limited to any time or place, that's its glory. Because it doesn't create illusion, because it resists the pleasure of showing appearances, it has the possibility of suggesting infinite amplitude, infinite space."

"You say that beautifully."

"I've convinced you?"

"You've moved me. Finish your story. What made you decide to talk?"

"A tutor my mother hired for me pretended to jump off a cliff."

"What a horrible thing to do to a child."

"I couldn't let him die. I had to speak." He stood behind her, almost touching. "But in my painting I returned to my silence."

Her eyes filled. She put down her brush, conscious of the heat of his body behind her.

"You are a man of contrasts."

"But you like them?"

"Very much." She turned from her easel to face him and put her arms around his neck.

"You know how I feel about you," he whispered. "Such a beautiful woman. You could be my muse."

She put her fingers on his lips. "Don't. This isn't like that."

"You are perfect."

"Listen, this is to be just once—just once, as a present, a celebration."

"What are you saying?"

"That it's just for now. I want to feel your moustache scratching my face."

"We'll visit Armenia, I'll show you the fountains where the village women rub their breasts against the rocks."

"Pretend I'm a village woman." She opened her blouse.

"Don't you want me to court you?"

"You don't have to do or be anything. I don't want you to talk. Don't even think." She took his hand and cupped it under her breast, relieved at how easy this was after the awkwardness with David. "Just enjoy."

"I can't understand you."

"Don't try." She pressed herself against him, wanting him to be quiet. She wanted simply the sensation of strong legs and pelvis pressing against her. Large arms, large hands exploring her body with a certain roughness. She didn't want to be anyone's muse. His moustache was coarse. It bristled against her skin, her face, her breasts as he began to kiss her. Good. Let it. He took her nipple in his mouth and pulled on it, sucking until it almost hurt.

It's all right, she thought, before she let her body soften. My painting is safe. I don't have to change it. I don't have to listen any more than I want to. She saw it glowing at her over his shoulder, just before she closed her eyes. "Hold me hard," she said, biting his shoulder. "As hard as you can."

❧22❧

Johnnie couldn't sleep. Even though his mother had a sick headache and had told him not to bother her, he went up to her room with the idea that she would make him cocoa and talk. He needed her to shut out the voices in his head that were whispering phrases from Hitler's *Mein Kampf*. "Pierce any abscess and a Jew leaps out . . . Jews are the black plague." Even before he reached the door he heard voices.

"You shouldn't have come, you know." Here the voice got faint and he couldn't quite hear. "Johnnie is. . . . What if he?" Then there was an angry mutter. A man's voice, it sounded like Walter. Then what sounded like objects being thrown down with a soft thud. Then his mother's voice, low, urgent. "No, please." Johnnie couldn't bear the strange sound of fear mixed with something he couldn't understand.

"No," she said again, almost a moan. Johnnie threw open the door and saw a man with his back to him, his mother down on the floor in front of him. The man had his hands around his mother's throat and was swaying back and forth, as if strangling her. Johnnie didn't stop to think, he ran forward and grabbed the man by the shoulders and pulled him back. The man exclaimed in pain. Agnes screamed "Johnnie, don't!"

The man tried to turn and fight back but he was hampered by his pants, which had slipped down around his ankles. As he stumbled, cursing and clutching himself, Johnnie, almost in tears, punched him. The man, having assured himself that he was still intact, tried to kick off his pants and fell to the floor, bare ass up, hitting his head on a decorative chamber pot as he went down. Johnnie stared at the white gleam of his buttocks, then kicked at them with one foot. It went through his mind that his mother shouldn't be looking at this. "Is he dead?"

Agnes was surprisingly calm. She knelt and examined Walter, took his pulse, her nightgown loose. "No, but he'll have a terrible bump on his head." She looked at Johnnie, her forehead wrinkled as if she were trying hard to think of how to explain this to him. "He'll be furious," she muttered to herself. "You shouldn't have hit him, John John. Didn't I teach you never to hit?"

"But he was strangling you."

"Maybe Lara's right, you're a fantasist. You thought he was strangling me? No, he was"—she stammered, stopped short, glanced around her. Her eyes rested for a minute on the chamber pot and suddenly her face brightened—"he was using my chamber pot," she said. "I think he was a little drunk, but you didn't need to hit him. I was helping him get his trousers zipped. The zipper stuck and then he couldn't get it closed. I couldn't let him go out like that with his pants open, could I?"

Johnnie shook his head. He started pulling up Walter's pants, tugging them over that bare white expanse. Walter started to stir.

"Go now. He's waking up. Don't worry, he won't be angry at you."

❦

The next day Johnnie tried to talk to his mother about what had happened. She gave him an odd smile. "You and Walter fighting in my room? What an odd idea," she said, straightening his jacket. "Walter's miles away in New York. You should get some fresh air, Johnnie. Sitting inside and reading those awful books breeds morbid thoughts."

"But Walter?"

"Please don't insist on this nonsense, Johnnie. I'm being as patient as I can. Go for a walk or a swim, something active. Put it out of your mind."

Johnnie wandered around the farm the way she had told him to, taking deep breaths and swinging his arms. He wondered why people kept trying to convince him things were different from the way he saw them. He knew Walter had been in her room and he knew Walter meant harm just as he knew that the Jews were in danger. Danger had a smell like burning rubber. It came at him when he read about Jews being beaten up in Austria just as it rose up from Walter's body when Johnnie touched him. A deep black pungent smell.

He stood looking at the vegetable garden for a moment to calm himself. Everything was innocently growing, unaware of the threatening black smell. The vines were heavy with ripe tomatoes, the beans clambering up their poles, masses of peas sprawled over their supports. He wasn't a dirty Jew, he thought. What he did was clean, innocent as these growing things in front of him. What came from love was good, he realized. Only hate was bad. He hated Walter. He loved his mother and Lara. And what you loved, you needed to be close to and touch. It was natural. He broke off a pod and opened it, scooping out the tender peas with his tongue. He wished he were an animal, so he could lie in the stables, his head against a warm flank. You saw the cows kissing each other, rubbing their broad quiet foreheads against each other's sides, their eyes placid. He imagined himself sucking his thumb the way he had as a baby. Nothing to worry about, lulled by the comfortable warm breath of the cows.

Johnnie saw Robin by the screened porch of the big house. The door was ajar. Sue, the intern, must have gone inside to the bathroom and not wanted to disturb Robin's play—she was surrounded by a large circle of blocks. But Robin wasn't building, she was squatting down, watching a yellow liquid drip down between her legs onto the ground. He watched her, fascinated. She pulled up her skirt so she could see the pee come through the white cotton of her panties like a sieve. She touched it with her fingers, pressed, put her fingers to her nose, to her mouth. He ought to help her, he thought, ought to take off her panties.

He approached her slowly, but she was so absorbed in what she was doing that she didn't seem to notice. When he drew her pants off, she was still looking quietly at the damp, dark patch on the gravel. She bent her head and looked between her legs gravely, poked herself for a moment, looked again to see if more was coming out. Her pubic mound was very white and he could see the little cleft and its red knob. He had never been so close before except maybe to Lara. He felt himself getting excited. She was so small and she didn't seem to notice him. Hesitantly he reached out and touched her softness.

"Mine is different," he said uncertainly, "it's bigger. I can put out fires with it. I can pee standing up. Do you want to see me do it?" When she didn't respond, he unzipped his pants and took out his penis. "See, I can make circles on the pavement. I can even write your name. See." He moved slowly, manipulating the stream of urine, proud of his control. But Robin only glanced up briefly then back at herself. Upset at having his offering ignored, Johnnie pleaded with her. "Why don't you like it?" He shook himself off, took her hand and put it on him. "It's silky. You can pet it like an animal." Her hand was inert. She began to look distressed. Still pressing her hand around his penis, he suddenly started to cry.

That's how Lara found him. "What in God's name are you doing?" she shouted, pulling Robin away.

"She didn't want to play," Johnnie said.

"John"—she held Robin close to her—"you're not a two-year-old. You're a man. You can't just. . . ." She stopped and stood there, her face red, no point in trying to talk to him, she could see that, but still she couldn't help being angry. "Zip up your pants, John. Hurry up!" She looked around her nervously. "Oh God, John, why do you have to do these things? What if it hadn't been me that found you? Do you know what they do to people like you? Do you? Tell me."

Robin, who had been calm until then, started to give little shrieks, hearing the panic in Lara's voice.

"Come on, Robin." Lara took her by the hand and started through the screen door. "We'll look for Sue and then we'll go

paint. Johnnie"—she turned and motioned down at his fly—
"your pants."

"Don't tell Mother," he said just loud enough for her to
hear. "Please."

Your pants, she signed to him, mimicking the action, close
your pants. When she looked back just before she went into the
house, he was standing bent over, fumbling with his zipper.

❧23❧

That night Johnnie opened Lara's door and went over to her bed. He sat down on the edge and took his shoes and socks off, then he pulled back the covers. She woke with a start from a deep sleep.

He put a hand tentatively on her shoulder, "Let me lie next to you," he said in a whisper.

"Johnnie?" she asked, still groggy. She couldn't quite remember where she was. "Wasn't the door locked?" No, it couldn't have been. She'd forgotten.

"I'll be good. I promise. I just want to put my head on your shoulder and smell your hair the way I used to. Don't be angry about the girl, it's you I want to be near." He bent his head close to her face so his hair tickled her cheek. She could feel his breath.

"You hurt me," she said, pushing his head away. He kept his hand on her shoulder and she could feel its warmth.

"Only once. I didn't mean to." The moon peering through the window was the moon of fifteen years ago—huge, pale yellow, it glimmered on their secret world.

Caught unaware, she felt tears on her tongue. "More than once." Back then, she had called her mother but her mother had just told her to be quiet and go to sleep. She had never wanted to listen, wouldn't listen.

"I couldn't help it. It happened by itself."

She sat up suddenly, fists clenched. "You still don't understand, do you? It shouldn't have. I was just a child. I trusted you."

"But you liked it before that," he said.

She shuddered. It was true, she'd loved the warmth, lying close, telling each other secrets, the fumbling child kisses, the power her small, breastless body inexplicably gave her over her big brother.

"You used to sing to me, remember? Into my ear. Guten Abend, gut' Nacht," he began in a sweet soprano, "mit Rosen bedacht . . . ."

She looked down at his long pale feet, whiter than the lullaby's lilies, and felt herself getting hysterical. "You've got to get out of here." She pushed him off the bed and got up. "Right now. Get out!" She didn't want to hear about the roses or the lilies, or slipping under the covers. She had a visceral memory of his erection pressing up between her legs.

At the door he turned and clutched her. "My head hurts," he said into her neck. She could feel him trembling. "Please let me stay. I'll sleep at the foot of your bed, on the floor, anywhere. . . ."

"Oh God, Johnnie . . . stop. . . . It won't work, don't you see? I can't. Now go . . . you'll wake Mother." Invoking her name hadn't helped back then. He'd always said, "Oh, Mother's on my side, she won't believe you," but now, she noted with obscure satisfaction, Johnnie looked frightened. He slunk off down the hall like a pale ghost, and she locked the door behind him with a click.

∽·∾

"Would you wake Johnnie?" Agnes asked Lara. "He's sleeping awfully late."

Ordinarily Lara would have told her mother to wake him herself but she had an odd feeling at the pit of her stomach. She went into his room—painted a dusty blue—walked slowly over to the bed with the model planes hung above it, and looked down at him. He was breathing, there was nothing to worry about—she'd been crazy to think that just locking the door . . . she'd been locking it for years.

She shook him gently thinking that she'd ask him to have breakfast with her on the terrace.

"John, wake up!" His eyelids were a peculiar bluish color, they seemed to lie heavily on his eyes. They didn't even flutter. The breathing that had reassured her before seemed too harsh. She shook him harder, hard enough to wake anybody, even if he'd been drinking, and Johnnie didn't drink. Finally she slapped his cheek. She saw the red mark of her fingers.

"Wake up, Johnnie," she said as loudly as she could, but he wouldn't wake up and his eyes, when she lifted the lids, were rolled back. A second later she saw the empty bottle of sleeping pills on the floor.

How could he do this? Had he imagined her finding him?

"Call an ambulance," she called to her mother. "Hurry! And get David! Johnnie's unconscious. . . ."

David ran to the bedroom in his robe, followed by Muriel.

The scene struck her as a scene from the new Buñuel-Dali movie, figures moving in a room that seemed unreal, actions that were really something else—like David taking Johnnie's pulse—in the movie his wrist would have metamorphosed to her wrist and then to a snake or a hose. "He took a lot of pills," she said hoarsely.

David's voice sounded ridiculously normal. "Pulse is weak but he's breathing." She saw him struggling to pull Johnnie to a sitting position and moved to help. But she didn't feel as if she were there. She was somewhere outside, watching while David opened Johnnie's mouth—the tongue was coated and swollen—and inserted two fingers down his throat. A little pale bile came out.

"It's no use. They'll have to pump his stomach. Get some more blankets," he said and Agnes rushed off. "We need to keep him warm."

"What happened?" Muriel asked Lara softly. "Do you know why he did this?"

"Later, Mur," David said propping Johnnie into a sitting position. "No one's coherent right now."

"I heard you arguing with him last night," Agnes said, coming back into the room with two of her afghans. "What did you do to him?"

Lara observed her mother from a great distance. "Can't you wait till you see if he's going to die before you start blaming me?" Could she be going to lose her father and her brother in one year? So close together. At least they'd seen the spring, she thought.

"But you. . .", Agnes began.

"People don't do something like this because of a little argument with their sister," Lara heard David's voice firmly cutting her off. "And blame never gets you anywhere. Let's get these blankets on him."

Lara looked at him gratefully.

For the moment she was saved.

∼24∼

A few days after Johnnie's suicide attempt, Robin collapsed completely. Wouldn't eat, wouldn't chew what was put into her mouth, just let it sit there. Finally she withdrew to her bed upstairs in the big house, in Johnnie's old room, her eyes closed, seeming not even to hear. Lara sat watching while Muriel cradled Robin's head on her lap as they waited for the young intern to arrive for her shift. If sheer goodwill could make things happen, Lara thought, looking at Muriel, Robin would open her eyes.

"She needs as much contact as she can get," Muriel explained, smoothing back the child's fine blond hair, plastered to her forehead by the late August heat. "David and I will have to take turns doing this."

"I could stay with her tonight, if it would help," Lara said. "You're already getting contractions. You don't want to have the baby early."

"I'm fine." Muriel's gray eyes were shining, but her face looked tired and there were beads of sweat at her temples.

"Aren't you afraid?" Lara blurted out.

"Of what?"

Of losing David, Lara wanted to ask. It wasn't just that he'd kissed her: yesterday she saw him eying Sue the intern's breasts. "Of labor," she said.

Muriel smiled. "On the contrary, I want this baby out. It's slowing me down."

"I could never have done what you've been doing with Robin, pregnant as you are," Lara said. She could still see Muriel soothing Robin at the pool after she'd bitten her.

Muriel's eyebrows went up. "I've stopped lifting her."

"I don't mean that. I mean the attention." It's what she wanted in her painting, the sense of an endless pouring out.

Muriel looked as though she didn't understand, couldn't grasp the fact that other people didn't have this endless generosity.

Sue smiled at them from the doorway and Muriel extricated herself from under Robin's head. "I'll stay nearby," she told Sue, giving Robin's limp hand a final pat, "just in case she wakes up."

They went through the small door into the adjoining room, and Lara again felt the shock of seeing her parents' bedroom completely transformed. Everything that had been dark and fussy was cheerful and practical. Muriel had replaced the old four-poster with an early American bed in warm maple. There was an array of green plants under the windows, a hooked rug, two soft comfortable armchairs.

"This might be a blessing in disguise," Muriel said, dropping into a chair and kicking off her shoes. "Maybe Robin didn't go back far enough with us. We hand-fed a lot, let her wet, but maybe she needs to give up her mobility, stop walking, even standing." She paused and stretched her toes luxuriously. "Really be as helpless as a baby."

"What good can that do?" Lara asked, horrified. Wasn't the idea to get better by gradually learning and doing more? She sat down in the other chair, facing Muriel.

"My guess is that unconsciously Robin wants to re-do something, do it better this time. I'd like to try it, give her a bottle, push her around in a baby carriage. Maybe then she can relax, relive a time in her early life that was obviously disappointing to her."

"But isn't she too old to be acting like a baby?" Lara pictured Robin scrunched grotesquely into a pram—it seemed like another example of Muriel going too far. "I've never really understood why she got sick in the first place."

"Probably due to a combination of inborn sensitivities and poor care." Muriel paused and Lara saw her belly lurch. "God knows Robin's mother had real reasons to be anxious and distracted when she was nursing her. Her husband had just lost his job, she was sick—but what matters is that we're left with a child who needs to be coaxed back to life. We've got to get her to want something for herself, even if it's just a suck of milk from a bottle." Muriel glanced through the door into Robin's room.

"But what if Robin's given up wanting to try?" Lara asked. Robin was still stretched out under the sheet, completely immobile. "What if we can't reach her?"

"I don't think it's as serious as it looks, Lara," Muriel said, leaning her head back against the chair. "She has made so much progress in such a short time, eating by herself, expressing anger, learning to masturbate—true, only analysts would consider this last a worthy achievement," she smiled. "It's probably sensory overload, a sort of short circuit. Besides, she saw the ambulance men come to take Johnnie. That probably frightened her."

Lara winced. "What if something else happened? I mean, something to upset her?"

Muriel looked at her, suddenly alert. "Did you see anything?"

"Well, I just thought, you know, all the hired men. Someone could have seen her, or made some gesture."

"Neither Gus nor Rider looks like a child molester to me. I think it's just overload."

This was it, Lara thought: if she was going to say anything, she'd better do it now.

"Johnnie exposed himself to her. I saw him." She got it all out in a rush.

Muriel straightened up. "You did? When?"

"The day before he took the pills. I guess Sue thought Robin would be all right in the garden for a few minutes."

Muriel looked at her with an expression Lara had come to recognize, of a sergeant taking control.

"Was there anything else?"

"You mean . . . ? No, he didn't . . . ," she stumbled over the words, "rape her or anything but he put her hand on him."

"Did he fondle her?"

"I don't know. She had her pants down but she was peeing."

Muriel had gotten up from her chair and started pacing around the room swinging her arms, her belly swaying. "So that's what happened. I'm glad you told me, Lara. Now I know just how to deal with him when he comes home."

Lara had expected outrage, blame, concern, anything but this. She felt her facial muscles stiffen. "But he's not coming home. As soon as he can be moved, the doctors want him to go to Battle Creek."

"That's a mistake. It's not at all appropriate. Look, these places, even the best of them, aren't good for people. The patients are confined, the regime is stultifying." Muriel picked up a magazine from the floor next to the chair and flipped rapidly to the picture of what looked like a manor house surrounded by a high fence. "See this? It's an asylum for retarded girls. There are no learning programs, no activities of any kind." She rapped the back of her hand against the page. "The children are treated as slaves of the state."

Lara glanced at the headline. 'Reporter exposes all at Letchworth. Delinquents turn deficients into criminals.'

"Battle Creek doesn't sound like that," she said weakly.

"No, of course not, but even there, doors are locked, there's a deadening routine of medication, other patients in turmoil, an arts and crafts program where they make little things. There's nothing really related to Johnnie's life or his problems."

Muriel stopped pacing and looked down at Lara. "We have to get him back home."

Lara looked at her, open-mouthed. "But they think he's dangerous," she stammered. "When he came to, he kept saying that Walter was trying to hurt Mother. They had to put him in restraints to keep him from running out of the hospital. He wouldn't believe she was alright."

Muriel waved this aside. "It seems ironic. They let potential murderers out of prison every day but if someone is emotionally distressed and shows too much concern, they tie him up."

"He was awfully excited. They were afraid he might run Walter through with a poker. And it was all mixed up with his ideas about the Jews."

"Ah! I'm beginning to understand," Muriel said. "Everything's starting to make sense. You see, he has sexual fantasies, he feels dirty, he thinks he should be punished. Then he projects all this onto Walter. I think if we attack the guilt directly, Johnnie's obsessions will disappear. Please don't look so worried, Lara. He didn't do anything so terrible. There was no penetration, he didn't rape her, he just put her hand on his penis. It's no catastrophe."

Lara's palms were clammy. "What if. . . ." She stopped, not even wanting to think it. She took a breath. "What if next time he goes further?"

"I don't think he will. You'll see, we'll work it out. Even with incest cases, I've found it's much better to have the two people together at home."

"Better? I don't see. . . ." She trailed off.

"If Johnnie has contact with Robin, it'll give him a chance to feel remorse. Take responsibility for what he did. I can help him talk it out."

Lara glanced again at Robin—she didn't feel reassured. "It seems pretty risky."

Muriel looked at her reprovingly. "Don't you want your brother home?" She started walking again. "Don't worry, I've handled worse cases."

Lara spent the night holding Robin and thinking about Johnnie coming home, wondering whether she should have told Muriel the things Johnnie had done with *her*. Would it have made a difference? She stroked Robin and offered her the bottle that Muriel had prepared. Robin didn't spit the nipple out but didn't close her mouth around it either. Toward morning Lara tiptoed downstairs and heated the milk on the stove, figuring that a warm bottle would be more comfortable. When she tried the bottle again, Robin pressed her lips lightly but perceptibly around the rubber tit.

Lara held the bottle still, watching Robin's lips. It almost seemed easier for Robin to change than for Johnnie—because Robin was starting from so little, any tiny movement forward was progress. But how did you undo a lifetime of wrong moves? Didn't they eventually take you into a street with only a blank wall in front of you and no way out, even if you wanted to find an exit? And she wasn't sure Johnnie did.

❧25❧

Lara had seen Johnnie in the hospital before, but she was still horrified by the strange wax-like pallor of his skin, as though it were a mask, not a face. She threw open the curtain so the sun streamed across his body huddled under the hospital sheet, then bent and kissed his forehead. "Hello, John John." He had an odd sweetish smell. The non-expression didn't change. She stroked his limp hand and arm.

"How're you doing? Mother and I brought you some roses from the garden." This damn room was so sterile, all cold metallic edges. How could they expect him to want to look at anything? She rubbed the flower gently across his lips. "Like silk, isn't it? The color is unbelievable." She wanted him to open his eyes to see the glorious red with the pink center, but he kept them closed.

"My favorite camellia got a blight," Agnes said. "It turned brown, just like that, from one day to the next." Lara nudged her. She stopped, looking down at her son with a pained expression. Then she began to bustle around the bed. "These nurses don't know how to fluff a pillow," she said angrily. "It's outrageous. They haven't even straightened the covers."

159

"Maybe he was resting," Lara said, pulling the sheet up gently before her mother could tug it, "and they didn't want to disturb him."

"Humph," Agnes snorted. "That's no excuse for sloppiness."

Lara saw Johnnie cringe at her mother's tone and imagined the words 'sloppy,' 'dirty,' 'bad' revolving slowly before his eyes in red letters. Lara pressed his hand reassuringly.

"Never mind," she said.

"What's to mind?" Agnes asked. "I'm just concerned with his comfort."

"You sound angry, that's all. I can tell it upsets him."

"But I'm not angry at him."

"It's the judgmental tone. Forget it. I'll explain another time."

"He always was a sensitive child," Agnes said, wondering why Lara always acted as if everything were her fault. She walked over to the corner sink and stood with her back to the bed. While she let the water run into the empty pitcher, she thought of what an exquisite child Johnnie had been, with his golden curls—almost like a little girl in his baby dresses. And so brilliant, too.

Lara turned back to Johnnie, concentrating hard. She felt as though he were a fish deep down in dark water and words were the only bait she had to bring him up. Her instinct told her they should be concrete, practical, sensuous.

"How about making a kite like a giant rose?" she asked softly, "a little like your dragon one. You know the one, with the gold-bronze scales. Except petals in reds and pinks." She thought she saw a flicker of interest. "When you come back home, we could work on it together." With Robin, she almost said, and stopped herself, stomach knotting. She couldn't let herself think of that now.

"I don't think I'm coming home," he whispered. "They've been talking to me about being translated to another sphere. I'm going to be translated any time now. I'm just not sure of the means of transportation." He gave a little laugh. "Remember when I put gin in the car instead of antifreeze? It ran, didn't it? So don't worry. If it happens, I'll take you with me."

"I know you will." To the moon or to a state of higher consciousness, wherever it was he thought he was going.

"Is it the spirits again?" Agnes asked, troubled. "Do you think that maybe someone is really trying to communicate? What do they look like, Johnnie? Do they have auras?" She wondered if his genius was taking a roundabout route to some new revelation. Because he *was* a genius, she'd never stopped believing that. She never forgot how the Russian mathematicians had examined him, sitting amazed like the elders around Jesus in the temple.

"Mother, please, I've begged you not to do this. You'll only make it worse."

"Don't shush me, Lara. I'm your mother. I have my experience, too." Agnes put the pitcher down on the bedside table. "My friend Edna talks to her husband's ghost through a medium—and she's as normal as you or I." He's the next Einstein, the Russians had said. It seemed to her that this was all a nightmare, that soon she'd wake up and find her brilliant boy again.

Lara bit her lip. "That medium is a charlatan. She took advantage of your friend's grief. It's pathetic."

"Spengler's right. This world's finished," John said suddenly. "The new one will be better."

"Prophets have always been misunderstood in their own time," Agnes said.

It was bad enough to have *one* of them seeing things. Lara felt like shaking her mother.

"Johnnie, Otis's black cat had kittens," she could hear herself chattering. "There is every combination, a spotted one, a gray, a pure black with white feet."

"I'm tired by it," John said, opening his eyes a slit. "It tires my head to think of all these things—cats, roses, even kites. They're no good anymore. I'm trying, Lara, but I can't. They seem like pictures at the wrong end of a telescope, all the light is out of them. They're dingy. Even my body doesn't seem real anymore. It's just dead matter, lumpen stuff, mud." Lara made a sound of distress.

"How can you say things like that?" Agnes asked. "You have a beautiful body. You always did from the time you were a boy." She pictured him as a slender adolescent with the light down of a man beginning on his cheeks, walking with his arm around Lara's shoulder. The horrible suspicion struck her that maybe, just maybe, he had done the things Lara had said he did. When she had cried and complained and asked her mother not to let him into her bed. "You read too many depressing things, that's all," she said, appalled at her own thoughts. "Too many heavy books." She didn't quite know what she was saying but she kept on babbling. "You should strengthen yourself. Walter has these wonderful exercises he does outside in the open air with dumbbells."

Johnnie moved his head back and forth agitatedly on the pillow. "We're all false forms. Pseudomorphs, like Spengler says. Not just me—you. The whole country. Rotten flesh."

"You've got to get rid of ideas like that." Agnes twitched a dust kitten off the coverlet. "Walter says vigorous physical movement. . . ."

"Mother," Lara said sharply. "I don't think this is a good subject."

Agnes flushed. She knew she shouldn't have mentioned him but Eugene was gone, there was no authority to cite anymore. She needed something to counteract what she was thinking. "Healthy exercise? What on earth could be wrong with it?"

"W a l t e r," Lara mouthed.

Agnes pulled a chair next to the bed and sat down. "Johnnie, sweetheart, open your eyes and look at me."

Johnnie shut his eyes tighter.

"Please try. You have to make some effort to help yourself."

He put his hands over his ears and started to intone, "Walter weather wretched wrenched wronged."

Agnes tugged at his hands. He held on ferociously. "I don't know why you act as though I'm hurting you. How am I? Tell me? Please."

"Wronged donged"

"Not now, Mother." Lara took hold of her mother's arm and pulled her away. "He's not ready for this. Forget Walter, John John, it's okay. No one's going to force you to listen to anything."

"Walter water." His voice rose, spinning out of control, "waiter weightman nightman frightman. . . ."

Lara felt herself beginning to panic. She pushed hard on the nurse's bell as the words blurred into a steady roar of sound.

<h1 style="text-align: center;">✦26✦</h1>

David made a buggy for Robin from scraps of wood he found in the barn. It looked like a piece of junk, but it was strong enough to hold her.

"I wish I felt this would do some good," Lara said doubtfully. Robin had opened her eyes and watched Lara when she moved around the room but she hadn't shown any inclination to move herself. She lay impassively even when they rolled her to the side to change the sheets.

"Do you want to go for a ride?" Lara asked her, bending over the bed. To her surprise, Robin lifted her arms like a baby wanting to be picked up. Strange as it might seem, maybe Muriel had the right idea.

David scooped Robin up, looked across her at Lara, and carried her downstairs. When he put her in the buggy, she made feeble efforts to curl herself into a ball.

"Our baby," Lara said with light irony as she maneuvered the lumbering carriage out the front door. "Beautiful but odd. It's appropriate, don't you think? That I should have a frozen child."

"I'm sorry I ever said those things to you," he said, putting a hand on the carriage handle and helping her push. "You have plenty of feelings. They're just not always the ones I want." The carriage wobbled and creaked. Gravel scrunched under their feet.

She steered the carriage up the main drive, under the shade of the maple trees. Every so often, there were gusts of hot wind.

"You see the leaves move, Sleeping Beauty, don't you?" she asked Robin, who was looking up intently at the changing patterns of light and shade.

"Might be nice to be pushed around in a carriage," David said. "What do you think? Not having to do anything at all."

"Did you like it when you were blind and they pushed you around in a wheelchair?" Lara answered sharply.

"Are you still mad at me?" he asked.

"No," she said quickly, shaking her head. "Well, yes, maybe, because you're as scared as I am, but I don't know what of. You're running away as much as I am. But what from? Is it Muriel? No, don't flare up," she said, seeing his forehead furrow. "It doesn't help. We've got to talk about her sometime."

"I don't feel as though I'm running away," he said quietly after a minute. She could feel his shoulder trembling against hers. "I love Muriel"—he hesitated—"too."

"I had a nurse, when I was a baby"—Lara stopped and wet her wrists in the brook alongside the road—"who had the most amazing big breasts. When I sat on her lap, I'd lean against them and feel perfectly secure."

"What's that supposed to mean?"

"It's nice to be taken care of when you're a baby, that's all. And some of us," she looked pointedly at him, "hate to give it up."

"You *are* angry at me. Is my persisting in loving you that offensive? Or are you still brooding about our quarrel?"

"You have Muriel to take care of you"—the words came tumbling out—"and now you want me for excitement." She glanced down at Robin, who was still lying tightly curled.

David's face went white. "Is it Johnnie that's making you like this?" he asked her.

"Like what?"

"Moralizing like some Florence Nightingale. Being right-eous all over again. I thought you understood something, but you're just the way you were before. What happened?"

"Nothing. My brother just tried to commit suicide, that's all." She made an ironic flourish with one hand. "My mother is acting like a fool with a man I despise. And I have florid night-mares about vampire bats."

"It's bad, but it's not the end of the world. You don't need to fall apart, too."

"I'm not falling apart," she said. She wasn't being fair to him. How could she expect him to understand if she talked about her nurse and mentioned suggestive dreams. "I guess I'm not being clear, David. Look, I don't want to hurt your feelings." She flushed as she realized that wasn't exactly true. "I like you as a friend but I don't want to be your mother." He started to protest but she held up her hand. "You were right about my being involved with my family, with Johnnie. I have a lot to figure out, and when I'm with men sometimes I'm not thinking about them, I'm trying to see how I feel about him."

He stopped short. "Ha . . . just what I thought."

"It's easy to be clever about someone else," she said, an-noyed. "You don't want a relationship either, David, you want an escape. I'm not sure why. I can't see into your bedroom. I have no idea what's going on between you and Muriel. But I don't want to be a surrogate nipple."

"Well," he blew out through pursed lips, "that's certainly clear enough. Physician heal thyself, hmmm . . . sorry, for being so slow on the uptake."

"No need." She suppressed a twinge of triumph. "Let's just forget about it."

A trickle of saliva came out of Robin's perfectly shaped lips. Lara wiped it off. Maybe Robin could get a second chance at being a baby, she thought, but not David, and not Lara either.

∽27∾

Agnes was doing yoga in her bedroom on the oriental rug while Lara sketched the tree outside the window. Lara didn't usually work near her, but with Johnnie in the hospital it made them both feel better, or at least Agnes felt better. She jumped up, came down with her feet apart and then bent slowly over her right leg, keeping her torso parallel to the floor.

The movement was calming. She needed it. Besides, she thought, I have to keep my body in shape. She breathed slowly, strained by the pose. Walter had been understandably upset by all this and she was determined not to lose him.

Agnes looked over at Lara, afraid for a moment she'd been able to read her thoughts—she wished Lara liked Walter. Maybe that was too much to ask. It was natural for a girl to be loyal to her father. And she knew Lara thought Walter was too young for her. But he had such energy, he made her feel beautiful. She thought of how he'd stroked her hair last night, petted her, done all the romantic things she liked. Her body was starting to come alive in a new way. She caught herself looking down admiringly at her breasts and hips when she dressed in the morning, seeing them the way Walter did. She was beginning to believe him when he told her how attractive she was. God knows, she thought, feeling the play of her muscles, stretching and contracting, maybe it was true. Maybe she was going to have a chance at happiness.

She touched her calf with one hand, stretched the other arm out next to her ear with a grunt of effort, and stood—wide-stanced—in a crude approximation of a triangle. From where she was, leaning over, she could see Lara's sketch pad.

"You're doing the tree house," she said, feeling restored, "where you and Johnnie used to play." It was too bad children had to grow up.

"I thought I'd take it to him." Lara looked out at the maple tree with its steps moving up the trunk. Like a shaggy animal. The platform only partly visible between the fat leaves. She was doing one sketch for Johnnie—another for her lesson with Gorky. It was lucky, she thought, that he hadn't insisted on sleeping with her again. He'd wanted to. He'd written her passionate love poetry. All about the fires that blazed in his bones when he touched her. She smiled to herself. It probably sounded better in Armenian. She suddenly noticed the beauty of the negative spaces between the branches. What wasn't there was more important than what was, she thought, shading the spaces to emphasize them.

It was too bad; Gorky was a sexy man. Thinking about his big hands on her body gave her a frisson of lust, but she knew if she wanted to keep him as her teacher, she couldn't have him as a lover. His accepting that, however grudgingly, made her freer to take his critiques of her paintings. Learn, listen, but develop them in her own way. She'd begun to keep some of her most egregious departures to herself.

She took another sheet of paper and broke up the shapes, moving away from the fact of tree and branch and platform. Gorky would probably have suggested she bring out more of the interrelated angles, look at the platform from the side and the back, but her imagination was stimulated by the negative spaces. One, in the curve of a branch, suggested her father's face—a leaf for a mouth. She was less interested in presenting a formal concept of what was out there, she thought with mounting excitement—oblong shape of tree, half curve of leaf

—than in using it as a door to some inner space, a space of symbol and fantasy.

"How's your father's portrait coming along?" Agnes asked, when Lara finally put down her pastels and wiped her hands. "I haven't seen you working at it for a while." She cradled her feet in both hands, working her knees down. She probably shouldn't have mentioned the portrait. If it was going badly, Lara would be annoyed—she always said there was a direct line from her mother's mind to her tongue. It wasn't kind, but it might be true.

"I've stopped for a while," Lara said, "I think I need to work out some technical things first."

Good. She seemed cheerful enough. Not even a nasty look. Maybe this trouble with poor Johnnie was bringing them closer. At least it seemed to be making Lara less critical. She actually seemed softer. Agnes wondered suddenly why Lara never criticized Eugene but acted as if he'd been perfect. The unfairness of it hurt her. What about *his* adventures? She put her forefinger and her thumb together, resting her hands gently on her thighs in the position of meditation. She sighed. Well, it wasn't for her to speak ill of the dead.

A few minutes later, Agnes uncoiled her legs, massaged the calves briefly and stood up.

"Oh my goodness," she sputtered, all quietness gone. "I didn't notice the time. I'd better put up my hair if I'm going to get to the city for my appointment with your father's executor."

"Why are you seeing Sol?" Lara asked.

"I need an advance on next year's installment."

"What on earth for?"

"Different things. Repairs on the roof, for instance."

"Oh."

"Don't scowl. It's all perfectly ordinary." She went briskly into the bathroom and shut the door against her daughter's curiosity.

❧28❧

Johnnie was home, sitting on the lawn in a deck chair under a big tree watching Muriel garden. She had seen him sketching some wing designs yesterday—he started them in the hospital—and had gotten out of him that he'd taken a degree in engineering, designing a wing with maximum lift. She thought it was a sign of returning health that he was interested in something from his academic past.

He sighed, watching her weeding around a giant sunflower. She had a low center of gravity, he thought slyly, looking at her belly, no wonder she liked the idea of flying. She glanced over at him and he noticed the intensity of the black pupil in her gray eyes. Sensing she had some plan for him, he sunk lower in his chair.

"How'd you get them to let me out?" he asked to distract her.

"I'm a doctor. I told them I thought you'd do better here."

He looked at her feet, brown and strangely innocent in their sandals. "And do you really?" Fine, better, best, he intoned to himself. Words without objects.

"I wouldn't have said it if I didn't."

That was true, he thought. She was all clear. The sun suited her, made her high cheekbones glow with a color that

173

Lara would have appreciated. But under his tree, he felt himself dimming, like a light about to go out. Muriel didn't seem to notice.

"I can't bend or carry as well as I used to." She smiled at him. "Will you help? Would you get the bag of fertilizer from the tool shed?"

He nodded, relieved that this was all that she wanted, and walked off slowly across the lawn. It was turning brown in spots, parched from the heat. He looked up longingly at the sleeping porch of the big house. If there was any cool breeze, that's where it would be. He remembered lying there with his broken arm, looking out past the garden and the pool to the wheat fields, listening to the whine of crickets and the harsh sound of the bullfrogs. He circled the house and got the red and white bag from the shed.

"The soil is fairly rich here but I always add some anyway," Muriel said when he came back. She cut open the bag, letting out a stream of musty peat. Then, crouching heavily, she cut it into the earth with the trowel.

"You have to get air in, let it breathe," she told him, digging her fingers into the soil, letting it crumble into fragments.

The smell was bad. He tried not to breathe it in. He took the trowel she handed him and held it at arm's length, making shallow feints at the dirt, sweat breaking out on his forehead. Muriel looked disappointed and he tried to smile at her, baring his teeth in what he hoped was a fair imitation of a grin. It seemed to work; she proffered him a handful of round yellow seeds.

"You don't like this much, do you?"

Maybe his grin had been a grimace. If he wanted to fool her—and he wasn't sure he cared enough to try—he'd have to practice in front of the mirror. He thought of a story he'd heard in the hospital of a woman who had convinced her doctors she was sane until she accidentally let slip that she had a corpse under the bed. He gave a snort of laughter.

"I like it all right," he said, when Muriel looked at him inquiringly. He put the seeds in one by one, poking them down with the end of his trowel rather than his finger, "but the earth has a fetid odor. Everything rotting together. It seems—promiscuous."

"Companionable, I'd say. But if you don't enjoy it, there's no reason to force yourself."

"I'm more interested in things that get away from the earth," he said, pointing to a hawk that was soaring above them in slow circles. "Look how that bird hangs in space. I'd give anything to make a wing like that."

But when the seeds sprouted a week later, he was obscurely pleased.

"I've been here every summer since I was born and I never noticed how this works. It's an engineering marvel!" he exclaimed to Muriel. He bent closer to examine the tiny furled leaves. "So from the root/Springs lighter the green stalk," he murmured, "from thence the leaves/More aery. . . ."

"Last the bright consummate flow'r," she finished for him.

But gardening wasn't all she had in mind for him. The next time she took him outside with her, Robin was there with the young intern, sitting on the ground tearing sheets of paper into long strips. Though she didn't look up, Johnnie felt his skin prickle when he saw her. He didn't want to be reminded.

"She started tearing again," the young intern said in a low voice to Muriel. As though Robin couldn't hear what she was saying. People talked around him that way in the hospital and he hated it. What did they think he was, a stone? He could tell from the way Sue said it that she thought tearing the paper was important just the way Muriel seemed to think his sketching the glider wings was important.

When he looked over, he saw that Robin tore methodically round and round her piece of paper—the way you'd peel an orange in one continuous strip, then she ripped the center out and threw it on the ground, staring a minute at the empty place, her small face full of disgust. Muriel and the intern exchanged a quick glance. He grimaced. The doctors had told him he over-interpreted things. Well, what did they do? He could imagine what their overheated imaginations were seeing in that hole.

Muriel sat down on the edge of his deck chair. "I know something happened with Robin to upset both of you," she said bluntly, taking his hand.

She caught him off guard. "Leave it alone," he said, pulling his hand away.

She gestured to the intern to bring Robin closer. Walking in her shambling way, still tearing, Robin let herself be steered. If he hadn't felt so humiliated, shamed like a dog for making a mess, he would have laughed to see how darkly concentrated she was on her vision, as separate from Muriel as he was.

"If you said you were sorry, I think it would make you feel a lot better. Come on, Johnnie, say you're sorry and really mean it. Cry if you like, give her a hug." She reached out, put her arm around Robin and drew her within touching distance.

Johnnie stared at her. "There are things going on in the world to be sorry about," he said, "terrible things." How could he explain to her that they made any gesture of his irrelevant?

"I know," she said soothingly. "But this is something you're responsible for. And you can do something about it."

"If enough people saw what I'm talking about they could do something about that, too." He felt himself getting hot. "What's happening in Germany can be stopped before it's too late. You could write letters to the press . . . you and David and Lara. Don't you see? What you're talking about isn't even real; this is real."

"If you could take care of your part, maybe the rest wouldn't seem so terrible." Muriel motioned to the intern to go away. "Look, you like Robin, you've been awfully good to her, helping her with the kites. And she liked being with you, trusted you. You probably wanted to get close but having her touch you wasn't the way to do it." Ah, so that was why Lara had been watching him like that, slanting her eyes at him. "I'm not telling you this to make you feel guilty but so that you can make a fresh start. You should tell her you're sorry, assure her it won't happen again."

"What's going to happen will be far worse." He'd seen it all in dreams—children with their skin flayed off, eyeballs popped out, testicles crushed. "I touched her gently," he said, "I wouldn't hurt her. I wouldn't hurt any one. Not even an animal." He felt like crying. It was all so senseless.

Robin had turned her head away, her hands still tearing out the centers. Muriel was looking so disappointed and sad he felt a melting in his gut. He could see the tiredness at the back of her eyes. How much she wanted everyone and everything to be fine. The effort it took her.

"I'm sorry," he whispered the way he had when he was a child before his father spanked him. Muriel smiled. It took so little sometimes to make people happy. And what difference did it make after all, if soon they were going to be drowned in a flood of rottenness. "I'm sorry," he said again.

✌29✌

Though it wasn't the day to see Gorky, Lara had the impulse to drop in on him, just to talk about her painting. But when she got to Sullivan Street he was out. She left him a note and took the bus to 57th Street to see what was new at the galleries, thinking about where her work would fit. Then, feeling refreshed, she decided to go over to her studio and see what her mother was up to. She had gone to New York to shop the day before and told Lara she was going to sleep over.

When she opened the studio door, the first thing that struck her was the smell of Chanel, the second was the disorder. Part of her pleasure with the studio was to have it spare and spotless. White, quiet and neutral. A place for her dreams to hatch. Now, she thought with a pang, it looked like a boutique. Agnes was piling silk blouses on the bed, matching them with light skirts. Green, gold, rose.

"You look very stylish. A new suit, your hair marcelled."

"Walter's taking me to Florida," Agnes said triumphantly. "To see some property. Then we'll go for a boat ride through the swamps. I've never had anything remotely resembling an adventure. I want to see the alligators, photograph them head on."

"Now? When Johnnie's so sick, when he's just come home?"

"Why not? He hasn't spent more than a few minutes with me since he came back. He's always with Muriel." She lowered her voice, her face pained. "Besides, the doctors in the hospital practically told me it wasn't good for him to be around me."

"He got upset after your visit, that's all," Lara said, suddenly aware that under her scatty brightness, her mother was suffering. "He was terribly confused."

"What do they think I did to hurt Johnnie, these doctors," her mother asked, her voice suddenly shrill, "besides loving Walter? I know what you all think about that." She looked at Lara defiantly. "But you know what? I don't care. It's enough for me that Walter values me." She paused, lifting her chin expressively. "He wants to marry me."

Lara's sympathy vanished. "You're not thinking of that?" she asked, flabbergasted.

"Yes, I am."

"But how can you?"

"It's easy. It's not just the doctors. You always act as if I'm doing the wrong thing. As though you're ashamed of having me for a mother." She flushed. "Walter thinks it's shameful that my family doesn't appreciate me. He's been wonderful to me. Taken me places, helped me to forget about you and enjoy myself again."

"I didn't realize . . . ," Lara started lamely. What didn't she realize? That her mother was a human being?

"Maybe when you get older you'll have a little more awareness of other people." Lara started to protest. "Please, I don't want to discuss it." Agnes knelt and pressed down on the lid of a brown calfskin bag filled almost to overflowing. "I'll send you postcards, Johnnie too. Oh, why won't this shut?" She took out a thick folder of papers and a green notebook and put them on the bed, then she tried again. This time the suitcase shut.

"What in heaven's name are you doing with this on your vacation?" Lara asked, picking up the green notebook with 'Accounts' carefully written on it in her father's hand.

Agnes took the book from her and slipped it into another bag. "Walter thinks I don't understand anything about money. He's helping me. I told him about Grandpa being banker to the

Kaiser," her mother said, cheerful again. "He was impressed. He said there was no reason I couldn't learn."

Lara felt a chill. "Mother, for heaven's sake, be careful. Have your fling if you have to, but don't marry him. He wouldn't make a good husband. He's not like Daddy. He doesn't want to protect a woman or any of those things you were brought up to think a man should do. He wants to have a good time." She wondered whether he'd really suggested marriage or if her mother was just deluding herself.

"You'll get to like him," Agnes said serenely.

"Mother, remember when he threatened to get engaged to that flapper, how upset that made you? You could go through hell."

"He was just doing that because he thought I didn't really care for him. He was testing me. Once I agreed to marry him, he," she laughed, "he let me write her, let me pretend to be him and tell her how much he loved me. It was immensely satisfying."

"But that's an awful thing to do to someone. And if he could do it to her, he could do it to you, have you thought of that? Mother, listen, what if I told you he flirted with me? That he would have done more if I'd encouraged him."

"I wouldn't believe you," Agnes said, her face darkening.

"What wouldn't you believe?" Walter asked from the doorway. They'd been so engrossed they hadn't heard him come in.

"Lara says you flirted with her."

He went to Agnes, knelt down and kissed her hand. "Never," he said. "I may tie you to the bedpost, but I'll never flirt with another woman."

Lara saw Agnes flush and had a sudden vision of her mother in the bedroom on all fours, being whipped around the room. It wasn't that Walter was "kind". On the contrary, there was a nasty tension between these two. God knows what went on when they were alone. It made her stomach hurt.

"Doesn't your mother look chic?" Walter said, getting to his feet and studying Agnes, then adjusting a wave above her ear.

He was like a parody of Casanova. How could her mother not see it? If she had another ten minutes alone with her, Lara thought she might be able to convince her. She wondered if she could ask her mother out for a pastry and tea. No, he'd come along. While she was thinking, Walter suddenly looked at his watch.

"If we're to get downtown in time for our appointment, my dear, we'd better get going," he said. "I don't want to be late." Agnes moved toward the mirror to check herself but he handed her her purse and took her arm. "Believe me, you look marvelous. You can finish packing when we get back. Sorry to cut short your visit, Lara," he added smugly. As he pulled her mother out the door, Lara thought her eyes looked frightened. But it was all over before she had time to even sketch out a strategy.

While Lara was standing at the window watching them hurry down the steps of the brownstone—her mother adjusting her motoring veil, Walter carrying the bags—the phone rang. It was Mortimer, he was in his club a few blocks away and wanted to come over.

"You've been promising to show me your paintings for ages," he said, "how about now?"

Ordinarily Lara would have said she didn't think he was interested, but right now even seeing Mortimer might be soothing.

She heard him running up the steps and opened the door to him. "When will you learn to put your tie on straight?" she asked him, but even his disorder was OK. Her mother's comments about her lack of sensitivity stuck in her mind. Well, maybe she could be nicer to Mortimer.

Lara set out a series of paintings of the kitchen table at the farm, with tea things, bowls of fruit, flowers, books, done starkly in the cubist manner. She got a certain satisfaction from seeing all the impossible angles she'd gotten into them. The sides of the tables were splayed out, and she'd made areas of transparency so the cabinets in back could be seen through them. All sides of the fruit and the teapot were there too.

He studied them with a look of surprise. "They're remarkably intelligent paintings," he said.

She smiled at him, let him look through some more.

"I'm glad you don't think I've been wasting my time."

"On the contrary, I can see what skill you have. You've learned a whole new vocabulary." He looked down at his shoes. "Lara, I have something I want to tell you."

What a bore, Lara thought, sucking on her bottom lip, he was going to start getting soppy.

"Wait, Mortimer. You have to see this one."

He smiled good-naturedly. Odd, he seemed more self-possessed today. Not devastated at all by her putting him off. No long face, nothing. It was, she noted, mildly disappointing. She took out her painting of the cow with her calf, wondering whether he would sense a difference between this and the other work. See that it was more strongly colored. The forms more organic. He peered at it.

"Cows," he said, finally. "At first I couldn't make them out, they're turned at such a strange angle." He seemed relieved to have "seen" what it was about. "To tell the truth, I can appreciate intellectually what you're doing but it makes me uncomfortable. I'm not sure what you want me to see, or what I should feel."

"You'd be happier with an old-fashioned painting of a cow in a meadow," she said. "A lot of people would be." Other men would have lied and flattered her. It was enough that he'd taken her seriously. Up until now he'd acted as if she were simply learning to paint decorative watercolors.

He was standing in front of her, his thick lips trembling with the fear that he had offended her.

"It's all right," she said taking his hand. "I don't mind your being honest." He put his hands around her waist and drew her to him awkwardly, kissed her cheek. "Lara," he started, "you know how I've felt about you. . . ." She turned her mouth to his, barely noticing the ambiguity. He had his lips tightly closed.

"Relax," she said, kissing him lightly again and again. He kept his mouth closed, his body rigid. This was sort of fun, she thought. If I don't make it with my painting I could hire out as an instructress for beginners. They had a lovely phrase for it in Italian, *nave scuola*, training ship.

After stammering Lara's name again along with a few unintelligible words, Mortimer stood quietly, his lips relaxed.

She kept kissing him but now she let her tongue softly explore between his lips. He resisted at first. She could tell it made him squeamish but then all of a sudden he opened his mouth and she slid her tongue inside. She felt his body jolt and the bulge of his penis against her thigh but she wasn't going to hurry. His body was still tight and rigid. "Suck my tongue," she told him. She felt him tentatively trying, then she withdrew her tongue and licked the tip of his nose, blew into his ear, bit the lobe. She felt him loosening up.

He turned his head for her to do the other ear and she laughed.

"You like that, do you? Good. It's supposed to be fun."

She led him over to the bed and felt his body tighten again. He was probably worrying about what to do next.

"Don't think," she said. "You don't have to do anything. Let me do it." She pushed him down gently, took off his tie and started unbuttoning his shirt. She could feel his heart beating violently. She took off his glasses and put them on the bedside table. His face looked very vulnerable without them. He was looking at her with an expression of almost pained concentration. She started kissing his chest, stroking his arms. He tried to stroke her too, but she stopped him. "Let me do it," she said again, and he lay back with a sigh. She stopped and loosened his belt, unzipped his pants. He lifted his hips and she pulled them down and over his ankles, took off his socks. Stopped to massage his toes, one at a time. Then she worked her way slowly up his legs. When she got to his thighs he began to groan. His erection was enormous. "I want you," he muttered.

"Soon," she said, pulling down his shorts.

When she finally straddled him and let him inside her, he came almost instantly.

"I shouldn't have let you do that," he said, after they had rolled apart and lain still for a few moments.

"Didn't you like it?" she asked, leaning on one elbow to look at him.

"I've never felt such sensations," he said in a low voice.

Some girl would thank her someday. She smiled at him, pleased by the thought. "Well then?" Mortimer's face was pale, his lips an odd shade of blue. Lara studied him dispassionately.

He turned to her, hesitated, took her hand. "I'm engaged," he said.

"You're what?" She choked, suddenly alert. "Is that what you were trying to tell me?" Lara had thought of a girl in some distant future. She certainly hadn't expected one to materialize under her nose.

He nodded sheepishly. "It was all very sudden. You didn't want me, you know," he said, fishing for his pants on the floor. "And you were right. It would never have worked between us— much as I wanted it to."

Lara took a deep breath and drew the sheet over her, then she reached for a cigarette on the bedside table. She noticed her hand was shaking a little. It's just chagrin, she told herself. Wounded vanity. But it was a shock all the same. Who would have thought it? Running along after her like a devoted puppy dog.

"She's a nice girl, I suppose?" she asked, rubbing a painful spot at the back of her neck. "And she adores you and doesn't criticize and tease."

"She loves me," he said simply. "I'd hoped you'd be pleased."

Lara had a sudden pang as she thought of Mortimer happily content with someone else. She'd imagined she could keep him until she was bored. Take what she wanted from him and then let him go. But no, he'd gone off on his own. Trotting briskly over to someone else's fireside. For once irony didn't help her. She lit her cigarette, inhaling the soothing smoke. The unpleasant fact was that she wasn't irreplaceable. While she was playing Lady Bountiful, Mortimer was probably thinking of his little wife-to-be. Storing up things to show her.

Lara looked at him with grudging respect. It was something she might have done herself.

"I was afraid to tell you at first," he was saying, "but you're always telling me how modern you are."

"Oh, definitely modern."

"And you're not angry?"

"On the contrary, congratulations!" She passed him her cigarette with a self-mocking gesture of homage.

"I'm glad it's alright, then," he said, his thick lips curving in a satisfied smile. "I'd hate to lose you as a friend."

∽30∾

Lara was in the craft room watching Robin play with blocks—made of a smooth, blond wood—that had been hers and Johnnie's. Since Robin had started to move around again, she'd been different. It wasn't that she was more normal—though Muriel had seen her smiling and with her perpetual optimism was sure she was nearing a breakthrough—it was a certain new purposefulness in her use of blocks and paper.

Robin lifted each block carefully and moved her fingers over the sides and edges before she put it down on the wood floor. She was building a line of blocks, placing them end to end with a little click, fitting them exactly so that no light showed. The line gradually curved around to become an oval. She's making a yard, Lara thought, our yard. She has even put in a garden shack. Or was it a body with a baby growing? The thought intrigued her, made her think of trying to paint a combined figure, a woman/yard. Wouldn't it be ironic if Robin developed into a brilliant artist—a type of idiot savant—and Lara bogged down in mediocrity? Maybe being a full person was actually a handicap.

Lara was watching so intensely she didn't see Johnnie come quietly into the game room.

"Look at her. She's reading them like braille."

Lara started. Her nerves had been on edge since he'd come home. But he seemed calm. He looked like some strange disconsolate bird with his hawknose and ruffled hair, his long wrists hanging down beneath his sleeves. She held her breath. What he said made sense—he'd been sounding sensible for days. But she didn't want him here.

"Yes," she said, "yes, she is."

"She's learning the wood's language. I know, I used to do that with my kites. Find out how they wanted to be balanced. What trim they wanted. You'd be surprised how picky some of them were. There was one that hated green—you know, my tiger. You haven't been kite-flying for a long time." He hesitated, shyly. "I'd like to take you, show you my new glider. I put the silk on the wing-frame yesterday. It's almost finished."

Her eyes filled. "Thanks, Johnnie."

"I'll take Robin, too." He gestured at her. "She's been watching me work." There was a faint pleading note in his voice.

Suddenly Robin stood up and shook herself hard like a dog coming out of the water; some hard brown balls fell out of her underwear. She glanced down at them for a minute as if she were asking, where did this come from? Then she went on playing.

"Lara, did you see that?" Johnnie spluttered. "She's doing her business on the ground like an animal. Like a dog."

"Shush, Johnnie, she doesn't know she's doing it."

"How can she not know? It's impossible. It's a first principle of philosophy, I shit, therefore I am."

Lara looked at him. He's not crazy, she thought, he knows what's what. His internal wiring is OK, he can read the signals from inside. It's what comes in from outside that you get confused by, Johnnie boy. For an instant, she pictured his mind filled with wires, all sending desperate signals of approaching danger.

A couple of the dark balls had fallen right next to Robin's block wall. She reached down and picked them up in her fingers, held them for a minute the way she'd been holding the blocks, then placed them carefully on top of her wall. If it

hadn't been so repulsive, it would have been funny. The ulti-
mate in decorative material. Squeezed from the gut. The
original non-exhaustible stuff.

"My god, this is too much," Johnnie said, a note of panic in
his voice. "She's getting it on her fingers. You've got to clean her
up or all her thoughts will get muddy. She'll see everything
through a muck of brown." He took a step toward her. Lara
held her breath and glanced anxiously at Robin, but the child
was engrossed in what she was doing and seemed not to have
noticed.

"Dirty," he muttered, "dirty!" taking a step toward her.

"Stay away from her," Lara whispered, "or. . . ." I'll have to
talk to David, she thought. I can't handle this.

"Everything needs to be contained," Johnnie said, his face
pale. "Especially filth. You should punish her, Lara. It's for her
own good. So people won't call her names, like dirty Jew. She is
a Jew, isn't she? People say Jews lack self-control. You should
spank her."

"No, Johnnie," she grabbed his arm, pulling on it to make
him listen. "Just because you were forced to do things you
hated, you don't need to do it with her. No one needs to." She
shook his arm a little. "Was Dad whipping you with his belt
good for you? Was it? Robin'll be clean when she's ready."

His face crumpled. He stood uncertainly, his long hands
dangling. Robin kept on playing. Thank god she hadn't heard
him.

"Oh John, I'm sorry, but"—Lara tugged him toward the
door, pushing with her hip—"I can't let you frighten her and
ruin everything we've done. Go now, please."

Somehow she got him out, locked the door and leaned
against it, trembling.

❧

When Lara came to the big house and said she wanted to
talk to him, she saw David's eyes light up for a moment with
an unspoken question. Then, as he looked at her, the light was
replaced by a slight motion of impatience. She'd obviously
disturbed him at his writing.

"What's the matter?" he asked, holding the door open. "you
look as if you'd had a shock."

She stood in front of him, cracking her knuckles. "I know I've disappointed you, David, but I have to talk to someone."

"It's all right," he said, steering her into his study—though the books on the shelves had changed, Lara still thought of it as her father's library—and pulling up one of his study chairs for her, "I've been doing some thinking too. I wasn't being fair to you—or to Muriel."

She nodded, acknowledging what he said. "David, you know I told you about the books Johnnie was reading."

He got up and put a hand on her shoulder. "You worry too much. Muriel says he's doing well."

"But David, he's reading those books again. You won't believe this." She held out a book and he glanced at the cover.

"*Mein Kampf*. Never heard of it."

"Well, he's mentioned it before but not recently. I thought he'd stopped obsessing. Then something he said got me worried. I went to his room to talk to him and found this"—she looked down with disgust at the book in her hand—"open on his desk, notes scattered around. He's obviously been studying it. What's so awful is that this man Hitler really does hate us. Jews, I mean. There were pages of perfectly mad rant about Jews being abscesses. It's disgusting. Crazy. I don't know why they let people print things like that."

"Most people would have put it down after a few pages or tossed it out."

"He seemed to be getting better," she said sadly, "but all the time he was brooding over this. I'm afraid I blew up at him. I made him show me the diary he's been keeping. Here, look!" She held out a gray notebook.

David opened it and she heard a sharp intake of breath.

"'Ways of Death'," he read softly, "'Drowning, shooting, pills, gassing, jumping from a height.' But what's this?" He pointed to the sentences written heavily in red ink opposite each method of death.

"He took them from that book. He explained it to me. Each phrase justifies the particular way of death. It's bizarre, horrible." She pointed to the sentence next to 'Drowning' and read, "'The odor of these people makes me sick'." I asked him how he could possibly believe such rot. At first he tried not to answer but finally he confessed that he realized everything Hitler said about the Jews was true of him, Johnnie, personally. They were unclean, they smelled bad, they were shy of water. It was a stroke of genius, he said, for Hitler to put all the bad smells in the world into one body and call them Jew. I yelled at him. I stuck my arm in his face and asked him if I smelled. He said it didn't matter, *he* was dirty. Before he took the pills, he tried to drown himself in the tub but he couldn't manage to keep his head down. Here's another one. . . ."

"Lara, do you really want to do this?"

"I can't believe that in a modern country people are saying things like this and no one is objecting. Maybe he's right to be frightened. Maybe. Listen, 'Here was a moral pestilence . . . worse than the Black Plague. And in what mighty doses this poison was being manufactured . . . like a sewage pump shooting filth into the faces of other members of the human race.'" She remembered Johnnie staring at Robin with loathing. Seeing himself.

"God, Lara, you're so sheltered. They've been saying much worse for centuries. Doing much worse." He took the book from her. "'Gas,'" he read, "'is the antidote to moral pestilence.' It's uncanny the way he takes in what Hitler says and then makes the punishment fit the crime. The poor man, he must be going through hell."

"I got Johnnie to tell me the other ways he'd thought of to do himself in—purifying himself, he called it. He told me he liked to think of dressing himself in Daddy's coat, this long dress coat with fur lining. He'd wear it naked—like a baby. He didn't think he was as handsome as our father, but he thought in the coat he'd look more substantial. He pictured Mother finding him in the car, in her nightdress, her hair undone."

"Did you ask him if he still . . . ," David began, then bit his lip.

"I don't know what he's planning," she said. "But he's learned not to alarm us. He wouldn't have told me all this if I hadn't barged into his room and confronted him. He told me he didn't try gas because he was afraid of the smell of the exhaust.

It reminded him of having a tooth extracted under ether when he was a child. They had to hold him down. He was screaming and kicking."

"So he decided on morphine because that was the easiest?"

"He wanted to sleep without dreams. He told me that first he imagined taking a bath, washing himself the way Mother used to when he was sick with fever, handling his arms and legs gently, respectfully, he said, with love. He started crying when he told me. It almost broke my heart. He said that he felt shut out from me and Mother by a kind of glass wall. That even when words came out of his mouth they didn't reach us, they curled in on themselves and sang secretly." She started to cry. "I got him to promise he wasn't going to do anything to himself."

"It must have been a relief to him to talk to you. He must have felt you heard him and cared."

"But I didn't, on the night he tried, I shut my door and locked him out. He was trying to tell me that he hadn't meant any harm with Robin. He wanted me to comfort him. He wanted. . . ." She looked at him, open-mouthed. She'd almost blurted it out.

He was silent, studying her.

"I was so angry at him and frightened that I couldn't help him. He stood at my door begging me to let him in, and now I've betrayed him again. I didn't mean to, but I couldn't stand walking around day after day waiting for something to happen."

"Of course you couldn't."

"And just now he wanted to spank Robin."

"What?"

"He didn't hurt her. I made him leave but Muriel's so intent on having them do things together and. . . ." She bit her lip. "I'm scared. It's too much responsibility," she finished lamely.

"You're right to tell me. He should go to Battle Creek. I don't know how I let Muriel talk me into bringing him home in the first place."

"But she said the routine was dreadful, they'd drug him and. . . ." Now that she'd told, she felt terrible. She pictured

Johnnie sitting listlessly on a chair in a bare room, turning away when she came to visit him.

"It's not going to be easy to get her to agree," David was saying, "but he can't stay here. For his own sake as well as Robin's."

❧31❧

On the day of Agnes's wedding, the sky over Miami was such an intense hot blue that it seemed like a burning phosphorescent liquid—Agnes had never seen anything like it. The night before, she dreamed that Eugene came into her room, took her in his arms, then turned and quietly walked away. She woke up with her face drenched in tears that she hid from Walter. It was as if Eugene had known and was coming to say goodbye. Taken off guard she was surprised by the deep yearning she felt, almost like pain, in her chest and throat. But it was impossible to be sad for long—the little maid brought her and Walter their coffee and rolls and they sat on the balcony in their robes, under a scintillating sky that gave off sparkles of light no matter which way you looked. Then the little maid helped her weave flowers into her hair and put on her brilliant pink dress, the color of flamingoes.

Walter insisted they fly out to one of the lesser Keys with a pilot who doubled as a minister. Walter was a Pisces, he said, and wanted to be married surrounded by his element. He'd shown her the island on the map where it looked like a tiny footprint. Flying in the bi-plane over the ocean, suspended between blue and blue, Agnes searched his face for some sign that he realized what a spiritual adventure they were having, but he was laughing with the pilot and when he sensed her looking only reached out and squeezed her knee.

"Doesn't that cloud look like an angel," she whispered to him, "with his drapery billowing?"

"You're my angel," he said without turning around, "always improving on reality."

They landed, bumping and jolting to a stop on a dirt runway in the midst of nowhere. Despite her queasiness from the dipping of the plane, the tropical foliage, the thick moist leaves and the soft air bathed her in a feeling of well-being. So she didn't protest when Walter spotted an even smaller island—barely a mound of sand offshore—and scooped her up in his arms to carry her off to it.

"Imagine you're being abducted," he teased. "You'll like it better."

She clung to his neck. "Don't ever give me back," she said, ignoring the sarcasm. And even though she felt it was mean, she laughed with him at the minister wading along after them with his pants rolled up, his shoes and the Bible held over his head. Absurdly colored birds were darting and calling in the leaves. She forgot about the perspiration that was making dark shadows under her arms and was going to ruin her dress. This brightness was what she had been missing, she thought. It made up in one blazing instant for so much pain: Agnes the ugly duckling, the dutiful wife, the mother of a boy that wasn't right in the head. The sky poured down blue that covered up all that.

"Queen Agnes Island," Walter announced when he put her down. "Yours." It didn't mean anything, of course. It was just a heap of sand, but she felt exhilarated all the same. It implied everything he wanted to give her. And above all it was fun. When the minister solemnly unrolled his pants legs, she and Walter giggled like children, hands over their mouths, but when he opened the Bible they both became very still. They exchanged vows while she brushed away the small soft insects that flew down her decolletage, sticking to her moist skin. She noticed Walter's hand trembled slightly when he put on her ring—he hadn't let her get one for him. She smiled reassuringly. Dear boy, he was nervous. She leaned forward, her heels sinking in the sand and whispered I love you in his ear. She heard the silky lapping of the water surrounding them and felt his kiss—his lips warm and salty—then it was over. They were married.

That night their lovemaking was more satisfying than usual. She'd known that being married would help, she told Walter. It made her feel secure enough to relax. They went to sleep in each other's arms in the half-built hotel on Miami Beach that Walter said was going to be the Shangri-la of Florida.

She woke up in the middle of the night to find that their room had been invaded by a swarm of huge locust-like creatures. Bugs big as roaches had settled on her face and the covers. She jumped up screaming and brushing them away. She could feel their feet skittering on her skin. She grabbed her pillow and swatted them off her body onto the floor where they whirred and fluttered, trying to climb back up her bare legs. Finally she mastered her panic enough to scoop them up in heaps with a towel and push them out the window. Where was Walter? She knocked angrily on the bathroom door—could he really have stayed inside there when she was screaming like that—but when she swung the door open there was no one. He must have gone outside for a walk and a smoke, she thought, calming down.

She peered out through the glass but all she could see was the moon staring back at her and she wasn't about to go out looking for him with those dreadful creatures waiting to fall on her. It was past two o'clock. She climbed back into bed and waited, rehearsing her story, trying to decide whether to stress her alarm or her bravery. Be angry? Pout?

It would be so lovely to have someone sympathetic to tell it to, she thought. Lara might just have told her it served her right for coming down here in the first place. The thought made her look uneasily at her watch on the night table. Three o'clock. She got out of bed being careful not to step on any of the dead insects and went into the alcove where Walter had put his suitcase on the rack. She knew before she opened the closet that his clothes would be gone, too. The cruelest thing was her jewelry. He'd taken even the gold locket with his picture in it and a lock of his hair.

She must have fainted. Somehow she managed to get herself back into bed and lay there, her teeth chattering feverishly, trying to remember what she had signed. She went over each event in order, trying to revive her memory. It was the day before the wedding. They'd had a good lunch and a bottle of champagne, though Agnes had told him champagne went to her head. Then somehow he'd started talking to her about merging their assets as a form of trust. He wanted her to have access to everything he had, he said, and he wanted the same from her.

The way he put it, he was the one who would be giving up something. He would be a very rich man soon, he said, with his Florida ventures. He wanted her to share his good fortune. While he was talking he stroked her arm. She'd tried to tell him that trust had nothing to do with assets. A man should respect a woman for taking care of what was her own. They would get along better if she looked after herself.

"That's your daughter's thinking," he'd told her. "You don't think that way. Lara's always been against me. You know that." And then he sulked, his handsome face turning dark. It had been too hard for her. Somehow, he persuaded her to go to a lawyer in a shabby building filled with flies and sign some papers. It was incredible to her but she'd done it. God knows what she'd given him.

She lay in bed most of the day slipping in and out of sleep. It was too painful to be awake and face what had happened. Finally an urgent need made her get up to go to the bathroom but as soon as she stood, her knees buckled and she fell to the floor. Her legs weren't working. Maybe she had been lying on a nerve and they had gone to sleep, she thought, massaging first one and then the other, but though she felt her hand, the muscles wouldn't respond. Her legs flopped, curiously limp. She hated the sight of them as if they were giant white worms, not belonging to her.

She managed to pull herself back into bed and lay there until mid-afternoon when the maid knocked on the door to ask if she could clean. There was no doctor within call of the hotel, the maid said after Agnes had told her her symptoms, but the assistant manager of the hotel happened to be a Christian Science healer. If she liked, maybe he would be willing to see her. The maid had no truck with that sort of thing herself—charlatans making all sorts of crazy promises—but if Agnes wanted. . . .

The healer was a round-faced ruddy man with neat blond hair and well-cared for nails, the image of cleanliness and probity. He sat beside Agnes and held her hand. She liked him. After a few minutes, he asked permission to examine her and felt her legs carefully, moving the joints. The sight of her white helpless legs made her physically sick. She wanted to take them and throw them off the bed. They didn't seem to belong to her.

"I can't move them at all," she said in terror, "Oh God, what will I do? I'm a cripple." Without meaning to, she started to tell him what had happened with Walter. "And the terrible thing is that I want him back. If he came through that door right now, I'd throw my arms around his neck and kiss him. Despite everything." She thought of the gold locket with his photo. How could he have taken it?

"And then?" he asked, with the barest hint of irony.

"And then?" she repeated surprised.

"It's all just a dream, you know," he said. "It must have been a very compelling dream to have held you the way it did. But now you have to let it go. Even if this man comes back, it would only be to harm you more."

"But he's not coming back," she said, tears running down her face, "even if I were dying . . . he wouldn't. . . ."

"Probably not," the healer agreed, offering her a large blue and white handkerchief; "meanwhile, why not try to help yourself?"

"Can't you see, I can't move," she screamed at him, pushing the handkerchief away. "Why are you pretending I can? Why should I? What do I have to go back to? My daughter . . . ," she pictured Lara, coolly furious, scornful, Johnnie confused and wretched. She sank back against the pillows, letting her sobs drown her thoughts.

"If you'll pray with me, maybe you'll be surprised," the healer said quietly.

"I prayed for my husband to live and he died," Agnes sobbed defiantly. "I threw my prayer book out the window."

The healer smiled at her. "You might look at this as another opportunity," he said. She liked him, he wasn't pompous, wasn't full of righteousness, and he had a sturdy sort of presence. She could feel this was a real human being.

"You're much stronger than you think," he told her. "Let yourself feel it. Turn all that misdirected energy toward healing yourself."

The word "strong" was what suddenly hit her. It made a small, clear place inside her head. From the center of that, she started to pray.

"Nothing's happening," she said to the healer after a few minutes. "I feel as weak as ever."

"You're too impatient. Let your mind relax. Don't force it. Think of times in your life when you've been resourceful or brave."

"I can't," she started but then she remembered, of all things, the summer she stepped on a hornet's nest when she was ten and, though her body was swollen like a sausage, she joked to reassure her frantic mother. And once when her brother had cut his arm and was bleeding dangerously, she'd rigged a tourniquet from her skirt. And she'd nursed Eugene. And . . . the memories gave her a surge of pride. She began to pray again with renewed energy.

After what seemed like a very short time she felt a prickling sensation in her legs, the tingle of blood awakening. "It's coming back," she whispered, swinging her feet over the edge of the bed. Tentatively, she touched the bedside mat, then gradually leaned her full weight on her feet. The healer offered his arm but she shook her head with a small smile. Her legs, back in her own control, moved her smoothly across the room.

❧ 32 ❧

When he was working on his giant glider in the barn, Johnnie forgot the hooknosed, pig-eyed faces in his cartoon book, forgot everything except symmetry, balance and beauty. A soft light seemed to emanate from its wings. He fitted on the wood bar and adjusted it so that by leaning to the right or the left you could steer with the weight of your body.

There was a box of feathers set carefully against the wall. Johnnie loved to sift them through his fingers, feeling himself drawn to slight variations of color or size. Slowly, painstakingly, he had covered the wings of his glider with feathers—multicolored but mostly tawny and edged with black. He had rescued the feathers from the taxidermist. Now he was almost done. It looked like some giant bird.

❧

Johnnie was standing by the pool with Robin, holding one of his new kites. Muriel had gone to the house for some lemonade, saying she'd be back in a few minutes. He considered her action carefully. He knew that she and David had been arguing about him. He had overheard them the other day when he climbed up into his old tree house and sat looking at the light through the leaves. David sounded very angry. He wanted

201

Johnnie put away somewhere. Muriel didn't raise her voice, but she insisted on keeping him a little longer. Weeks, he wondered, or days? It didn't matter, really, he was almost ready for whatever was coming.

Strange to say, he was the happiest he'd ever been. Muriel wasn't wrong to have left him alone with Robin, he thought. He had no wish to touch her anymore. No wish to touch anyone.

He sat down on the grass and started writing strings of numbers on the kite's surface, covering every possible inch of the surface. Codes for a new age, he thought, if people only knew how to read them.

Robin pushed his hand and darted away. She wanted him to fly it, but he could tell there wasn't quite enough wind. He was just rolling up the string when a dog wandered up to them, a collie with beautiful markings, a white ruff and delicate pointed nose. Johnnie patted it idly. Animals interested him less than birds, and the way dogs sniffed the earth and each other's droppings disgusted him.

Robin was squatting next to him and when the dog nosed at her she squealed, frightened.

"Shoo"—Johnnie pushed the dog away—"go on, go home." He stamped his feet and the dog wandered off. When he saw it in the bathhouse, sniffing around at the damp suits, Johnnie went over and shut the door. He hated to see Robin scared. Her squeals hurt his ears. Inside the dog whined and scratched to get out, then quieted, and Johnnie forgot him.

He heard the boys before he saw them. They were whistling and calling "Hey, Bud," banging at the hedges with their sticks as they passed. There were two of them in worn overalls. Boys didn't really describe them; they were as big as men. Close-cropped blonds with red faces and big square hands. He vaguely remembered them from the neighboring farm. One was chewing tobacco and had a green bandanna around his neck. "We're chasing down our dog," he said in an unpleasant nasal voice. "Saw him go up your drive. You seen him?" He looked at the kite on the ground with suppressed interest.

"I put him in the bathhouse," Johnnie said hesitantly, motioning toward the little white shack. They had such huge hands. "He was scaring Robin."

"You were just going to leave him there?" The boy spat tobacco in his direction. His friend ambled over to the bathhouse to let out the dog, who came bounding over, leaping at them playfully. Robin started to squeal again, jumping up and down with a high-pitched eeee.

"He's not going to hurt you," the boy with the green bandanna said, holding the dog by the collar. "See, I'll hold him and you can pet him." Robin started whirling in circles, her fingers in her mouth.

"Hey, what's the matter with her?" Green Bandanna asked. The other one made a circling sign at his temple.

"Can't you see, she's weird. Kooky."

"Don't do that," Johnnie said, wishing Muriel would get back. "She doesn't like being called names."

"She doesn't know what's going on. Lookit." Green Bandanna waved his hand back and forth in front of her face. She just kept on whirling. "They should lock you up instead of the dog, girlie, or you'll be getting into mischief. Pretty hair though, like Goldilocks."

The one holding the dog suddenly noticed a cut in back of its ear. "Hey, the dog's cut alongside her head. You been throwing rocks at our dog?"

"No," said Johnnie, frightened. He suddenly remembered seeing the boys tormenting a cat in front of their barn as he was walking past one day, tying tin cans to her tail.

"You oughtn't to have. He's a full-blooded dog. Not no mutt. Didn't you see the collar?"

Green Bandanna opened a pen knife. "I bet Goldilocks threw them rocks. I'm going to snip me a piece of that pretty hair." He stretched out a hand toward Robin.

"Leave her alone," Johnnie shouted with such ferocity that the boys backed off, pulling the dog with them. "He's tetched too," the other one said. "Remember Pa said they was making this into a nut farm. Pa'll come back with us next time," he yelled, "burn this whole place down. Put you in the state hospital where you belong."

When Muriel got back, John was singing softly to Robin, who was walking around holding the kite against her chest.

"Thank you for taking care of her," Muriel said after John blurted out what happened. He could tell she thought it was bad luck. She didn't realize that nothing happened by chance. Especially things like this. If it hadn't been the boys, it would have been the gypsies looking for chickens to steal.

Muriel brought them back to the kitchen and gave them both cookies and lemonade. As though we're both her children, Johnnie thought. After a few minutes she started to find positive aspects to what had happened. She praised him again for standing up for Robin. "You're beginning to care about her," she said. He had noticed that care was one of her favorite words.

"What if they come back?" he asked her anxiously. "What if they come back with lots more—in a big gang?" He was sure they had guns for hunting. Most of the farmers did. "I couldn't manage then." He was trembling. "They said they'd bring their father."

"They won't, John. It's just boyish bluster. They're insensitive, but not dangerous."

"They thought we stoned their dog. They are the ones who do things like that." He stopped, frowning. "I'm sure they thought we were going to make a blood sacrifice, bleed the dog and mix its blood into our sabbath meal. You know, people say the Jews do that with babies, sacrifice them and eat them at their religious feasts."

"Johnnie, don't let yourself think that way. It had nothing to do with your being Jewish." Her face shut down. He knew she didn't approve of his thoughts, wanted him to stop thinking them. But he couldn't. "Did they call you names?" she asked him.

He wished he could explain to her that things connected. What they did to Robin, they also did to him. "They called Robin names," he said.

She bent toward him, over her big belly, as if she were trying to reach him with her physical presence. "People don't understand mental illness. It frightens them. Being different frightens people."

"They said she was weird. Ought to be locked up." He stared at the wall. He could see thoughts forming in their minds or minds like theirs—different, weird, crazy, sheenie—

the thoughts were forming everywhere and the tragedy was that people like Muriel refused to see them.

That night in bed he read the *Frankfurter Zeitung*. It was weeks late as usual but at least he'd gotten it. He knew before he even started to read that there would be some terrible news—the incident with the dog was a sign that a crisis was coming soon.

Sure enough, on the second page there was a piece on the union of the German moderates with the radical right. For some time he'd been watching the farmers' discontent, their gradual shift to the right. But it had seemed isolated until now. He had an image of two strands of colored rope meeting in the air, twisting together to form a noose. Who was the leader of the radical right? He had known, of course: Herr Hitler.

His flesh turned to a mass of tiny goosebumps. He read it carefully. The cool black letters and the tone of the article gave no indication of danger. The reporter went on about the plebiscite, the Young plan for reparations, Hugenberg—but what the man failed to see was that there was no turning back from this moment. What had been just words had become power. Hitler had latched on like a leech to Germany's body and was going to drink until he burst. All the political details were simply incidental. A pretext for fate to unleash what she was planning for the Jews.

Johnnie put down the newspaper and thought about the things Hitler said in *Mein Kampf* about Germany, the father-land—the need for working men to have jobs, to be able to bring up their children in peace. It was hard not to agree with that, though it was a little chauvinistic, a little too narrow. But then, Johnnie remembered, the tone had gotten more sinister. Something was keeping these good things from happening, society was sick, the jobs were being taken away, something or someone was at fault. Here, when he thought about it, Johnnie tried to stop what came next from unrolling in his mind—the someone was him, the Jew.

He thought of the blond boys. It's not our fault, he said aloud, we didn't do it. It was the Great War, the economic disaster, not us. But as he said it an image from the book of cartoons he'd been reading flashed into his mind—the captions were in Gothic type difficult to read—of a family of blond, healthy-looking Germans, threatened by a hideous hooknosed Jew with a big potbelly. He hated having that image in his mind, it made his head hurt, so he tried to shrink the bloated features and change the tiny rat's eyes back to those of a normal human face, but he couldn't. Instead, slowly, as though he were being sucked into a whirlpool, he got drawn into the image and felt his own features swell. His nose grew so he could hardly see over it, his fingers were tipped with long nails, he had a lowering brow, a thick drooping lip, swelling ear-lobes—all his features were fat with liquid as if he had dropsy. He tried to think of a future where he could manage to keep his face normal despite these images but he couldn't. They were too strong for him.

❧33❧

Lara finally felt she was ready to go back to the portrait of her father that had stumped her for so long. She felt free of Gorky, that was the main thing. Gradually she'd developed her new way of seeing the things around her as jumping-off places for her imagination. The finger painting that she had done now several times with Robin was an added stimulus. If Robin—who was only the barest outline of a person—could get herself to do what she'd been doing, surely Lara could manage to finish this one portrait. She thought this time she would try it in pastel and crayon.

She took the last version, an oil, out of her studio closet and looked at it. Then she searched for the photograph of her father in the worn album. As she turned past a photo of her mother in an ostrich plume hat, she felt her stomach cramp. Agnes had been gone for weeks, it was October already, and there'd only been one silly letter about the Florida swamps, notable for what it didn't say. Better not to think about it.

She found the picture of her father she wanted and put it next to her painting. He was dressed in a linen summer suit and vest with a watch chain. She was standing next to him in a simple white dress. He was looking away from her at some point beyond the photographer, fingering his gold watch chain.

Her colors had sentimentalized him, she thought. They didn't add a dimension, they falsified what was there. By their warmth they suggested a corresponding warmth in him. This time she was aware of a gaunt wariness in the photograph, a tension around her father's eyes. Some of this must surely have been pain, and the fear of his last illness. But was that what she wanted to show? She wasn't sure.

She sat down in front of the photograph, adjusting herself in the chair, with pillows behind her because her back hurt, and made herself study it. After a minute she began to fidget restlessly. Why should she want to show her father's pain? Or some weakness of his that was lurking at the edge of her awareness? She had wanted to portray the best of him—his courtly manners, his love for history, the way he searched for the meaning in things. She remembered how once when she asked him some question about Christianity he sent her to all the churches in Princeton to learn the differences for herself. She'd been so grateful to him for thinking she would be able to do it. But why so grateful, she wondered suddenly, looking at the high forehead with the sandy hair combed back and neatly parted? Did she imagine herself as stupid? In the photo she was looking at him with burning intensity, willing him to notice her.

The implications of the photograph were too difficult to grasp all at once. She forced herself to concentrate only on his head. In her mind, she divided it into the significant planes of forehead, cheek, chin, neck. The trouble with her earlier tries had been that she didn't go far enough. It was as though her father was somehow fighting back, resisting her efforts to see him. But this time she was resolved to push. He was dead, after all, she thought half seriously, he couldn't take hold of her hands. She concentrated on the plane of his forehead. She looked at it neutrally and let herself feel how high and broad it was. It was simply a shape now. It had nothing to do with her.

He was an aloof, mental man, she thought with a start, despite the sudden temper tantrums, the nighttime adventures with maids. She realized that the haze of passionate love that surrounded his memory was hers. She didn't really know what he felt for her. He was too hidden. Maybe the pain she needed to get into the painting was partly hers. It hurt to think how far away he had really been.

She began to work on his mouth. What if after she shaped it, made it as soft and sensual as she remembered it, it suddenly began to speak and told her everything she'd been waiting to hear since she was a child? "Hi, Daddy," she said aloud. But of course he didn't answer. Who did she think she was, Pygmalion?

She kept working at the mouth, trying to make it yield its secrets. Suddenly, on an impulse, she picked up a stick of lavender pastel from the open box and rubbed it over the lips, destroying the hard outline. This time the effect of the color wasn't sentimental. She felt as if she'd indicated a possibility. If you watch Daddy you could learn something, she thought. How to soften your edges. The thought was crazy, it made her laugh. Then she took a light green and worked over his forehead, watching the way it came alive with a strange, slightly sinister glow. She imagined his brains inside there, coiling mysteriously like white worms and for a minute she wanted to paint them. Then she shook her head, telling herself no. There's been enough of his thoughts—enough of him she almost thought— riding herd on her life. What came out now had to be from her. She felt her pulses race.

Unexpectedly she found herself cracking open the planes of his head like the carapace of an insect. New forms started to appear as they do in dreams—as they had when she finger-painted with Robin—tumbling out so fast she had trouble keeping up with them. She let them come, half flowers, half bodies, sprouting from her father's head, like a multitude of Athenas. More quietly, she started to elaborate on the fantastic shapes—petal-arms, breasts like strange fruit.

This was what she'd been looking for, the gateway to something new.

When she looked at her composition from a certain angle the whole thing seemed like a spherical bowl or vase or even like a torso. His eyes in the portrait were also breasts, and his mouth a purplish, open sex. I've done it, Daddy, she thought. I've made you see me. Looking at her work, she felt closer to her father than she ever had when he was alive. Her breasts and his eyes were interchangeable, his mouth and her sex. He couldn't open his eyes without seeing her female self, or his mouth without being aware of her sex. He and she were mingled one minute and separate another. She was both part of him and not him. And it was not at his will, but at hers. He would have hated it, been disgusted, aghast, but, she realized she didn't mind. For once she didn't care what his opinion was. It even added to her satisfaction.

She looked at the sun going down outside her studio window with a feeling of exhilaration. For the first time she felt she truly existed. She was the person who had done this.

For the next few days, she worked in her studio almost without stopping, doing canvas after canvas, trying to master her new vocabulary, including more of her own experience, going down deeper but also out farther, toward the organic pulsating forms of nature. She had the sensation of exploring hidden territory—deep feelings inhabited and lit the forms from within.

She redid her painting of her father's chair, concentrating first on the feelings bound up in the colors. A breath of green chill air. Fear first came into the painting through the window as green light illuminating his chair. But somehow that was wrong. She took a tube of red paint and squeezed it from the tube directly onto the chair seat using her fingers to form it into fiery shapes until there was a huge roaring fire where her father had been. Where were you? she asked him. Where were you ever? At least she'd been able to tell her mother about Johnnie, but even the thought of telling her father anything was ridiculous. He simply wasn't there. She wiped her hands and started on her father's pipe on the side table next to the chair.

Carefully, she made a calmer area around it, where anger didn't enter. Looking at the pipe, it seemed empty of the things she wanted to put into it. She shut her eyes until she could almost smell her father's tobacco, the rich fragrance of the smoke when he first lit his pipe in the morning. It announced him in his study, in the other rooms of the house, lingering on his clothes, on his fingers.

She opened her eyes and picked up her brush. The bowl of the pipe began to transform itself into the bulb of a plant, the stem sprouted buds—not full leaves yet, but red-tipped buds just pushing out.

✃··✄

Finally, she decided to ask Gorky over to see what she'd done. She put her new paintings out around the room. He was so quiet, she was afraid he didn't like them. He stood in front of first one, then the other, stroking his black moustache with a big hand and making small sounds in his throat. Her stomach ached with the strain of waiting and finally she removed herself to the bathroom and stood over the sink splashing cold water on her face.

"These are very good," he said soberly, when she came out. "They're not done the way I would have done them, but they're good nonetheless."

Patronizing as usual, she thought, but it was all right. He probably thought he was conceding a lot. She'd been foolish to expect him to be as excited as she was. She turned slightly away so that he wouldn't see her disappointment. "I'm glad you think they're competent," she said wryly.

"Better than that," he said. "I didn't say it well." He looked at her for a moment. "Perhaps it's not so easy for me to see you moving in a new direction."

"Perhaps not," she said, smiling at him.

"But the work is a great advance over what you've been doing, and this," he stood in front of the portrait of her father, "is wonderful." He'd regained his characteristic liveliness and was gesticulating at it. "It's not as if you've totally rejected cubism. You can see it in the sophistication of the planes of the face . . ."—he paused and this time she could see him struggling to be satisfied with the traces of his teaching that he found there—"and then there's this completely unexpected explosion of energy." He put his arm around her shoulder and squeezed it. "I'd like to show it to my dealer. I can't promise anything but we'll see what he says. You need a few more paintings, but I think you're ready to show."

∞·34·∞

Lara was walking by the barn and she saw Johnnie sitting in the hayloft under the roof—the big doors were wide open—dangling his legs, smoking a cigarette. It had been one of their favorite spots in the late summer because of the sweet smell of the newly harvested hay, and the fact that it was always cool. She waved to him.

"You shouldn't smoke up there," she called. He shrugged. The stairs to the loft were at the back end of the barn and were dark and covered with bat droppings. As she went up she felt the hairs on the back of her neck rise—she hated being confined in the narrow space, thinking of bats hanging from the rafters above her. But it was the gauntlet she had to run to get to the sweet hay.

She settled down next to him at the edge of the loft, her back against a bale, feet over the edge next to his. He was wearing open sandals and his feet seemed especially long and white.

"I think I finally finished Daddy's portrait," she said, with a hint of challenge in her voice. She imagined him saying "So you got the old man!"—with light irony, as though they were conspirators. But he just looked at her, the cigarette hanging loosely from his mouth.

"He was awful to you," she said, irritated by the slackness of his mouth.

Johnnie looked surprised, his blond eyebrows arching in his thin face. "Hard, yes. Demanding, but nothing to be so indignant about. He wanted a certain kind of son and I disappointed him. God knows, I tried. . . ."

"That didn't give him the right to fly into rages." She had a sudden memory of her father's flushed face, the way the strap came down on Johnnie's bottom. Herself watching, biting her lip, wishing her father would care enough to spank her, too.

"He had the right," he interrupted her, suddenly fierce. "Being our father gave him the right to do anything he pleased." He inhaled the smoke deep into his lungs, held it for a long moment, exhaled. "In his position, I might do the same. I hope I wouldn't but I might. . . . But it seems like an academic question, doesn't it? I'm not about to be a father."

"Is that why you find one unsuitable girl after another? You don't want it to work? You always have reasons not to do things. You can't excel because people would notice you're a Jew, you can't live a normal life because you might turn out like Daddy."

"You sound like Muriel," he said, "as though people were instruments and you could tune them to normal. Mmmm. . . ." He tapped his head with his finger and a column of ash fell off his cigarette down onto the gravel below. "Woops!"—he put his hand to his mouth—"bad boy!"

"I have weird ideas too," she said, thinking of how much she'd wanted her father to touch her, even if it hurt. "That's why I'm scared." She attempted a laugh. "And it's easier to tell you what to do than to tell myself."

"I know." He stubbed out his cigarette carefully against an exposed beam and reached out and took her hand. She let him hold it. The family was something they shared. She imagined them as two transparent creatures bound together by the feet but leaning off in different directions, thick looping veins of blood running between them.

"Why was Daddy always going somewhere?" she asked, after a minute, thinking that because Johnnie was a man he might understand.

"Business . . . what does it matter?" he answered, distractedly.

"It matters because I'm trying to figure out whether we meant anything to him. If he wasn't off on a trip, he was in his study, behind those thick books. . . ."

He squeezed her hand hard. "Stop it," he said, "it's pointless."

He was right, she could see that she wasn't going to get any further by talking to him. He was finished puzzling about their past, had given up on it, and she was just starting to break through the fog that kept her from seeing it. It was better to be quiet, she thought. To simply sit there, with her feet warmed by the sun, feeling the pressure of his hand.

Without any warning she felt her hand thrown back into her lap. "You shouldn't have shown them my diaries," he said abruptly. "They were private . . . my private thoughts that I was sharing with you." His voice was matter of fact. "Why'd you do it?"

She flinched, curled her hand on her lap. How did he know? It was hard to believe Muriel had told him. "I was worried. . . ."

He turned to her, she could see his thin lips tremble under his moustache but otherwise he seemed calm.

"Do you think I'm crazy too?" he asked, his voice suddenly shrill. "Is that why you wanted to talk to me? Or is it because I'm your brother and you thought I'd understand better than anyone else what it was like growing up in this family of ours . . . what did your Muriel call it, a hotbed of neurosis?"

"I was afraid you were going to hurt Robin—you don't remember how you were that day. You frightened me."

"And so you had to call in outside help? Were you really that frightened?"

She took him by the shoulders, not knowing whether she wanted to shake him or hug him. "Swear to me that you won't hurt yourself, or her . . . and . . . I'll talk to them."

"It's funny," he said, removing her hands. "Prospective murderers are listened to, they form political parties, people vote for them, but when I try to warn people, they want to lock me up. Doesn't it strike you as odd?"

"Oh Johnnie," she said, almost crying. His face had clouded over. "Why do you make it so hard?"

Lara had been out making studies of the cows in the back field when she looked up and saw what seemed at first a giant dragonfly moving up the water tower ladder. As soon as she realized what it was she started running. She could just make out Johnnie struggling up the rungs, the glider with its wings bumping along behind him. By the time she got within shouting distance, he was almost at the top and as she ran—panting with the exertion and the heat—she saw him step across to the playroom roof and drag his glider with him. Now he was walking along the ridge toward the chimney where they'd sat as children and told each other their secrets. She called to him but the little figure kept moving the way things do in nightmares. She ran harder, her throat burning. She knew he wanted to get to the chimney because it was the highest point on the farm, the place where they'd made their wishes. When she was ten she had wished never to grow up, he had wished for a hooded falcon. From the chimney you could see the fields stretching back to the woods and beyond them to the blue mountains that ringed them. They had wanted to run away together. Now he was strapping himself into his glider. She was near enough to see the sun gleam on the feathers. "John," she shouted, her breath coming in painful gasps, "it won't hold you. Wait." He heard her, peered down at her for a minute, smiled.

"Don't worry," he shouted, "I'll be back for you." Then he looked up at the sun and pushed off. The wind picked up right then and it seemed to carry him. The glider drifted, hung. Lara felt her heart pounding. He floated, arms outstretched under the feathered wings, legs straight behind him like a diver's. It was working, she thought, he'd done it. He'd drift to the ground, be alright. There was a look of absolute triumph on his face.

Then the wind dropped.

The glider plunged straight down.

Lara covered her eyes.

When she opened them again she saw him lying face down next to the open stone fireplace where they'd had their barbecues. One of the wings was under his head and she prayed that it had shielded him from the impact. People did fall two stories and live, she thought, as she started toward him again. He was still in the position he'd fallen. She knelt beside him, trying to turn him over. Though she knew you weren't supposed to move people, she couldn't stop herself. She felt as if he couldn't breathe, that somehow the wing was suffocating him, and she had to give him air.

She lifted his shoulder, the upper part of his body turned grudgingly toward her. Then she saw the blood and started to scream. It was pouring out of a jagged hole in his forehead and streaming over his open eyes, going into his eyes, covering them with a bloody film, trickling down into his mouth. The blood was such an amazingly deep color, so vibrantly alive.

She was barely aware that David and Otis had run up and were kneeling on Johnnie's other side. David knelt and put his head on Johnnie's chest. Then he took her arm and tried to make her get up. She shook him off impatiently and started to rip off Johnnie's shirt. Otis and David exchanged horrified looks but Lara ignored them. She had to stop all that rich blood from pouring out. She took a piece of linen and stuffed it in the hole. Then she wiped Johnnie's face gently. His skin was warm, his lips were warm. She put his head on her lap and sat there, cradling it, blood all over her dress, feeling his cheek cool by hardly perceptible degrees.

❧ 35 ❧

There were so many details to be attended to the next day that Lara didn't have time to feel anything but numb. First she had to tell her mother. She couldn't bear talking to her on the phone, describing what had happened, so she cabled her in Florida at the last address she had for her. It was cowardly but it was all she could manage.

Then she made a list.

Arrange funeral, she wrote in block letters on a page torn from her sketch pad. Then she stopped. She saw Johnnie being taken off by the undertaker in some sort of sack like a dead animal. Death would have to be prettified now, she thought. The hole in his forehead would probably have to be patched. What did they use for that sort of thing she wondered, putty? dyed clay?

Lara took a deep breath. She couldn't seem to get enough oxygen into her lungs; she was always either sighing or yawning. She scribbled drawings of flowers in the margins of the page, underlined the word "funeral" twice with harsh black strokes. The hardest thing would be to decide on the kind of ceremony and who would officiate, so she decided to leave that until last.

She thumbed through the leaflet the undertaker had left with her, describing the kinds of caskets available with their prices. That was relatively easy. No velvet, no baroque decorations. A simple wood box. But suddenly she remembered that her father's casket had been left open so people could pay their respects. The thought sent small fingers of ice creeping up her spine. She'd seen enough . . . couldn't imagine Johnnie's face anymore without seeing the blood gushing from his forehead. Red against white. Red over blond. Red over. . . .

She stared at her paper. Though she'd helped her mother arrange Eugene's funeral just half a year ago, she felt paralyzed by doubt. Not just the question of the casket. All the details seemed equally impossible to decide on. Who would she call, for instance? The same family friends who had come to her father's funeral? Sol, people from the office, her friends, Mina, Mortimer. Come help me celebrate my brother's suicide.

In more severe times, suicides were put outside the walls of the cemetery, their graves unmarked. People probably lied about cause of death, she thought, trying to pass. The worst would be to be left uncovered, exposed. She thought of Antigone sneaking out in the night to bury her brother. Throwing dirt over his naked body, keeping it from the vultures. She imagined Antigone in bright yellow against a black sky. She had long fingers almost like claws. Could Antigone have been relieved that her brother was dead? That now she could have her father's affection. Now she was the only one? Now finally he would notice her? Did that thought make her risk her own life to bury her brother?

Lara looked up at the clock and was amazed at how much time had gone by. After several hours, she was still obsessing over small details. What's the worst that can happen if I make the wrong decision? she asked herself sternly. Is Johnnie going to come back to complain? She heard herself giggle.

She took her pen and wrote 'Choice of service.' Her father had wanted a rabbi even though for years he hadn't been near a synagogue. Johnnie had never expressed any preference. Where did this leave her? Reasons for a Jewish service, she wrote.

1. J. was obsessed with being a Jew
2. We are in fact Jewish

Reasons against

1. Mother would hate it

2. I wouldn't like it either

That surprised her. She knew her mother hated being Jewish. But this wasn't the same—at least she didn't think that it was: the whole mumbo jumbo simply meant nothing to her. She'd been to a synagogue once and the mass of swaying praying men left her bewildered. Now, she realized, she felt openly hostile. Johnnie's obsession with Jewishness had killed him.

She'd like to get someone inclusive, she thought, a Quaker or a Unitarian. People didn't need more awareness of their differences, they needed something to show them what they had in common, their humanity. But as soon as she'd written 'Unitarian' she crossed it out. This wasn't her funeral, after all, it was his. She felt inappropriate laughter welling up inside. So she'd been confusing them again. She'd really have to get it straight. She drew a stick figure and self-mockingly labelled it 'Johnnie', then another one and labelled it 'Lara'. Then she wrote

Reasons for a Jewish service

1. Johnnie thought it was important to know who you are.

He was afraid to be Jewish because it meant he was in danger.

There is no more danger.

Ergo, he can be as Jewish as he pleases. Have I got it right, Johnnie?

What to do was suddenly obvious. She decided she'd call her father's friend Stephan who was a famous reform rabbi in New York. She didn't know why she hadn't thought of him before. He was a man she respected, he knew the family, she'd ask for a spare service at the grave. Maybe she'd read something from the psalms, she'd always loved the images. She'd tell very few people. Only people who mattered in some way.

That night she received a garbled cable from her mother—their wires must have crossed—hinting at some disaster and saying she had been very sick. It sounded as if she needed to be rescued but Lara couldn't deal with it now, so she just shut it out. Later, she told herself, just one thing at a time.

~·36·~

Agnes hired a car to drive her from the station to the farm. Miraculously, no one saw her when she arrived; they must have been inside checking over the last details for the funeral—and she went straight to her room and lay down on the bed. She ought not to be afraid of facing Lara, she thought, but she was. She could imagine the look of scorn on her face when she told her about Walter but she knew she shouldn't think about that either.

And poor Johnnie. Dead. It was hard to believe. When she called after the telegram, all Lara told her was that he had fallen off the roof. But Agnes knew from the way that she said it that Johnnie had jumped. For a moment she felt the impact in her body, the sickening thud of hitting, the pain, the breaking of bones. Lara hadn't told her any details but there must have been blood. Agnes saw it mixed with his fine blond hair—the hair that was still like a baby's hair. What made him do it, she wondered—her stomach heaving. Crack his head like that on the stones?

She thought of the night he had caught her and Walter together and the way she had lied to him, how she'd taken advantage of his ignorance. She remembered the confusion in his eyes. She would have done anything, said anything, not to have him know what his mother was doing. She had been so disgusted with herself, with the dirty, filthy thing she'd been doing, that for a moment it seemed quite alright to make it seem something childlike and innocent. But Johnnie must have known it was a lie, that his mother was . . . . And then he'd gone and touched that little girl.

She started to cry. The faith healer had warned her that she would have relapses, that what she had done wasn't forever, that she'd have to keep renewing her faith. She knelt down next to the bed and tried to find that still place inside her mind where her strength came from. It was hard. Inappropriate thoughts kept slipping in, like Walter holding her in his arms, kissing her hair, telling her she was his precious, beautiful love. Go away, she told the image. Thin air, that's all it was. The thin air of illusion. He was a liar and a scoundrel.

That worked. The image vanished.

I was a foolish old woman, she said to herself. I should have seen through him from the beginning. I should have listened to Lara. I haven't been fair to her either. What a thing to see, her mother simpering and coquetting . . . at my age. Agnes was overcome by a feeling of humiliation. Then she remembered what the faith healer told her. Castigating yourself is a waste of energy, he said, the energy you need to move forward into your life.

She tried to concentrate on what had been given back to her. The use of her legs, her health. She was whole in body, and with work she could be whole in mind, too. She stopped trying so hard and just let the difficult thoughts go through her mind the way the healer had instructed her. She saw Johnnie lying on the ground, Walter's betrayal. The idea struck her that this was the price she had to pay for understanding and she started to cry again. It was too much, too hard. But she stayed there feeling the hard floor under her until the pain lessened. The thoughts still came as she imagined they would come for years, for her whole life maybe, but they were less intense. She could see a time when they would be bearable.

When she finally got up, she caught a glimpse of Eugene's photograph pinned against the corner of her mirror. He seemed to be looking at her with a sort of rueful tenderness. If you'd lived, none of this would have happened, she thought, remembering how he'd come to her in her dream. She supposed now that he'd been trying to warn her.

"I never grieved for you properly," she told him. "You know how I always hated being sad."

She pictured herself quite suddenly as running fast over a green lawn in a frilly muslin dress, with her hands over her ears, not wanting to know how she really felt—about Eugene, about Johnnie, about anything. She washed her face with cold water and combed her hair. I look like a different lady, she thought. This is Agnes. This is who I am. Then she changed into a black dress and went downstairs for her son's funeral.

❧37❧

They had the ceremony by the grave—in the country cemetery—just the way she had planned it. Sol was there and one or two close friends of her father's and mother's, and David and Muriel, Gorky and Mina and Mortimer—Mina, irrepressible even at a funeral, wanted to gossip about Mortimer's engagement. And, of course, her mother, who stood by the open grave under the old trees, looking around her with a slightly dazed expression. Sol, Eugene's executor, held one arm, afraid she was going to crumple. Lara heard him say in a whisper to David: two deaths in less than a year. A terrible thing.

But, in fact, her mother not only seemed strangely calm, she looked completely different. She'd left chic and glowing. She wasn't exactly dowdy now, but she'd lost the sexual glow. She'd cut her hair and stopped dying it blond—it was back to its original dark brown with streaks of gray—and she was wearing a severe black dress with sensible black shoes.

Sol didn't seem to notice any change; he kept peering anxiously into her face, while Stephan—Lara didn't think of him as a rabbi but only as a compassionate man—remembered his long acquaintance with their family, noted Johnnie's brilliance and gentleness, his promise cut short. Stephan had the

eyes of a dreamer, Lara thought, while he intoned the obliga-
tory prayers for the dead, mournful chants filled with guttural
syllables.

When he finished Lara read the psalm she had chosen,
standing very still, trying not to cry. "Yea though I walk
through the valley of the shadow of death," she read, "Thou art
with me . . . Thou makest me to lie down in green pastures . . .
Thou restorest my soul."

The leaves on the old elms rustled, lifted by a rising
breeze. A hint of cold to come. They were beginning to turn
yellow and orange. It would have been comforting to believe
the words of the psalm, Lara thought. Even reading it and
thinking of the refreshed soul gave her a certain peacefulness.
For a minute she wished that she believed in redemption and
rebirth. In something or anything outside her own lonely and
frightened will.

When it was finished, they had to file by the grave, each
with a spadeful of dirt to throw onto the coffin. Lara and her
mother headed the procession. When her mother heard the soft
thud of dirt against the top of the coffin, she gasped and stood
looking at it, tears running down her face. Lara shuddered. She
realized why she hadn't wanted the casket open. She had some
illogical hope that he wasn't really in there, under the flowers
and the dirt. She put her arm around her mother's shoulders,
murmured into her hair, until she moved on, still crying.
Gently Lara took the spade. When she dug into the dark earth
piled up at the edge of the grave, it smelled rich and loamy like
the furrows at the farm being plowed for winter wheat. She
had a sudden sense of her own aliveness. Her future, not neces-
sarily happy, but full of smells and colors. She started to cry
and her mother took her hand.

Muriel, hugely pregnant, came up to them as they were
walking back to the car.

"I wanted to tell you how sorry I am," she said to Agnes,
her earnest face distressed. "So sorry . . . this . . . happened."
The words squeezed themselves out. "It oughtn't to have . . . I
really misjudged." Lara couldn't remember seeing Muriel at
such a loss. "When you feel better, we must talk," she finished,
touching Agnes's arm.

"Talk didn't keep him here," Agnes said, raising her veil and looking straight at Muriel, "and it won't bring him back."

Then she lowered her veil again and got into the car.

When they got back to the farm, neither of them could sit still and they walked around the freshly mown lawn under the huge maples. Agnes blew her nose hard several times and wiped her eyes. Lara waited for her to break down and cry again, but she didn't.

"Well, these things aren't so important, really," she said after they talked for a few minutes about Johnnie's jump from the roof. "There's no death, you know, only change. Johnnie attained a higher consciousness, after all. We should be happy for him."

"I'm glad he's at peace," Lara said, "but I'm also very sad."

"I was sad too at first," Agnes whispered. "You know what I did to fight it? Recited all the poetry I knew by heart. By the time I finished, all the negative thoughts were gone."

Her mother ended up talking all through the afternoon.

Lara couldn't begin to process what she was hearing. So much had happened in such a short time. Just listening made her head spin. She felt dizzy. She hadn't even known her mother and Walter had been married. The wedding, as her mother had described it, sounded so bizarre, more like a Valentino movie than real life. Walter flying them out to some remote island in the Florida Keys. The marriage surrounded by exotic birds and water. Agnes's brilliant pink and fuchsia wedding dress. If it hadn't been so pathetic, Lara would have laughed thinking of the minister wading ahead of them with his shoes and the Bible held over his head, then solemnly unrolling his pants legs, and Agnes swatting insects during the ceremony—they were flying down her decolletage, her mother said, and up her skirt.

When Agnes got to the end of her story of the wedding night and the giant bugs that invaded her room, she was silent for a few minutes.

"Before he left, he asked me to sign some papers," she said finally.

"Papers? What kind of papers?"

"I don't know, dear. I trusted him. But I'm afraid I signed over a portion of my stock."

"Didn't you read whatever it was?" Lara looked at her aghast. If they were really married, her mother would never see her money again.

"I'm sure I did, but, well, we'd had champagne and. . . ."

"You got tipsy and signed something without reading it. I can't believe it. It's crazy." Lara felt the blood rushing to her face. She could picture herself out on the streets.

"It's cheap to say I'm sorry," her mother said simply, cutting her off, "but I am. Deeply sorry. I wouldn't have hurt your and Johnnie's chances in life for the world."

Lara had been about to say, I'll never forgive you, but something about the dignified way her mother spoke made her stop and stare at her.

"Is there anything I can do to get it back? I don't care how humiliating it is for me. I'm prepared to tell the whole story."

Her mother had never sounded so rational. Lara felt herself calming down.

"I don't think you could have given him our money," she said after thinking for a moment, "it's in trust. Yours is, too." Maybe her mother had only given Walter permission to withdraw the cash in her account, whatever she'd been able to persuade Sol to advance her. "I'll talk to Sol about it in the morning."

"I want to do it," her mother said softly. "I have to learn to manage my affairs sometime. And I suppose the sooner the better."

❧

That night it was warm and neither of them could sleep, so Lara got a flashlight and they went for a walk. For a while they circled the cottage garden without saying a word, listening to the frogs and the crickets.

"I wasn't a good mother," Agnes said suddenly. "I know that. I didn't have enough inside me to give."

Lara couldn't see her expression in the moonlight but her voice was thoughtful, ruminative.

"Don't castigate yourself," she said, surprised.

"I'm just trying to face facts for once," Agnes said calmly. She opened the back gate by the tree house and they headed past the vegetable garden with its dark shadows of cornhusks and the remains of the pole beans, toward the pool. "Johnnie's dead. Even if he's better off, he's gone from me. Removed. There's nothing I can do to alter that. And I've made a fool of myself with Walter and I've lost my jewelry and purchased some fairly worthless land and signed away heaven knows what." She paused and Lara held her breath—maybe now she'd hear exactly what Agnes had done. "But I've found something to do with the rest of my life."

They passed the foot of the ladder to the water tower and Agnes looked up for a moment at the innocent round shape covered with gray shingles. "I'm going to take that piece of land and drain it and build a center for Christ Science."

"You can't be serious," Lara said. It was just another enthusiasm, she thought, a way to forget Johnnie.

"I am. The assistant manager of the hotel where I was staying is a Christian Science practitioner. He saved my life. He's already put me in contact with some of the elders. I hope they'll help me with financing." She put her hand on Lara's. "I've never had a real life," she said quietly. "I was always in someone else's power. First my mother, who made me stay in bed while my pinafore was washed. With all the money we had, she only thought I was worth one dress. You can't imagine what it's like to be made to sit in one place like a doll or a whipped dog for hours. It crushes your spirit. But I'm not blaming anyone." She moved slowly up the grassy incline where Johnnie used to fly his kites. "I just want to explain. Then your father who took care of me in his way, was gallant and sweet but, well, you know what he did with the housemaids." Lara made a motion to stop her. "It doesn't matter." Agnes removed Robin's cork life vest from one of the ghostly lounge chairs at the pool's edge and sat down. "That's how men were brought up in our day. They could give their hearts to serving-girls and waitresses and actresses and then turn around and marry someone of their own class. Not very fair, if you ask me."

She wasn't dowdy, Lara thought, flicking on her flashlight and looking at her. She was simply sure of herself. Her features all seemed pulled together. It was amazing the sense of unity in her face. "I didn't think you knew. . . ."

"I knew." She put up her hand to shield herself from the glare and Lara turned it off with a murmured apology. "But I couldn't let myself believe it because I depended on him for everything. Where could I have gone? I didn't realize I had the spirit of Christ inside me that could make me, weak as I am, as strong as anyone. I didn't realize that my sense of lethargy and inertness was only an illusion. Something that could be overcome by right thinking and prayer."

Lara winced involuntarily. Why did it have to be religion? Lara had always prided herself on being a free thinker. It seemed so retrograde. "Just because Walter ended so badly doesn't mean you have to become a nun." She toyed with the flashlight switch, wanting to turn it on again and see her mother's face.

"Christian Science doesn't have nuns, Lara." Agnes got up abruptly and started skimming leaves from the water with Robin's bucket. "But some people aren't meant to be happy in love. The thing is, I know I'd do it again. I wouldn't mean to but I'd make a wrong choice and get hurt again. It's much better for me to give it up." The soggy leaves, drained of color, lay in a dark pile next to her. "Weren't you always telling me there was more to life?"

Lara crouched down next to her, looking at the moon in the water. A leaf was floating in it like an eye. "Yes, but not. . . ."

"There are moments in life when you just know something is right." She shook out the bucket and put it down. "When the assistant manager came into my room, I was crying my eyes out feeling sorry for myself. My legs wouldn't work. I thought I'd gotten some terrible disease from those insects. He sat and prayed with me for an hour, holding my hand. Told me my sickness was only as real as I let it be. That I didn't have to let it win. I could be the victor, not the victim. And there it was, absolutely simple. Before night I was able to get dressed and walk out of the room with him, at the end of another hour was well enough to have dinner. By the next day I knew what I was going to do. Believe me. If I hadn't found this, or, if it hadn't found me—because that's really how it happened—I'd probably have been a hopeless invalid. I would have come home in a wheelchair and lain around in bed demanding that you take care of me. Would you have wanted that?"

"No, of course not." Lara realized with a shock that part of her did want just that. For her mother to cling to her. It wasn't just Agnes that was holding on. She started to shiver even though the night was still warm. "I hate you thinking you've been the subject of a miracle when it's just some kind of suggestion," she went on. "You weren't really crippled, you had a physical reaction to Walter's leaving you. Then the faith healer. . . ." Lara had a sudden macabre vision of herself having a stroke, of it happening to her. Was it that disorienting to have her mother detach herself?

"Don't try to explain it away," Agnes said severely. "There are some things I don't want to listen to. Everyone has his own way of dealing with disaster. This is mine. And it seems to me it's every bit as good as this psychoanalysis of yours. It didn't save Johnnie, did it?"

"It's just at the beginning," Lara said, holding her hands out and pulling her mother to her feet. I am, too, she thought. She had a sensation of empty space that would have to be filled. Not just canvases. Parts of herself that had hardly begun.

Suddenly she wanted to go back to the water tower. She pulled her mother along past the back of the flower garden, past the big house and the cottage. When she got to the foot of the ladder she kicked off her shoes and started up. Her mother had to take off her stockings first, rolling them neatly and putting them in her shoes, then she followed her slowly. When they got to the place where you had to take a step over to the roof, Lara went first and held out her hand. Her mother stood awkwardly with one foot and one hand on the ladder and reached out. For a minute Lara was afraid she'd slip and pull them both down but she didn't, and they set off slowly across the slanted roof.

"It feels like a pilgrimage, doesn't it?" Agnes asked.

Lara didn't answer. She just wanted the feel of the roof shingles under her bare feet and the moon on her shoulders. And she wanted to help her mother up onto the chimney and sit with her looking up at the Big Dipper and the Little Dipper and the evening star.

❧38❧

Sol stayed the night at the farm, and the next morning he explained to Lara—with embarrassment because as executor he ought to have seen what was coming—how much money Walter could have gotten away with. Lara felt immensely relieved. Two years' income was a lot of money and the jewelry too was worth a good deal, but the stocks had been protected. Her mother had been lucky, she'd gotten off lightly.

As for Johnnie's wish to leave his share of his own money to Lara—Sol said that was already stipulated by her father's trust.

That afternoon Lara asked David and Muriel over to the small living room in the cottage to hear the rest of Johnnie's will. It was scrawled on two pieces of paper that he had given to Sol when he came to visit him at the hospital.

Sol read it.

It started off simply. Johnnie wanted his portion of the trust to go to Lara. He hoped it would help to keep her safe, to do her paintings if that was what she wanted.

After that, there were small bequests to the caretaker Otis and his wife. Johnnie's drawings of birds in flight went to Merle. How isolated he'd been, Lara thought. No friends, only them. She could see her mother leaning forward hoping for some word. But there was nothing for her except his math books and school trophies.

Instead there was a rambling letter to Muriel. Johnnie had left her his papers, all his journals and his diaries. Considering what was in the death diary, it seemed a cruel gift, but Lara imagined he didn't mean it that way. She tried to follow the stream of images. "When I look in the mirror," he wrote, "I see through to the bones now. There is no further to go. You think my health is disturbed by my brain, that my thinking is clouded. But the clouds are elsewhere."

Here he went off into a digression about thought and Lara only caught part of it. Suddenly it occurred to her that he was comparing his and Muriel's views of reality. Yes! That was it. "Your face becomes a shining star when you talk to me about secret traumas," he wrote. "But are they any more real than the darkness I see outside? Where are your shattered bones, your blood?" It was so like Johnnie Lara smiled despite herself.

The last part of his "letter" seemed to be about love or sex. He called it desire. "The kite desires the wind that lifts it, desires the sun it leaps toward, the flesh desires," he wrote, and stopped, crossed out. While Sol struggled to decipher what came next, Lara wondered whether it would have changed things if Merle had loved him. His images were so full of yearning, but without bodies or touching parts. "Don't you see," he went on, "desire can't be bad? It is only a wish to be safe. To be saved. What is dark and dirty and heavy is hatred. It gathers inside, pushes itself out through the skin . . . destroys everything it touches."

"I am too tired to say much more. I've collected these news-papers and accounts for a year now. It is all there in black and white: the pictures, the accounts. My notebooks explain the increase of danger. Give the dates, the tendencies. Name the people that must be watched."

"I don't know why you couldn't hear me. I sensed you wanted to help me, you trusted my goodness. Maybe my physical presence distracted you. Made changing me more important than listening. But even if I were mad, couldn't what I'm saying be true?"

There he broke off, signed his name.
"P.S.
I would like my kite collection to go to Robin."

Lara was painting a mural on the wall of the baby's room—Muriel had asked her to do it. It was the only thing that made sense to her now: opening tubes of paint, squeezing the clear colors out onto the palette, measuring the surfaces with her eye—controlling her world.

She painted a forest filled with huge sensual flowers. While she was doing it she didn't have to think about the money her mother had lost, or the hole in Johnnie's forehead, and what it all meant to her, Lara.

"I love it," Muriel said, coming in and standing in front of the wall Lara was working on. "It's innocent but not senti- mental . . . just what I'd want a baby of mine to look at."

"Maybe I should put in a couple of mangroves," Lara said, sensing an undertone of distress—or was it apology—in Muriel's praise, "a touch of the Florida swamps."

"Is your mother really going back there?"

"Wild horses couldn't keep her away," Lara said, thinking how she'd come on her mother that morning smiling at her graying image in the mirror. "She's stopped posing. I can't say I understand it but I like her better too." They had spent the morning going through Johnnie's things together, deciding which to keep and which to give away.

Muriel looked out the window at the yellow and red leaves of the maple blown against the window. "I thought I could do everything," she said, her lips compressed in a bitter smile, "find a companion for your mother, cure your brother, make a terribly sick child good as new. I even imagined Robin graduating from college, white dress and all." She smiled again, grimly. "At least I haven't harmed her. But your brother. I'll never forget I was the one who brought him back here."

Lara knew she should say I don't blame you, you tried, but she couldn't. Not yet. What came to her mind was: The road to Hell is paved with good intentions. She stroked in black stripes on an orange tiger.

"I'm not sure I like this," she said, suddenly leaning back to look at what she'd done. "He seems to be peering out of a thicket, not shining at all—a ridiculous tiger."

Muriel leaned forward, studying the tiger's face. "He has an air of comic puzzlement. It's almost as though he's wondering how he got into such a fear-inspiring body."

Lara felt her tiger's confusion. She added a touch of white to his eye. "Johnnie did the same thing to me that he did to Robin," she blurted out suddenly—then stood there trembling, her brush dripping paint. She had never thought she'd hear these words aloud. She waited for some extraordinary event—a lightning bolt or an earthquake, but all she heard was a soft "Oh!"

Lara sat down on the floor. "He used to crawl into bed with me and kiss me, touch me." She wondered how this could possibly sound. "He said he was going to marry me."

Muriel lowered herself down next to her, crouched back on her haunches. "These things happen," she said. "Children are no different from the rest of us."

Lara raised her face. "I didn't sleep with David, you know." She didn't know why she said this just now, but there was a pressure at the back of her head.

"You don't have to tell me this," Muriel said gently. "We're both free adults. What David does is his own business."

Lara wiped her brush distractedly on a rag. Muriel might say that, but Lara knew that much as she tried to hide it, she'd been jealous. "But I didn't, that's the point. I didn't. It's the first time I've ever restrained myself."

"And did you with Johnnie?" Muriel asked.

Lara nodded.

"And now you're telling me."

She nodded again. She hoped Muriel wasn't going to go off into her professional mode. Start giving her interpretations. She wondered whether if she said 'I'm telling you because I like you,' Muriel would stop looking at her in that penetrating way.

Suddenly, Muriel leaned over and gave her a hug. "Well, I'm glad, glad that you didn't and that you told me. I wish everyone had the same restraint."

For a minute Lara didn't understand, distracted by the sensation of the baby kicking against her stomach, then she thought of David's eyes on the intern's breasts and flushed. Muriel obviously suspected he was having an affair.

"What are you going to do?" she asked after a minute.

"Don't know . . . I'll decide after the baby is born." Muriel gave a sudden laugh and got up. "This has been some exchange of confidences, hasn't it?"

Muriel seemed surprised by what she had said and wasn't going to discuss it further. She probably prided herself on being able to handle things herself, Lara thought, but it had been a beginning of sorts. The balance had changed between them. Maybe now they could be friends.

Watching her wearily collect some toys and prepare to go off and do something with Robin, Lara remembered how Muriel had come striding into the house on her first visit, gray eyes shining, notebook ready, full of plans.

"Don't blame yourself for what happened to Johnnie," Lara said, "there were so many things pushing him." She couldn't quite say 'it would have happened anyway.' But it had been enough: she saw Muriel's shoulders straighten, and just before she left the room she turned and smiled.

∽39∾

When Lara and Muriel took Robin into Johnnie's room to give her his kites, Lara was afraid she would start to howl or collapse. But she didn't; she walked slowly around touching the kites with her fingers, tapping them gently; then she took Muriel's wrist and tugged her toward them. Together Lara and Muriel carried them over to the big house—it was clear that was what Robin wanted—and Robin set them up around her room like guardian spirits. Then she sat down next to her favorite blue one and put her face against it, and tears started to trickle down her cheeks.

The tears clearly startled her—she had always been dry-eyed—but when she touched them, her face had such a look of sudden understanding that Lara almost cried too.

Afterwards the women sat together on the lawn and Robin skittered around them with her kite. She began a game. She tapped Muriel on the arm, then she ran off, holding the blue kite to her chest.

"She wants to be chased," Lara said with a shock of pleasure. It was the first time Robin had initiated something with another person. Muriel pulled herself to her feet and lumbered after her over the lawn. Robin zigzagged back and forth, barefoot, blond hair blowing, looking almost normal, but it was clear that though she wanted to be chased, she didn't want to be caught or held the way a healthy child would. It was a chase on her own terms.

After a while, Muriel stopped short, breathing hard, and Lara noticed that she grimaced, then looked at her watch. Lara walked over to them.

"Are you having contractions?" she asked. "Should I do anything?" Muriel shook her head.

"It's probably a false alarm. I've been having them for weeks."

"Hey, Robin," Lara offered her arm to be tapped. "Can I have a turn?" The child ignored her. She pinched Muriel's arm and pulled her wrist, darting away toward the garden with its mounds of russet chrysanthemums starting to fade, then coming back. Finally she stood on tiptoe, drew Muriel's head down until her mouth was close to her ear and made a sound.

Lara saw Muriel's gray eyes widen. "Robin, did you say something?" she asked, her voice uncertain.

Robin whispered again. It was unmistakable this time, Lara heard it too. "Chase you!"

It sounded like a deaf person's speech, Lara thought, odd and flat, and Robin didn't have the grammar right. She'd made herself and Muriel into one entity, "you," but it was definitely words. Lara felt like applauding.

"Of course I'll chase you," Muriel said. She had just time to shoot Lara a triumphant glance before Robin set off, whirling and flapping toward the pool hill in back of the flower garden. Lara went after them. The wind had come up. Good kite-flying weather, she thought. She wondered for a minute if Robin expected to find Johnnie and get some help with the kite. Could she understand he was dead? Or did she just notice his absence?

When Robin got to the top of the little hill she stopped and smiled at them. Muriel put out her arms and Lara could tell that she wanted to grab the girl's skinny body and hug her, but that wasn't part of the game, so she just smiled back.

A few minutes later the intern came—Muriel asked her with a grimace if she'd mind telling David she needed him—

and when Sue had gone off with Robin, Lara walked Muriel back to the big house.

"Can you believe she actually said, 'chase me'?" Muriel asked as they were going up the gray porch steps. She still looked exhilarated.

Lara smiled at her. "I heard it with my own ears." She thought of how the child's face had changed when she said it. How the huge blue eyes, the beautifully formed mouth suddenly came alive.

"I'm glad you were here." Muriel reached over and put her arm around Lara's shoulder, then doubled over, grimacing with pain.

"What is it?" Lara asked, supporting her. "Has labor started?"

"I think so," Muriel said. "But don't worry. In between pains I feel great. I've never felt better."

"Well, let's go, we have to get you into town. Do you have stuff packed, a suitcase? I can run upstairs and get it. We'll pick up David on the way."

"It's already in the car but I don't think there's time."

"What do you mean? Isn't there a lot of time with a first birth? Aren't you supposed to time the contractions and then. . . ."

Muriel grimaced again. "I was timing them," she gasped as soon as the contraction eased, "but then I had to chase Robin. There wasn't anything else I could do, was there? After she said those words. I guess it speeded things up."

Lara thought she'd better get Muriel inside. She opened the front door and walked her through into the hall.

"Tell me when you feel the next one," she said, looking at her watch.

"Now." Muriel leaned against her, clasping her belly. She was sweating, her bare arms were glistening—and Lara was aware of a sweet-sour smell.

Lara peered at the watch dial. "About a minute and a half. Isn't that very close?" She cursed herself for being so ignorant of the birth process. The nearest she'd gotten to a baby was to kiss a cousin's forehead while it snuggled in its mother's arms.

"Very." Muriel giggled. "I guess I'll have to have it here. If you'll help me."

Lara was amazed to see how carefree Muriel was, as if she had taken laughing gas.

"You look as if you're enjoying it," she said, taking Muriel's damp arm and leading her into the living room. There was no way they were going to make it upstairs.

"I am. I feel . . . it's indescribable."

Suddenly Muriel looked down. Lara followed her glance and saw a flood of liquid gushing down her leg. Her first thought was that it was blood and she felt a wave of fear, but Muriel seemed unconcerned.

"It's the water," she said, bemused, "it's broken. My goodness! There's so much of it. Like a river. Look, Lara!" She stood there smiling and holding her wet skirt.

"There must be a gallon of it," Lara said smiling back—the festive mood was strangely catching. As if they were on an adventure together, shooting a rapid, or climbing a mountain. She maneuvered Muriel over to the sofa.

"It's going to make a mess," Muriel said. "I ought to go outside and lie on the grass."

"I'll get something to put under you." After the next contraction, Lara ran to the linen closet and got a blanket and a clean sheet.

"Don't worry," Muriel said, when she came back. "I'm still fine between them." She pulled her shift over her head and Lara helped her lie down and position herself comfortably with her knees raised. Muriel's belly, when she peeled off her underwear, looked as though it was going to split open, it was so taut. Lara felt a moment of panic. She thought of her own tight sex. Could the baby really get out of there?

"Should I heat some water?" she asked, not wanting Muriel to see her fear.

"No, stay with me. Hold my hand, can you? I think it must be going through the transition." Muriel started to pant rapidly.

"Does it hurt much?" Lara asked, fascinated by Muriel's total concentration. Eyes hooded, staring inward.

"Yes," Muriel said after a minute, "but it's a good pain, like music. You can't believe the rhythm of it. The way it starts out so softly. . . ." She stopped and Lara watched her begin to pant again. She could sense from the way her breathing quickened that the pain was building until Muriel's whole body clenched and her bottom was lifted up off the sofa as if by a wave—then just as Muriel's face became distorted with what seemed like excruciating pain and Lara felt certain she was going to scream, her body relaxed and she opened her eyes. They were perfectly calm.

The whole thing made Lara think of a seizure. It struck her that was what artists were imitating when they depicted prophetesses writhing in front of the oracles of Apollo—birth-pangs. It was an astonishing thing to see. Amazing to think her own mother had done this. Not once but twice.

Lara wiped Muriel's forehead, damp with sweat, but Muriel hardly seemed to notice. She was so concentrated on what was going on inside. Just then David came running up the porch steps, opened the door and burst into the living room. Lara motioned him back.

"I think it's almost here," she said, "don't worry. Everything's fine but we'll need some water." He seemed relieved and soon Lara heard the pots clattering in the kitchen.

"I feel like pushing," Muriel said suddenly. "Lara. . . ."

"I'm here." Her hand was gripping Lara's with such force she was afraid it was going to break, but she didn't try to pull away.

Muriel held her breath and bore down, her face suffused with blood.

"Can you see the head?" she gasped. "Look and see."

Lara bent and looked between Muriel's knees. The opening was terribly distended, the lips purple. As she watched she saw a patch of damp, dark hair beginning to push its way out.

"I see it," she shouted, "I see the head, it's coming." Each time Muriel pushed it moved out a little further and then sank back. Lara wanted to help it come but she wasn't sure how. Tentatively she put her hands out. "It has black hair like yours," Lara found herself laughing. There was something so touching about that thick black hair. She put her hands under it, cradling it, helping it emerge. "Come on, baby," she said softly, wondering if it was afraid, pressing along that tunnel in

❦40❧

The day after Muriel's baby was born they had an early frost that killed all the remaining tomato plants and most of the flowers. The next day, the end of October, Gorky called to tell Lara he had good news. He'd shown the portrait of her father to his dealer, Julien, and Julien wanted to have it and some others for a show. Gorky said he'd bring him to her studio to see them the next week. Together they could choose the ones for the show.

Lara was suddenly afraid she didn't have enough, so she worked feverishly all that week. She'd go to bed exhausted and would wake up after an hour or two with images flooding her mind. One after the other, brilliantly lit, powerfully colored. There was no way of stopping them to go back to sleep, so she would get up and paint, turning on all the lights, trying to capture the colors. She painted without really knowing what her subject was, but after a few nights she realized she was making image maps of the farm, of places she and John had been together. Only one had figures—the painting of the night he had first come to her bed showed two slim terracotta figures embracing, not clearly either male or female and "Je ne puis prendre ni l'une ni l'autre joie" painted under them.

But the majority of the canvases were pastels. She wanted the velvet richness of the color of animals and flowers and birds. The cubist style had been harsh, abstract. She had liked it for its coldness but it wasn't her. She had been afraid to be labelled a woman artist rather than simply an artist, but now she saw that passionate intensity was her strength. She used color freely to express emotion, made her bulls blue-black or startling red and set them against flagrantly open white lilies as big as the bulls.

It was safe to paint the poetry of sex, she thought with a touch of her old irony, safer than living it. That would have to wait—she simply didn't have the energy to do both at once, not yet. She thought about David and Muriel, wondering what would happen to them. Whatever happened, Muriel would be alright, but if she stayed with David she'd have to tolerate his childishness.

Lara realized she wanted a stronger man. I don't want much, she thought wryly, just everything—a man with the brains of Mortimer, the sensuality of Gorky, and David's compassion—and of course he can't interfere with my work. She imagined herself saying this to her composite wooer, when he proposed to her, and laughed. Better just keep painting. What was wonderful about painting, she thought as she worked on a peacock's feather that was also an eye and, if you looked at it still another way, a flower, was the way you could mix the elements to suit yourself. I'm a prickly person, she thought, hard to get along with, demanding in the extreme. But here I'm in my element. She stood back and surveyed her glowing canvases lining the walls.

Gorky came with his dealer Julien, a dapper little man half his size, who looked as though he had a sharp eye for business. Gorky strode around excitedly looking at her new work.

"They're beautiful," he said. "I should never have tried to stop you from doing what you wanted." He went up until his nose was practically touching a pastel of cows under a tree. "Look at that touch of violet on the tree branch," he said to Julien, holding up a hand. "It brings the whole painting into focus and yet manages to be pure poetry. You've found your path."

"I think there may be a market for these," Julien said dryly. "They have a female sensibility. Very lyrical."

Lara winced. It was what she'd been afraid of, being pigeon-holed. But she'd have to get used to it. Maybe she could turn being a woman painter into something less derogatory.

"You don't have enough for a one-man show, your paintings aren't large. But as I told Gorky, I'm having a group show in the winter. I think these would fit right in."

Lara put out her hand. There was so much she wanted to ask. Who else would be in it, did she know them, were any of the others women—she realized to her surprise that she didn't know any other women painters—but there would be time to find out. She didn't want to seem over-eager.

"I'll be in it too," Gorky said, answering part of her question.

While Julien and Gorky looked through her paintings, making the final selection, Lara sat on a stool and watched them. I should leave the farm, she thought, as they stood shoulder to shoulder discussing her canvases. I can't live at home anymore, even if Mother's off in Florida. It occurred to her that she could go to her old high school in the city—they'd always liked her there—and ask if she could teach part time. That or take a few beginning students. She didn't think living completely alone would be good for her. She needed some regular contact with people. The rest of the time she'd paint. She'd get a slightly bigger apartment. It all suddenly seemed so easy. The glue that held her to her home had come unstuck.

One of the last things she did before leaving was to make a picture map of the farm, starting from the stone gates at the main driveway. The map wasn't hard; she found she knew every part, every path as well as she knew her own body. She tried to make separate pastels of the details she wanted to remember. The color and texture of the pebbly gravel in front of the main house that brought back the sound of her father's boots in the early morning, the way the clods in the plowed fields broke into rich folds, the glint and dance of the brook, the droop of the willow tree that was planted when she was born, the room where her mother and father had slept, with its view over the garden, her room with its tree filling the window with shades of green and gray, the hayloft where the yellows and ochres brought back the sweet smell and harsh texture of hay, the bright modern blue of the swimming pool with its neat white bathhouse, the red clay tennis court where her father ran after the compact sphere of the ball, the deep red of the roses along the white picket fence, the Rembrandt dark of the grain bins with their smell of cool decay. . . .

In the end she had to stop, overwhelmed by the sheer pour of details, more vivid and real than the things themselves. But her final image, a painting, was of them all—her and Johnnie, her father and mother, Muriel and David and Robin—in her mother's garden with its profusion of colors. In the background, like a double image, a small overheated child struggled from a woman's lap to grasp a wildly improbable orange poppy.